PENGUIN BOOKS

# THE LOST CHRONICLE OF EDWARD DE VERE

Andrew Field is Honorary Professor at Griffith University in Australia, where for many years he taught biography and writing. This is his second novel, and he is currently at work on his third. He is best known as the author of artistic biographies of Vladimir Nabokov and Djuna Barnes, about which the Scott Fitzgerald biographer André Le Vot has written: 'Andrew Field's life of Djuna Barnes is a study of the first order [and], as in his remarkable work on Nabokov, Field does not hesitate to place himself on stage and allow his own personality and subjectivity to come face to face with his own subject . . . His is a method which is both mimetic and original.' Field travels widely and has spent considerable time in Cambridge and London while working on this novel. He lives in Australia with his wife Meg.

# ❧By the Queene.

FOrasmuche as the tyme wherein common Interludes in the Englishe tongue are wont vsually to be played, is now past by tyll Allhallontyde, and that also some that haue ben of late vsed, are not conuenient in any good ordred Christian Common weale to be suffred. The Quenes Maiestie doth straightly forbyd al maner Interludes to be playde eyther openly or priuately, except the same be notified before hande, and licenced within any Citie or towne corporate, by the Maior or other chiefe officers of the same, and within any shyre, by suche as shalbe Lieuetenaunts for the Queenes Maiestie in the same shyre, or by twoo of the Iustices of peax inhabyting within that part of the shire where any shalbe played.

AND for instruction to euery of the sayde officers, her maiestie doth likewise charge euery of them as they will aunswere: that they permyt none to be played wherin either matters of religion or of the gouernaunce of the estate of the commō weale shalbe handled or treated, beyng no meete matters to be wrytten or treated vpon, but by menne of aucthoritie, learning and wisedome, nor to be handled before any audience, but of graue and discrecte persons: All which partes of this proclamation, her maiestie chargeth to be inuiolably kepte. And if any shal attempte to the contrary: her Maiestie giueth all maner of officers that haue authoritie to see common peax kepte in commandement, to arrest and enprison the parties so offending for the space of fourteene dayes or more, as cause shall nede: And furder also vntill good assuraunce may be founde and gyuen, that they shalbe of good behauiour, and no more to offende in the like.

AND further her Maiestie gyueth speciall charge to her nobilitie and gentilmen, as they professe to obey and regarde her maiestie, to take good order in thys behalfe wyth their seruauntes being players, that this her Maiesties commaundement may be dulye kepte and obeyed.

Yeuen at our Palayce of Westminster the xvi. daye of Maye, the first yeare of oure Raygne.

## Imprinted at London in Powles Churchyarde, by
*Richard Iugge* and *Iohn Cawood* Printers to the
Quenes Maiestie.

*Cum priuilegio Regiæ Maiestatis.*

ANDREW FIELD

_____

# THE LOST CHRONICLE OF EDWARD DE VERE

LORD GREAT CHAMBERLAIN,
SEVENTEENTH EARL OF OXFORD,
POET AND PLAYWRIGHT
WILLIAM SHAKESPEARE

PENGUIN BOOKS

This edition is for Meg, my first reader,
who does not believe anything too easily
but who believes in Edward de Vere.

PENGUIN BOOKS

Published by the Penguin Group
Penguin Books Ltd, 27 Wrights Lane, London W8 5TZ, England
Penguin Books USA Inc., 375 Hudson Street, New York, New York 10014, USA
Penguin Books Australia Ltd, Ringwood, Victoria, Australia
Penguin Books Canada Ltd, 10 Alcorn Avenue, Toronto, Ontario, Canada M4V 3B2
Penguin Books (NZ) Ltd, 182–190 Wairau Road, Auckland 10, New Zealand

Penguin Books Ltd, Registered Offices: Harmondsworth, Middlesex, England

First published by Viking 1990
Published in Penguin Books 1991
1 3 5 7 9 10 8 6 4 2

Copyright © Andrew Field, 1990
All rights reserved

The moral right of the author has been asserted

Printed in England by Clays Ltd, St Ives plc

# Publisher's Note

The manuscript here published as THE LOST CHRONICLE OF
EDWARD DE VERE was discovered by chance in April 1990
at Shipton-under-Wychwood in Oxford. It came to light in a
secret drawer of a desk being treated for severe woodworm.
Although its authenticity has not yet been established, it purports
to be the autobiography of Edward de Vere, Seventeenth Earl of
Oxford, and dates from the early part of the seventeenth century.

*Far fly thy fame*
*Most, most, of me belov'd, whose silent name*
*One letter bounds.*

John Marston, *The Scourge of Villanie*, 1599
[A.F.]

Am I then such a fool as to bid myself farewell twice? It would appear I am. Here I desert my own counsel and conviction to navigate with a backward hand in prose which sails close to my sonnets. Long have I known the villainous inconstancy of my own disposition, which turns like the wind and has all tempers. Pride made me silent, now it bids me speak.

I have a Monarch who is a poet as well as a King and who warmly smiles on me, but Death does, too. Elizabeth of late no longer can mind. They say the embalmers fear'd to pierce Her belly. They practised their craft only on Her cheeks and so She was a Virgin Corpse, fully embowell'd and embossed. Painted death is frightening to behold. The monstrous crack of Her thick-oak'd coffin like a lash from Heaven laid all Her ladies-in-waiting into prayer and fainting on the moonless night before the burial. They'd let Her lie a month in state. That was an error. Another coffin fit for a Queen was no problem. There were several stacked at the ready in the Revels Room, I recall. But the sea of white ostrich plumes surrounding Her black velvet bier was half ruined with muck, and there were no more to be had in England at short call.

Humble-visag'd Shakspeare, who minded our costumes, tied the horses and played the parts without words, foremost head in our every crowd before he helped move and manage The Globe, will not much mind if the true name of de Vere is at last used after his death. He's been paid out above any player and is a shareholder now. He is innocent altogether of the serpent called fame. After all, I never left my work completely unsigned and even shoved my secret E into his name when it was forced on me. Now I'll have no more puzzles. I shall speak plain and to the purpose. But how much time do I possess? My head is hot as molten lead. Sometimes my tears are hotter still.

Here's the risk. Could my name be better protected by a true account than by stubborn silence before the slander of my foes, which, let it be confessed, is sometimes half-right anyway? I fear not, though what they've said has laid stains upon the very stains. Once I wanted my name to be buried with my body. Now the name must fend for itself. Authority is not keen to bury the plague-sore and is hard-press'd to find men even to stoke the graves. Tinkers do the job and seem to live.

Silence? No. My woe will not be mobled. Let it stroll uncovered in the crisp night of some distant time.

Pray then my plague, if it be more than *pestelentia minor*, will pause until this tale is told. And if I do not finish? Half my poetry and all my life are broken lines. The hearth can always be lit even in an English May to burn this parchment if need be.

I'll speak of Court, of a Queen who in my youth kept me dancing with creaking shoes and sour heart on Her wax'd masonry for all the prospective princes of Europe who in vain came to be King, while I wanted only to be in the lands from which they journeyed. She called me My Turk, first for my luxurious costume and my manner, later for my interest in the place. When I travelled and was twenty-six, She gave me place and honour, though always frugally as was Her wont. I was at Court too long.

These were the busy years. With John Lyly at my side, we organized the pageants and the plays. He assembled stories as I directed, from chronicles and foreign tales. The enterprise grew like the broad but humble English mulberry, full of fruit though often maculate and not refined. I established a company of players. They named themselves Oxford's Boys, though they were mainly men. We rented Blackfriars. John and I began to nail together the Plantagenet plays in those years and in time others sat there at the long refectory table near the fire with its in-turned charred legs as we re-chronicled the whole stormy history of the island. There was Anthony Munday, who could please the pit, Thomas Kyd, the master of swordswipe lines and gestures. There were Rob Greene and Thom Nashe, both my sort of common men though dangerously rash, and Peale and Thom Dekker, who was more than a pamphleteer. There was satirical Marston, and George Chapman, who wrote in two hands, English and Italian, and was my friend in spite of the purple of his faith and his passion for no other writer save Homer. I forget how many others there were. Yes, Marlowe, who was a great talent at the table and so such a loss in that tavern brawl, though he suffered from envy. At first we drew our ragged wits from Shoreditch, which was then the theatrical well of London, but ere long they drew themselves from everywhere. Over all this passing company presided my patient old Thomas Churchyard. He'd been already many years ago in my employ, went over to Leicester after we quarrelled, but then he came back. I see him now with his long steel pointing needle circling the writers' table and knitting together all the stray pieces so you could not see the join.

I was their patron, with my own talent and gold, and the Queen's money, too. I was more than willing, I was almost drunken with the business. But the cost was the heavy drift of such Oxford lands as had not already been stolen from me by Leicester and by my guardian, father-in-law and Lord Treasurer. I speak of the eminent Lord Burghley, Pondus, Polonius, Pandarus, too, in *Troilus and Cressida* – all these in the one portly person.

My income was and is still by right a thousand and more pounds a year. That is plenty for all but a few of the Queen's subjects, you'd say? But of my own assets my former guardian had most so entailed in his cunning net that there was insufficient income in hand to maintain an Earl of Oxford. I forgive him everything but the covering kindnesses he did throw around me, which confused and compromised my young and overtrusting senses. Even though I was young, I do not forgive myself that I let myself be incited to popinjay deference so easily. I saw at least and at last that the name and lands of de Vere were to fall full into the estates of his obedient daughter Anne, my unloved wife, and her daughters. If I had foreseen how soon she'd die.... If I had foreseen how short of breath Pondus himself was.... I did see though that those three pelican daughters of hers had little de Vere but much Cecil in them and, being raised under the direction of good William and fiery Mildred and Mildred's own ever-living mother, the cold snake-eyed Elizabeth, Lady Russell, there could be little hope of filial obligation or tenderness from those daughters. Sooner whistle the ivy to come from off its wall; though it may rustle as though it were about to take flight, it will not budge.

This turn has put me out of tune. I'll drink some sour eisell against the plague and rest and carry on tomorrow. Pray sit still, unborn reader.

## 2

I am subdued if not renewed. Sleeping I am again a king, waking, a man near his end. There were then some eighty properties in my name. I let them run in like petty streams that must service a great running debt. Who could have known that there is not much between the cost of building mighty castles and running small theatres? Translations were sponsored, plays were adapted, players were trained, costumes were sewn, tours were made. The dish was called ruin.

I was a poet whose lines were known by heart and praised by all the world. But something happened amidst the hurly of our efforts. The patron became a playwright and sometimes even a player. I found I had in me an exchequer of words to spend. Lyly saw the path we had to take and gathered a school of like-minded poets. These were the Euphuists, whose creed was softness, but I soon found I had to lead and teach the teacher as well as supply the school house. They were all my friends, yet I could but smile at their way with words. Still, they first raised the alarum against the Puritan creed in our land. Call us radicals and Italianish then. We wore those clothes gladly.

Lyly and I worked together on his plays. *Sapho and Phao* was nearly good. And then he gradually ceased to write for himself and began to service my own conceptions.

The Plantagenet plays seen off the stage and from afar now seem to me a broad blanket of art and prattle patch'd up with cloths of many colours. In places there are shining lines that blazon poetry and history. But they are sword-play instead of music, and they roll on and on as though we wanted to make a tapestry to stretch back from Dover to Calais. Some of it is linsey-woolsey. There were near a dozen plays: the *Richard*s and the endless *Henry*s and the one *John*. That single Henry alone, the seventh, who let my clan be impoverished, I would not have. He enjoyed the full contempt of my silence. The only other silence was the Magna Charta, which was left out of *King John*. That was the pleasure of the Queen.

The *Wars of the Roses* play again to both the people and the Court in a passing rhythm of kingly power. More than half a century and kings as far apart as eagle, frog, cat and horse to contemplate. Further ancient lessons were later taken from Roman times and Castiglione's *Courtier*, my favourite always against Machiavel's book. But let me say it once more. These plays are but endless pageant talks of our nation, with arresting blooms of true poetry along the road. Advice to a Monarch, pomp for her people. I was a very young man and a young poet. By the early plays I gradually learnt to furnish the craft of playwright, lowliest of all the arts, with proper costume and manners. The rhythms of my drama grew more complicated. With the years She had no greater passion than Her plays. If playing earns Sidney's contempt, thought I, yes, the poet will go in disguise and wear the cloak of playwright for awhile.

The Queen was in Her theatrical habits King Henry's daughter. She merely used me wisely and well, and added plays to Her father's staged Revels of state. Had not the Oxfords kept their players since 1492? Her progresses and our plays eventually webbed across the country in diverse directions. The same plays were performed in different styles, nay, almost different languages, in Blackfriars and at The Globe, Inns of Court, and in the Royal Court at Whitehall and at Greenwich. Every city and large hamlet saw them. They laced together green England's Red and White, her high and low, with supple gold strings. The state's portion of the cost was a thousand pounds yearly at my full command and accountable to no one but the Queen Herself on the day before the Accession Day Tilts. She never challenged me, nor was there reason to do so. Not being lame of sense, I had clues that Walsingham had his spies follow after my men even as they purchased cloth, and so, though I was grandly given exemption from account, it was scarcely needed. I would complain that there

6

was not sufficiency in what She gave for what She wanted. She smiled. Though not enough, it was Her most generous dispensation and all She could give, She averred. This temper was but Her grandfather's passionate humour of meanness still peeping out at the edges of her cuffs and collars.

So I lived and wrote for more than a decade, silvering many mirrors to show all the masks of life. I grew ever poorer and ever richer. My riches? The occasional flash of a pheasant thick and soft as French velvet from the field. Just one perfect line from time to time – *The multitudinous seas incarnadine* – by which new life and flight and poetry and power would be bestow'd on poor Seneca's or Tacitus' awkward birds. It is no secret that all true poetry is not new but translation from without or within.

I've lived too long. My way of life has turned to yellow leaf. Old age should be accompanied by love, honour and troops. Of none have I enough. The thirst increases daily with the fever. How will it end? I have only the perfect word, the words, the dry words. They are cold and succulent as pearls and so must comfort me in my fever.

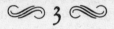

Soft then, here follows prose. The tide laps in, withdraws, returns. It's come at last, has it, to that rough shore? Perhaps this is the progress of every poet. I fear this maturity. Something of death wafts from prose. Yet were I fit I could wheel and go coursing after Montaigne perhaps. It is stuff, after all, for art like any other, and its manifest imperfections may be used to good effect as the Frenchman used his gall stones. So here sits my life at the water's edge scratching itself like a sullen bear who's escaped the dogs and is brought down by fever. Very well then – I hope at least there will be truths for me as well as fleas hidden in the damp fur. What needed two hundred sonnets I thought could be put fairly on a single scroll or two in prose. 'Tis the other way round. There is neither time nor parchment enough to do the job properly. How to describe all that has happened, all that has been thought all these years? On stage how often I let a character give lip-service to high ideals unbelieved, and those thoughts shadowed, burst into dark flames and consumed him. Here there must be no such distance between the thought and the word, no soothing rhythms, no fancy figures, just the truth itself. I see I seek any excuse to hesitate.

What man would not gladly see a beautiful woman naked? What poet would gladly show himself so naked? Now I shall draw the curtain and let you see my picture. Who, I wonder, are you? Not my wife, I trust. The false panel of this desk should see me secretly through this generation. Edward and Henry, sons and brothers unknown to each other, both skirmish in the Low Countries and might not live to be my readers, or care to be. When Francis and Horace return I'll give the desk to them with instructions that it be opened in a hundred years. They'll know to arrange it.

8

I must image you then myself: a recusant poet in some distant time and place, silent and not in favour in your monastery in Mexico or Bermuda or, yes, best of all, in ancient Andorra, the little country without history. Though well-born, your job perhaps is lowly in their sight, say, to sort old manuscripts. You bathe in papers and silence, and, not happy in your fate, what is there to stop you in your fancy from setting sail for a distant shore, which is your lost country and my fate? Welcome then, brother reader. You'd not have troubled to make the trip if there were not something for you here. Your English, really, is quite good. You are sympathetic but far off. If you are a lower looker-on, I shall not notice and pray you read forgivingly my own lesser moments. I'll hope some family elders once at least did pay to watch the tilts, and you were told in your childhood. Please to have some small smattering of our English blood or, if not, of our spirit will do. Let us have it thus: I shall assume you know and understand much, yet still want help, which I shall endeavour to remember to furnish you. If you know only half of what I say, that will still be a sufficiently sad and instructive story. I dally; it's time to start this tardy-gaited tale.

What is the very worst they say? They say he sent his patrimony flying. No, say rather that my whole patrimony was my father, John, the sixteenth Earl. There will not be a man like that soon again in England or abroad. Death took him early and so he lives evermore in my bright boyhood eye. Why should he change?

Henry fined my father's uncle, his most devoted noble, the heaviest penalty that any noble line of England had ever known except through loss in war and exile. That crack'd his life and our line for nothing. That was in 1498, before the title passed to my father's side. What was the fault of that Earl? That he hired two thousand retainers to meet their king in gay costume along the road. A fine opportunity to restrain his nobles from the habit of private armies, and how better to speed the message throughout the kingdom than to tax so your truest friend and loyal supporter?

My father spoke to me of that Henry's visit when he was arranging for the arrival of the young Queen to Castle Hedingham in 1562. All around us his men and women and their children were deck'd by the score in Roman garments and cloths through which the Essex sun shone so that twelve-year-old imagination could see behind those fabrics as he spoke to the even brighter hues and weaves of that other pageant, worn by thousands for love of the king. You'd have thought that fatal far-off day was the most ordinary one in our family's history. I recall not one sour word. His only judgement was, 'If our Majesty's affections be forfeits of men's estates, we must endure it,' which exact words came ready-coiled to the roots of my tongue when I heard that the Queen had died nearly forty years later. My mother, the only woman in Essex who did not love my father, scowled when he spoke of that Henry without rancour. But that indeed was my father. I am different. That unjust impoverishment is the first fuel beneath my flaming wrath. Though it had quietened, the historic flames leap higher as I die in shame, almost a commoner in my means.

He had a rotundity of love and warmth for his fellow man save that one dark spot at the centre, his wife. I had long passageways of love between poetic meadows and dark nights of the spirit. Perhaps we were not that different though. Three years before I was born he caused a breath of scandal to go throughout the kingdom when he had his players stage a farce at Southwark in February even while the dirge for Henry VIII was rolling out of all the wide church-doors of England. That was as near as he ever came to being critical. *It was my mistake*, he said, smiling like a hayfield at Summer solstice. I went with him by coach one June when I was very small as he visited the inn at Plymouth to watch a play in rehearsal. The system was the same. During the Summer months they played for fees in the courtyards of inns and then performed them somewhat more fair-acted at the castle in Winter. In theory the fees of Dover, Ipswich and Barnstaple would carry the company costs for the year. In practice, of course, that never happened. When the Queen died two years ago, I, too, was caught up in a tempest of writing and rehearsal, so the Lord Great Chamberlain was woefully unavailable to participate in the funeral procession. It was my privilege.

My life sailed between the straits of two Annes and two Elizabeths. Father's had two Dorothys and a Margery. His first wife died early, providing me with Katherine, a half-sister, and some stories. She was a Neville, of good birth, and they loved each other. The other Dorothy was but my half-sister's nurse, though not nurse-like in her bearing. I knew her well. That was the love of his life. She was no common customer, it will be understood, though it is said that she could go off and on easily like a glove, first cold and upright like a statue, then offering her body in intemperate lust while the servants still waited at table. The Nevilles were outraged at her low station and complained to Court that my father dishonour'd their dead daughter in his intent. The Nevilles chose to forget, let us suppose, that though they descended through Westmorland and Buckingham, noble homes, they had all the same popped a seam when they reached up to the de Veres. It seems they wanted still further social elevation even beyond the grave. The Earl my father was a well-horsed and gallant bladesman, but he was not sword-tongued and fell back before the kill-gentle scolds of the Court. There was no marriage, though I do not know how the story ended. I know only that my mother was always offended by any talk of any Dorothy and took but little time to return the insult when he died at end of Summer: she'd remarried before the pudding could be served at Christmas.

My father'd secondly married this woman Margery in Essex. She was the daughter of John Golding of Belchamp St Paul and the ceremony occurred in August 1548. The match took place after Lord Wentworth had withdrawn his daughter's hand from my Father, first freely given, because of just fears about the de Vere fortunes. The Goldings had been at Court, though in a modest corner, and had managed well through export of all the harvests of the de Vere and other estates to Moscovy. Margery had exceeded her family and become Maid of Honour to Queen Mary. The high Nevilles were thus contented for their dead daughter's honour, but only just. When I look in the mirror, I see an extra narrowness in the chin, a certain thinness in the mouth and my eyes are not set apart as my father's were. That is the Golding on me. But the mirror cannot reflect the blood that flows beneath, and that is the strong current of de Vere. My mother's greatest dowry was held for me in her brother Arthur, who, between his grain accounts, was the greatest scholar of Latin that England had and my constant tutor. I knew Ovid's erotics by heart when I was still a lad, and Uncle had permitted me to publish bawdy stuff in my English translation under his name and against his sister's pleasure. Ovid has been ever and always my first love.

In most things I had the finest master, the Earl my father. To learn to handle the hawk and the horse, to shoot an arrow that finds its roost like a rapid swallow, to follow the fox with superior craft, all this he taught me. And best, the special ritual of de Vere, to hunt the blue boar and stand calmly before its charge with the boar-spear ready. He did that. I did that, as did all my forebears, one even gored to death. The fighting de Vere spirit was steeled with this sport. The blue boar is our crest.

The sun was shining in the English sky when I faced my boar. The party flew with fear into thickets, while I idly waited for victory or death. The sky had never been so blue, nor blood so red, nor death so moist and close. The fields were merry and rejoiced then, and I was only sad that he'd not lived to see me do that deed.

In poetry and plays I've tried to catch those perfect early days in the country with my father but never could do it well enough. What hope is there now in fevered prose? He used to call me Hap, and I was happy then. I can see his horse and the blue scarf and his black leather back and the wind combing the grass in the meadows as we followed the hunt over the hill. But no matter how richly I image it up, it is a painting in my most private gallery, not the thing itself, nor of public use.

Did my father suffer the plague, too, then? I did not wonder, but think about it now. Though still out of season then, the plague was a prophetic visitor in those years on occasion. Of a sudden all the castle doors leading to his quarters were barred to me by servants. I railed against them on the stairwells, but they would not be moved. There were glimpses of their seriousness through the window-bars of their eyes. When I grew desp'rate, wild and furious enough, they called in Sir Thomas Smith. Though later he was Elizabeth's private secretary, he was then my chief tutor, with eyes severe as a swordpoint and a beard as formal as a battle standard. He bid me go back, and I went, bent over by years of his sarcasm and fear of adverse reports to my father: *Recite your lesson now for me, my young Lord. IF you have bothered to learn it*. On this occasion it was his kindness that disarmed me: *You will be called* was all he said in a strange soft voice. My mother was nowhere.

Still a wayward lad, I laid my plot with easy cunning. A roll of hemp from the castle keep storehouse was carried to the top of the western wall, and there was an easy escarpment by which to lower myself to his window. I could not be sure that the shutters would be open, nor could I be sure that the rope would reach the ground if they weren't. I came down the wall in lurches and burnt my hands through having remembered to get the proper boots but forgotten about the gloves. The shutters were open, and I found foothold at the casement of the chamber window. My father was in his great bed, from which all the curtaining had been piled up on the canopy like a cluster of coloured cloud, doubtless to provide better air. The strange thing was that I knew no one of the small crowd gathered round the skeletal bedframe.

Father saw me at once and raised himself up on one arm. His nose and cheeks were festooned with what might have been bloodsuckers. Doctors, then. Where would they all have come from? Father did not smile or reach out. In my horror I could not see if he shivered or merely shrugged. He said, *Honour snatch'd*, and watched the officious little men run together to the window to slam the shutters against me. The fools had lost themselves and thought they were in their surgeries, where any ass could poke its head in through the window. They'd have pushed the lad to certain death if it had not been for the rope around my waist. Cut by fate to leave not a spare thumb, the rope let me hit the gravel with force enough to tear my flesh but not my clothes. When I arose the pain was in my heart. My tutor was right. I should not have seen my father thus.

Through all my life there has not been a month in which I have not dreamed that dream. Half-dreaming, half-feeling, I come to the end of my rope, and then I fall through the ground, with my father standing at the window of his chamber in the castle, which ever floats above me, and I fall again, and I fall again. There is no end until I wake. My father shrugs and notices nothing strange to see his son fall away endlessly, while from the sky come leeches like leaf-sized shiny black snowflakes. They arc always back and forth too slowly ever to touch me. And besides, it's always Summer in the dream. The dream has rubbed away the reality, until there is almost a comfort in the friendly old horror. After all, I know how it ends; I am always safe. The ground is always pitiful and hurts me not. The rope begins to twist and turn into a whirlpool that smells of vinegar and clove, and then I wake. The dream is but the rehearsal for a day. On all the other nights I dream of him as he really was and wake with some vexation that 'twas a dream and flat.

There was a happiness fell close to madness. Best leave it stored in the silence of the past.

The servants informed me that my father's wife was gone the night before. Was she a prisoner or a guest at Castle Hedingham that she left so quickly? Good lady Margery, she did go! Whatever the reasons there was a lack-love both for her husband and her son. Dear reader, believe it.

# 4

I became an elderly lad that day and was indeed lord of the castle for most of the week. It was little bother to summon up seven score fine horse. I allowed only those with well-developed chest, not too wide or too deep, with a windpipe full and loosely attached to the neck. The fetlocks needed to be large, the pasterns strong, the barrel deep and straight. I could have had more had there been time to dress them, but there were not enough sempsters to be had at any price. You would not have thought there were so many shades of black, but that was quickly turned to advantage as the different hues of dark cloth were blended to make trims and crests as though of different colours but still of black. The meadow was dotted with horses and tailors fitting the funeral coats to them.

Messengers came to confirm the death from London and were surprised that the burial was not to be at Essex, and that the procession was in fact near ready to come to the Queen. I'd worried that the Queen would not see fit to come to Colchester, and perhaps I sensed that Castle Hedingham would not be hallowed ground for him. For myself, when once gone, I never returned, and of all the many Oxford lands I ever sold, it was that one I disposed of most lightly.

There were two-score Old English Black Horses, half of them on suffrance, and six of the best of these pulled the funeral carriage, which was all draped in cloth and had no driver. I led them from father's horse alongside. The Blacks stood seventeen hands tall and were as massive as they were intelligent. No hand was needed on the bridle. Only a dozen Pages had to be in train. Following them came a lesser number of Scottish Clydesdales, still massive but slightly smaller and not all of them were black. The numbers had to be made up of Yorkshires and Cleveland Bays, some of them chestnut but most with either black legs or heads. No horse was smaller than fifteen hands.

On the carriage there were large bunches of dark rubied cherries sewn into clusters like grapes on beds of broad purple leaves, for father had once told me in jest that he'd have his coffin thus draped. As we marched slowly to London I watched the faces of everyone to see if anyone would dare laugh at the fruit, but, though some did point, the procession met with courtesy and respect enough even through Ludgate and Cheapside. I remember those places as a boy barely able to see through the carriage window when the strumpets stood at the kerb and flipped their skirts back over their heads to display their wares and good-humoured contempt. Word flew ahead of us, for when we reached Whitehall, the Court seemed camped outdoors on the steps, and soon the Queen Herself came on to the top landing, which was no ordinary thing. I knelt before Her on the steps. *Sovereign, I have brought my father to Your care*, I said.

*O, little Lord Oxford, it had been much better to wait*, She told me and bent to kiss my cheek. I flushed with anger, and She kissed me again. Even in my grief it was painful to be so kennell'd in my youth. Until I saw the glist'ring in Her eyes and cried myself. She assumed Her regal tone. *We shall condescend to care for you and your dear father. But first We would that We review'd your horses.*

Though the Queen's fashion was for carriages, She followed Her father in love of riding, and no one who was there will soon forget the grace with which She rode on pillion to St Paul's. We talked long into the afternoon about the virtues and particulars of the Old English, or War Horses as she called them. *Now they peacefully plough the fields*, She said, *but wait patiently for the sound of trumpets again. Glad We are to have them, but let them stay at work awhile. Rooms are being prepared for you. We expect to have your company at Court. If all my Earls behav'd as you, England would be an even more difficult kingdom than it is.*

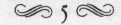

## 5

I see that I am not mastering my task, this fierce abridgement of my life, which grows too many circumstantial branches. To pause then and drink the old conserve of rose and hazel-nut. Let it expel raw humours and venomous vapours while I keep myself in bed. My loving wife Beth attends to all but at a distance, a distance that I myself have purchas'd. 'Tis bitter cold in my heart, which is pulling like a lodged anchor at my pen. When I am better, I shall again pick from the worm-holes of long-vanished days. I've said too much already, though there is much I still have hidden. Words fly up, thoughts remain below. The rose begins at red, it peels to purple, then to black. When will the last petal come? That's now not such a hard riddle to crack.

I was first three months at the Court and liked it well. My country skills were good enough to pitch my price quite high among the beauties of the chamber, who noticed the fancy of the Queen with my wit and dancing. There were fresh cups, sweet words and finally soft beds. After some weeks I had bed-work with two comely young Ladies of the Chamber, each of whom thought to seduce and teach me. Though I'd then had only one lass at Earl's Colne, and that but once and not long ago, they seemed abash'd that one so young was yet no innocent and more when each discovered that she was not alone in attending to my education. Both were long-legged and large-breast'd. One did not bathe overmuch; the other, whom I liked better, was always fresh and sweetly oiled, and her enjoyment had less calculation. She is now a grand dame of the realm and well deserves her renown, say I. To whisper and jump at night and otherwise pretend indifference at sight. Thus did I quickly become a polished and well-refin'd courtier.

My tutor was brought to Court but paid less attention to me

than to the Queen. His scholars knew less of many subjects than I, save the Italian Guido, with whom I spoke for hours every day and learned much. The Queen's Italian was also near to perfect from her youth, and towards the end She would pass side comments to me, playing Her own satiric jester in front of those who stood before her but could not understand the tongue.

On the first of November I was told that my mother was marrying secondly. I heard it as a good joke but guessed it was not. The will had not yet even proceeded to the Crown. Her bridegroom was Charles Tyrell, being a mere Gentleman Pensioner, as he was the last of many sons of Sir Thomas Tyrell, our Essex neighbour. This Charles was well known in the shire for his scandalous marriage with Agnes Odell, a queer woman whom I remember well, large-handed, her face over-larded with dun powder, and having massive legs and hips that gave unneeded buttressing to a bony trunk, and narrow head with scarce sufficient room for little eyes and nose. The poor woman had not one good feature, and yet she always had a sneaking smirk of self-assertion and unwarranted superiority, to what or whom one could scarcely guess. They are a deep mystery, these shallow people of such smugness. Tyrell was more pleasant in several respects but had learnt her smirk. There was a tale that had one of them chasing the other around his manor house with a knife, though it remains uncertain who held the knife. No matter, he soon lost the smirk and their marriage was annulled by the Court of Delegates. King Henry imported Eastern divorce to England and in recompense cast out wine-making when he crushed the monasteries. Tyrell was having profit from both circumstances since he strove to fill the holy breach by cultivating vineyards. There was not much promise in his project since the proper ways and best bushes had perished, but there was some gold to be harvested in copper grains for quick sweet wine dispensed directly into the villagers' hogsheads, and perhaps my mother had hope of that in her connection. Theirs was a sweaty haste without purpose though, for in not too many years they raced each other to the grave. Our claret was once as fine as any to be found in France or Italy, but now a bowl of good wine in England must flow from a narrow-mouth'd bottle brought from other shores. Our English onion bottles are not good enough.

One other bit of good cheer I had that November. The Queen, who seemed to know as much about my situation as I, told me that it was my father's wish if he deceas'd that I should reside with his good friend William Cecil. That proved that my parents' rift had been long in place and not of the moment, and that I was my father's son. Cecil had never pleased me as a boy, though I could never lay hand upon a reason. His double-warmth early pushed me back and finally caused a chill in me. When he came to Castle Hedingham, I would flee to my kingdom in the keep. With his robes and furs even in warmish weather, the man look'd to a small boy like a cargo ship, sufficient to be looked at from a distance. It was not till many years later, as Lord Burghley, that it became clear how much he co-actively also ruled England.

He was Her man of management all his days. There was no denying the sense of Her proposal, which, after all, began with my father, who, no more than I, was never entirely successful in his friends. What a prolixious man that Cecil was. Though he was the substance of several living statues in the plays, he was the only model I ever had who defied my powers of memory. Often I had to dart out and note down his wondrous silly phrases. Was this really English he spoke, or Hungarian? I had him best I think in Pandarus, just as he once berated his daughter in front of me: *Well, well! Why have you any discretion? Have you any eyes? Do you know what a man is? Is not birth, beauty, good shape, discourse, manhood, learning*, mummery, mummery – I'll find that later – *and youth the spice and salt that season a man?* One understands every word and some general thrust, and yet it would all fly away like musty weed seeds in his wind. I don't remember too clearly how I first heard him when I came to live at his various houses. Doubtless as a well-meaning man with some secret disability.

Cecil was more intelligent than his words showed and made a stellar career of his queer blend of craft and devotion. The root of his life's tree was the charterhouse he kept to shelter the nation's noblest orphans and those who'd been safely rechristen'd in the Tower. The Keeper of the Wards. His most illustrious pupil was, of course, the Queen herself, who was released from the Tower to his interim custody at Hatfield House. She told me that while there She still signed all her letters Elizabeth Prisoner, and yet there was peace and comfort in his keeping. Rumour has it that he fought wars to get Her, though it was only proper since Edward VI had also sat there awhile awaiting His Accession.

She observed how deftly Cecil served his present and his future together. He, She said, was the first to treat Her as his Queen, while an [in spite of A.F.] shows of personal distaste at the task, he nevertheless had Her followed everywhere she turned, and every word She spoke was listened to from behind curtains. These skills pleased Her then, which later made me mad-brain'd. Here for Her needs was a courtier who could serve two masters and be false to neither. A wonder of nature: *We saw that if We learned to stay him, We could both rule him and, when We chose, let him rule for us with safety, which is a rare comfort to any ruler.*

To my eyes now he was a damnable both-sides rogue, who made honesty go abed with soft exactions. An opportunist at the first and to the last. He and his lackeys gave competition to the wind behind the curtains. Low benches on stumps were everywhere installed behind the curtains in both manors to let, said they, the air through and prevent mould and damp. To prevent the shoes of the spies he sent from poking through under the hems, 'twas.

So many of my early years were so curtained that I draped my plays with them. Not just Polonius but murderers and saucy Falstaff, all stood before or behind the arras. I, too, was caught behind bed-curtains, but of that in a moment. Shall I speak now of Walsingham? No, 'twould strain the floor of any stage to have them both attending one another at once with silver basins full of flowery lies and useful notes. Shortly. I'll grant that England's avoided civil war for some forty years, but it's been a peace effected by a war of spies and crawlers. All hail to Lord Burghley and Secretary Walsingham. Their pain-beguiling sport could bark the honour from the trunk of any man. Were a life under twenty locks kept fast, their spies and lies broke through and pick'd them all at last. Calumny comes from behind in white hate or for puny gain, and no mortal can escape it. Is there sash enough to tie up all the slanderous tongues of England? These new men are the knights with great belly of our tin and pewter age. England will both survive and perish of just such men.

## ∽ 6 ∽

I've been speaking in my later voice. To be honest, I first tried to love Cecil, failed, and then even tried again. That is my principal fault, that I am cramm'd full of impulses that are strangers to each other. Divide one man into a thousand parts, and there I am. When I speak there are seven other voices with prompt-books bidding me to say it differently, hissing me for a moon-calf and a knave at once.

Cecil purchas'd my affection quite amply, for those were still his generous days. The best tailors of London came in a steady trot to chalk and pin me up with habiliments and haberdashery from Italy and France. In truth my father was not better arrayed. Only in time did I learn how the payment was arranged. My costs, including clothes and every mouthful that I ate, never less than hundreds, sometimes a ripe thousand pounds a year, were set by my guardian against properties. He did not exactly steal the money, but a piece of land might be mortgag'd below its true value and tied to other sales of Cecil's own and more to his advantage. It was in this way that the second slide of lands fell away from the de Veres, mostly to Leicester.

The rest involved no money, simply a personal lien against the land or village done both by and to my guardian's own name. The trick here was that I would bring a dowry to his daughter when he'd snar'd me, as he did indeed. For when the marriage to Anne was being settled, Cecil promised more dowry than he gave and then shar'd the considerable cost of my boyhood caps and boots from that very middle sum. I think he liked me well enough for what I was and for his daughter, but what he really wanted was a high-born noble name for his family. Though he was rich and stood beside the Throne, the best that he could see looking over his shoulder was a father who'd grown wealthy in parliament and a grandfather who'd been a sheriff. And after that the woods grow thick. He wanted his daughter's husband to be high-born but was cunning enough to strive to limit the freedom of spirit that accompanies such station. I was to be not so much married as annex'd and at a thrifty price, too.

That meanness was a strong bond between the Queen and Her High Treasurer. 'Tis said that when he became Lord Burghley and succeeded Powlet to the Chancellery, he grew more peevish about money and at last fully distanc'd his reputation for mild temper and discretion. But I was there from early days and can give witness: he never changed – the matter simply grew more evident and could no longer be conceal'd by purposeful extravagances.

The Queen would later jest – I did not laugh – that She and I were rare graduates of England's two finest universities, Hatfield House and the Tower. It was a queer joke, since She had sent me to both places. She reminded me that, while waiting for Her Crown, She had chosen to lodge again in the Tower.

*We were different sorts of prisoners though. You were Prometheus with the torch, I rested on the cliff-face. My motto was* video et taceo. *I did not say all that I thought there, though I never said anything I did not think. My main lesson was Cecil himself. To grasp how this good Catholic supporter of Queen Mary would be a stalwart Protestant for Queen Elizabeth. What I envy you in your time was the Latin, for you had Golding, whereas I was more fluent than my poor teacher, Ascham, from the beginning, and so now I fear that I may speak false Latin and be laughed at by the scholars. I am cross that I was confin'd to Caesar and Livy.* In this way She would reminisce about both our childhoods, saying that memory of those days filled Her with melancholy. In truth it was Her French that was very bad, because, after all, She had been taught it by an Englishman and thus spoke the language with a ridiculous drawling accent: *Paah Dieu, paah maah foi.*

The financing of Princess Elizabeth's stay at Hatfield House was a curious thing. It could not be done as it was with me, of course. Cecil solved his problem and dispensed some favour by allowing Leicester to give Her many gifts. As regards those two,

Cecil and Dudley, I never could get to the bottom of their common purpose. I know that Cecil frequently instructed the Purvey of the Queen's Goods to supply Leicester with free stone and wood for the work on his many mansions, but I cannot see quite who was the cat and who the mouse in this game.

The Earl of Leicester was the most obnoxious in his private character of all who were shown favour by the Queen. It was he who brought the low craft of poisoning to England. All, including the Queen, finally came to suspect him on good grounds of the most shocking crimes, which he, however, long affected to conceal under high pretensions to piety. I did use him for my plays, and not once. Later, when She saw his face full-on, I would tease and tax Her with it, and She defended: *We only showed him favour because of his goodness to Us when We were in trouble during the reign of our sister. Remember that he even sold his possessions to provide Us with funds.*

*It was a good wager,* I'd say, and She would frown. She kept me near Her at the end to make Her frown, as once I'd made Her smile.

But Leicester, for all his other sins, does not stand in the line of those who helped stage the marriage of Edward de Vere and Anne Cecil. There is a school of thought which holds that my cousin Charles Howard did some stair-work to put the match together, in part out of one of his queer humours, in part in shrewd calculation that that match would be the best means to limit my favour. I can't know if and how Howard might have been involved. I do know that the whole lot of Howards have been the most difficult relations imaginable, sometimes too likeable to cut, but too mischievous to bind yourself with, for they were the falsest cousins that ever blood made kin. Charles Howard was a scoundrel. Perhaps he was in it. There are many ways and humours by which men hurt their enemies and their friends.

No, the main culprits were myself and Cecil working against each other but in perfect unison towards the same end. He gave signs that he smiled upon another match, with Sidney, when he was fifteen and she thirteen, and that was enough to focus my attention upon Anne. Which he well knew. She ran away from me, but I'd now wager it was also a careful instruction, if indeed she even needed that. The little bird looks to sing as its parents show it. My only true, though unknown, ally in my own best interest was venomous Mother Mildred, who always hated me with a true passion because I would not play the ward. In opposing the match, to appearances he mollified his wife and still had his way. More than anything I wanted to see the wares and ways of Europe and was being restrained even then. Here was a way to have parental leave to be abroad. My youth was nimble but too truant and too calculating. Let Cecil and Howard and even Anne stand aside, the blame for it belong'd to me alone in the end.

## 7

Their trap was twice set in bed-curtains. The situation was each time worthy of great stage business, but all in all so very painful to me that I never used it in a play, though several times I prepared to set a bed and did not do it.

The first time was our first assignation, late at night in a bedroom in the guest wing at Theobalds when her parents were away in Surrey. We each had well-trusted Pages and Maids as sentries on our way to the meeting. She was already on the bed but not between the sheets when I drew the curtain. Her knees were folded under her to the side and with her long dishevelled hair there was something of the nymph about her. It was a promising start. But I realized suddenly that she had come along all those long halls in just her night-gown, and that gave me unexpected pause rather than passion, for it was as though she'd grown confused like a child and turned the wrong corner on her way to nightly prayer.

*You've come, magnanimous mouse*, I said, for mouse was her pet name, and placed my hand within her gown.

I have not yet said that she was pretty. There's no denying that, and I was crazy with the thought of her for a time. Later I was astounded at the short season of that blossom, though it did last long enough to make the Queen jealous and sorry She had allowed the match. Anne had the zest of youth and a conviction that flew backwards to find pretexts. Her smiles came out of place but with such sunny assurance that they season'd their own reason. She was passionately in love with love, and the game of danger provided good nurture. I am unfair again. The love was real enough until it was taken to bed. The worst I shall say is that she was very young at the beginning and the end and never managed to fly from the nest.

Here is what happen'd. Without a word she turned into me and thrust her breast into my waiting palm. She was in a cold sweat, alarumed even for a virgin. I could not see to the end of this adventure but had not an instant longer to wait. The curtain swept back, and there stood Cecil with three attendant servants holding large candelabra behind him. O no, he was not in Surrey. Time went elsewhere for that moment, and flick'ring fairies danced in fright around the still bed. I still had her little dug in one hand, while the other rested on an exposed thin waxen thigh. And there was I, in a mouse-trap.

Immediately Cecil began his strolling judgement with attendant candle-bearers and the mouse-of-virtue-still-clad-but-in-tatters running behind us.

His daughter was young, wise and fair. Though I disclaim'd her lack of pedigree, he said, that is for all intelligent men a foolish measure of virtue, and anyway she soon would share my family chart. There was much more in that vein without a single syllable of reproach. His gist was of the wedding, and would the Queen approve? Then suddenly Mouse-Anne shot forward, doubtless worried by my wordlessness to proclaim like a merchant at Wednesday's town market: *And will you, nill you, I will marry you! Marry you! Marry you!* she shouted at the end. Everything about her said slave to her parent, and yet she feared her master's weakness in the deed and so exceeded him in the heat of her frenzy. All this in the presence of the servants who were there to bear witness as well as tapers.

Spurr'd on by this outburst he began to threaten me as though I had reneged on my obligation and my honour, though I had still not said one word. The scene, in truth, was interesting, and part of me withdrew for safety to watch it as spectator. I must smother my disdain or be thrown away from his protection for ever. I must marry or reap revenge and hate loosed upon me without a pinch of pity. Such possibilities loom'd very real I will confess.

*Speak! Thy answer!*

*I'll take her hand* (at this Mouse-Anne rushed forward) ...

27

*formally and in due course.* I swiftly withdrew my hand from her grasp and rushed off to my bed in horror, pursued down the hall by the shadow'd frenzies skipping along the walls. There is one thing more, but later.

The marriage was in the week before Christmas, 1571, at Hatfield House. I was twenty-one, my child-bride, fifteen. The Queen attended but did not smile much. Her two brothers were there, the nouveaux first Earls of Salisbury and Exeter, to watch their sister snatch the young and ancient Earl. Sidney sulked. About Mother Mildred, I need not write. Lord Burghley was relieved his job was done. The Howards were gay beyond any guessable cause. Anne cried and smiled throughout the day. I accepted my fate. What was I to do? Bolt away into the hedge-mazes of Hatfield's gardens where Anne and I had often hidden innocently three years before? It was a fine wedding, and I was Edward Prisoner still and again.

I'd been in all nine years in his care. Perhaps it was the finest school, though that could be lean praise if you think of all the others too attentively. Sir Thomas ran his noble orphans like an army camp. It was up in darkness for a cold bath, followed by dancing lessons until seven-thirty on the Dutch clock. Only then was there breakfast, also cold and often dark. From eight to ten it was French and Latin, and then rhetoric and drawing until prayers, followed by a better lunch, though there was still only time to chew and not to talk. From one to two we studied cosmography, for some years with the celebrated Dr Dee, which taught me to rely upon myself more than the stars, though I eventually had use of those lessons as well, and one never had time to entertain disdain in his sharp-witted presence. Then two hours more of language, this time Latin before French. Fortunately, I had the French and so had the time to contend with my Uncle's harsh demands for Latin. I devis'd a simple system of hands on my coat that aided floundering Rutland with many verbs and declensions. In time I mastered most of the poets and historians. Then calligraphy until it was time to dress for dinner at five-thirty, which was but another hard lesson of wit and manners. Four hours for preparation of the next day's lessons and to bed before midnight with all one's manuscripts, books and dancing patterns laid by the Page at the ready for the next day's Star Chamber.

The sweetest was the last, Saturdays and Sundays, when we hunted and learnt, too poorly I saw later, sword-play. For a time Sir Thomas introduced Greek on Saturday morning, but it interfered with the hunt and so none of us acquired more than parcel-Greek. In Princess Elizabeth's time the Greek was better. Sunday's music lessons, which came directly after chapel, were also not to the highest standard. Our music teacher was dispos'd to triumphant displays, a deep-seated fault still present when the Queen played the virginal in later years. She would thwack the keys competently but as though beheading all the jacks.

I am dying and pause to play critic of the dead Queen on the virginal. The right side of my face is laced with lumps within, my head and body burn while my feet are icy. Otherwise I have some woes but no complaints. The eisell seems to have little power over the tides of pestilence, but I keep drinking it for want of any better. I train myself not to look at the sores on my body. My blood is ink. I'll lock these papers away and take repose in hope of greater strength to start again tomorrow.

Taken in a sweep, that was how I spent nine years. Though I do cavil at him in all other ways, I give the man this: he had me trained to the standard his friend my father would have wanted. The houses shifted often – Hatfield, Theobalds, Cecil, Audley End in Saffron Walden – but the only real interruptions to the scheme were the yearly manor-cleanings for Hatfield House and Theobalds, near to one another a comfortable day's journey from London, which had to be evacuated of man and bed for several days each year and smoked to drive out the vermin and unlicens'd rats just as we used to do at Castle Hedingham. They were vacations from routine. These smoking-outs were timed mostly not by season but before the visits of the Queen.

I went to Court, but Court more often came to us. Cecil had the Queen for protracted visits at Theobalds in Waltham every year save one while I was his Ward. The royal progresses would last from three to six weeks on average, and it can be said precisely what they cost because Cecil went about in an ecstasy of moaning o'er the costs.

*This visit*, he'd say, *will cost me two thousand pounds, or even three, but my love for my Sovereign and my joy to entertain Her and Her train is so great that no trouble, care or cost is too much provided that all is bountifully done for Her recreation and content. It is surely a minor matter if these freely accepted duties lay financial ruin upon me.* And more in this spirit, delivered without prejudice and at length to everyone from coachman to Privy Councillor. He did it well, in fact, so much so that the Queen would arrange to receive embassadors and foreign delegations at Theobalds. There were ways in which Lord Burghley's entertainments exceeded those of Court, largely thanks to the acres of fine gardens, which offer'd a dozen stages for masques, shows, devices, plays and tilts. It would happen that an entertainment was planned and constructed in secret, so that the Queen would be surpris'd and amaz'd by the actors or musicians standing ready to start from the moment she appeared at the planned point on her walk. *The old fool,* She told me, *I knew his plan whenever he announced a rest day and then offer'd to take me for a stroll to see some Italian statue or plant from Africa newly install'd. But I'd pretend to be astounded and in truth was almost always delighted.*

She knew the dangers to Her realm in drama, and She tried to remain cold-hearted to it, but in the end She had to make peace with Her passion. When the plays ran, I would not be held to my lessons.

Cecil knew Her temper and always kept things within those borders. What She most detested was the taint of flattery, or, rather, She wanted it as much as any woman but cleverly concealed. I was with Her at the fulsome masque arranged for her by Essex. At moiety She gave a swirling upward signal with Her hand and left the show with Her entire retinue muttering aloud, *If We had known so much was to be said about Us We would not have been here.* Never before and never since, I think, has an entire audience exited a theatre in such fashion. The players became statues with slack jaws while poor Essex's mouth was so tight that he appeared to have only a wrinkle above his beard. Could it be, I wonder looking back, that Essex began to go down from the time of his shabby masque?

Eliza did not use many words, but She did not fear to voice Her power. I heard Her twice stop the players as they shouted and waved their arms in windmill fashion. I fought that same battle in rehearsals for many years and rarely won. And once She even shouted out at St Paul's when the sermon seemed to slide into matters of Her manner of governance: *Leave that alone! To your text, Mr Dean! To your text! Leave that!!!*

To my own text. I still slip away from the main things, though 'tis curious that I have more vivid remembrance of the peripheries of my past life than of the centre. What I must show is canvas that is rolled and cracked and dusty. I feel my cheeks cool and my hand quicken, on the other hand, as I think of things past and to the side. The darker story looming can wait for the morrow. One never knows which insignificant memories will lodge and grow gigantic as we remember, though they stay petty still. My writing becomes as bitter as my medicine.

I loved the Queen best when I was still a lad dancing before Her and even with Her at Theobalds. Her head was heraldic then, with its dawn of red hair over two emblematic jewels and a scimitar mouth when the turns amused Her and She laughed out loud. I remember well how strange the desires stirring in me felt when we first danced. I remember the intensity of Her eyes.

Dancing was then the greatest of all my skills, and it was not too much work to outdance the entire Court. That is not to boast, for Cecil had brought Arbeau, Europe's greatest dancing master, to Theobalds for nearly a year. An evening would invariably begin with a stately processional played to bass music, which would pass to lighter and then more vigorous dances. The festive sonorities and musical pulsing would continually grow until finally the very finest dancers came forward for the bravura dances with swords. Not always but occasionally there followed the Volta, which the older courtiers never liked, claiming that its swift closeness and leaps were a danger to a virtuous woman's honour and health, even though the Queen would sometimes wink and dance it Herself. She would have little breath when I turned my last neat *révérence* towards Her and the final oboe's reedy and pungent note trailed off sonorously.

Her flirtations were many, and mine was but one of them. She'd lightly given assent to my wedding but soon regretted it. Anne, who'd never sit in the Tower, was too much the toy in Her eyes. She was a girl, and the Queen had only recently felt the first slight drafts of ageing. She gave Her Treasurer's daughter swift dark looks when she spoke, trading like her father in homilies, too much and too brightly. When I was first in Court the Queen stroked my light beard and called me Peachfuzz, which was affectionate. When I was married, She stroked my beard and let Her long white fingers stay on my cheek, which was more than affectionate.

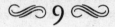

## 9

This was a time when I had two lovers of disputed title whom I neither loved nor touch'd, but each of them had great power o'er me. Was I Eliza's lover? I was not. She promis'd me that if I were not so contrary I could be Her king in all but name. We sat in Her private quarters and talked of Ovid. She'd excus'd Herself and vanished for the longest time. When I got up in perplexity and open'd the doors to the inner chamber, I found it was a small room, which contain'd nothing but a large bed and a Queen sitting on its edge.

*You're very slow, My Turk*, She said. *I've been waiting for you a long time*. She drew me to Her with flowing arms and kiss'd me deeply.

*Is there fear then in a Vere? I am a woman, too. Do not be shaken by your scruples*.

Her passion, however, was uncertain, for when after a moment's hesitation I reached to undo Her belt She gave a powerful shiver like a mare being led from her warm stable into a wintry night. I withdrew my hand, but then She kissed me fiercely once again. She spread her excellent soft armour wide and drew me upon Her, whereon I could feel Her works of love thrust and shift with great rhythm and passion for some minutes until She gasped for air and pushed me away violently. Then there was a comical popping of air, which I had to pretend not to hear.

*Are you not sorry now for what you've done?* She asked. It was a queer question from a queen in the circumstances. The part She'd played was in Her own mind and body, having little to do with me. She quickly recomposed herself, fixed Her clothes and strode into the next room, indicating with Her fingers opening like a fan that I was to sit beside Her at the parlour fire. No woman ever used her fingers so artfully or incessantly. She carried on reciting Ovid's love lines as though nothing had happened, which from

33

one point of view was perfectly true. As we parted She said: *Gratia mea sufficit*, and *Don't lose your head over this, My Turk.*

Essex bowed down for ever at thirty-four. He was the closest She'd ever come to a proper lover. He was the son of one of her most trusted followers and the grandson of one of her only true friends. They were close by blood. No matter. His head rolled, too, though it must be said the Queen let Her cup of exasperation overflow before She did it. Perhaps She had played with him for a decade as She played with me that once. Perhaps She did indeed die the Virgin, albeit most certainly not the Faerie, Queen. It's not for me to know. Essex died because the cloth that hid his lust for power was rent to ribbons. It did not help much that he'd wearied of the Queen's games and took Sidney's widow. That put Her in anger! But She had herself to blame. She made what I still think was a most sensible choice, but She chafed at the price as the years slipp'd by. It was good for the daughter of old King Harry the Eighth to say of the marriage that Her Ministers always were rushing to make: *I do not choose that my grave should be dug while I am still alive.* It was even better that She saw Herself, as once She calmly confided, fated to stay single, because Her mother had been beheaded by Her father, who then died pox-ridden. Why then did She not take a quiet willing lover like every other English monarch and noble has for six centuries? The willing part would have been easy, She said. She let herself be violated by Her own cult of Virginity. That would have been a play! In my dramatic scheme of things She was Herself only as a babe in arms in *King Henry VIII*, though hidden references to Her flitted everywhere like Monarchs in Spring.

I would not, however, write one line in open praise of Her alive or dead, though She and the burning questions of our time were never long absent from what I wrote. This was the invisible razor's edge on which I balanced and surviv'd unsliced, and this was why at Lord Burghley's order I became simple Shakespeare. What was poetry by Shakespeare would have been instant sedition by de Vere. Instead I came close enough to make the Court swallow gasps, and even She sometimes pulled back Her head like a swan. That was what She wanted of me and what I above all the men of England could give Her: calm art, boldness and indifference.

Twice I nearly went too far. Long after our clothed tussle I dared recast it in a poem for Henry Wriothesley, with lines as lewd as they were accurate. Venus pursues uncertain Adonis and proclaims:

> 'Fondling,' she saith, 'since I have hemm'd thee here,
> Within the circuit of this ivory pale,
> I'll be a park, and thou shalt be my deer;
> Feed where thou wilt, on mountain or in dale;
>> Graze on my lips, and if those hills be dry,
>> Stray lower, where the pleasant fountains lie.'

which, I daresay, affronted her less than the lines which went before:

> She would, he will not in her arms be bound;
>> And when from thence he struggles to be gone,
>> She locks her lily fingers one in one.

The other time was an open challenge when I confronted Sidney on the tennis courts before the Queen and dared to scorn him as a Puppy. 'Twas Her chamber name for him, She'd told me Herself. That was a quiet instant, but, as I foresaw, the waves would have been too great, and so the pond swallow'd the stone without a ripple. I had the tennis court by rank. His cheeks were redder than the richest curtain of Italy. Now I regret that dramatic moment, for it put a crack in the clear glass of the Queen's confidence in me. We were never quite the same friends again. But I was so tired of the Court, so very tired.

She was one of my pair of fatal maidens. The other was my wife Anne. Here's the thing. Cautious Cecil for once in his life moved too fast. I did not have my tarse in her. I was not her lover and refus'd her baby thighs even after we were married by design that was not mine. Her father, knowing that the marriage was not consummated, went to work afresh. This time the same mouse-trap caught me fast. I'd been observed to follow a strapping Yorkshire wench who watered the flower-beds. She boldly tucked her skirt sides up into her waist to save herself from splashing mud and freely showed her fine strong legs. Twice she caught me with pails of water when I came too close, but the third time she bantered gaily over our meeting place.

*Surely, milord, you'll not take me here in the flower-beds? The violets will blab. Strain yourself to find some shadier, drier place for your pleasure, milord.*

I picked that same deserted bed and found I'd loos'd myself on mouse-in-disguise instead. When I later cried that the child was not my daughter I was told that thus screams every courtier. But it was but one time and not set properly to produce the child that followed. There was a plot. Never does a wife run more passionately to a husband than immediately she has been unfaithful to him.

Thus began my time of troubles. I went to flee England without the Queen's permission and was stopped. I tried again with more success but lingered too long in one place. Travel had already been withheld for many years. When at last I had the Queen's permission to go abroad, there was occasion to send for me once again. I am sure that this time the errand was Leicester's rather than the Queen's or Burghley's. On the third try, and with Royal sanction, I was brought back by a message I was not expecting.

A fat little fool in a strange suit with a small ball of a belly and cushion lips stepped up to me and lisped: *My name is Nym, and Thidney loves your wife.* He affronted my eye as much as my ear.

The home of slander is always succession. I showed no anger to the knave, dismissing him with small coin for the beggar of other men's lies and lives he was. The news gnawed at me, however, and I ripped my trip and went back to France. It took me only four days to cross France, and another to be in England. Fury was my spur. Pondus and the mouse met me gravely at the pier. I swept past them darkly, and they had shame enough to stand back with lowered heads. Neither was game to indulge in bear-baiting, nor did I want to engage in light chat with a cuckold-maker and his double-dealing daughter. I went direct to Hampton Court to face the practised sighs and mock'ries of Court. Only my presence and scornful glances, I knew, would keep them in order.

The Queen was in good humour at this turn of events and showed me especial favour in every way. There was no trace of anger o'er my flight to France, or, if there was, it was wiped away by the presents I'd brought Her, the few that were left of many more that had been stolen. The custom was strong even in those days to present more jewels to the Queen than even Her horses could wear. It was artful and voluntary taxation but taxation all the same. I had a letter, written to me in vexation by my sister, who'd given Her a carcanet of gold with twelve arms and many intricately set small rubies and pearls. It was outshone by diamond buttons, nests of bracelets and a silly crane with opals, diamonds, rubies and pearls.

My gifts that year had no such value, and yet they brought unbounded, almost childish delight far above Her great gifts mostly destined to be worn once and given over to fatten the Treasury. I'd brought Her gloves of a sort She'd never seen. They were not of cloth but cut from the skin of unborn calves, pink and perfumed and softer than a rose petal, with tiny seams and artful slits to show Her fingers to advantage. There were cloth buds at the fingertips. She marvelled at their perfect fit. I'd had to buy six pair to be sure I'd have the right ones and had taken intelligence from a paid Maid when Her hands were being powdered and oiled. There were two bags of oriental sweets nearly transparent and smelling powerfully of mysterious berry essences that affected Her strongly, and a bouquet of roses done in silk with subtle shining craft. When I handed Her the bouquet whipped from under a silk cloth, She came forward and kissed me on the mouth with Her mouth still full of soft sweet like an amiable squirrel. My value at Court rose so sharply that all thought of slander was buried.

It had been in the Queen's intelligence that I was about to go over to the Spanish, which was an exceedingly foolish morsel of news that came from a double-dealer who introduced me to a Spanish agent and then reported me for knowing him. It was true enough that Norfolk's execution for plotting on behalf of Mary Stuart had placed me in despondency. He was my friend. He did plot. He ought not to have been executed when who in London was not accepting the favours and the company of the Spaniards and the French? I'll admit only that I had to know that my closeness to Norfolk and my natural Catholic sympathies would at the very least have meant a short conversation with Walsingham in the Star Chamber. England is a proper country, is she not? Then *of course* she must have her own *chambre ardente*, her own Inquisition Hall. That sped me on, but it did not cause my flight. All this I may write now without fear in the reign of Mary's son, King James. The bragging Spaniards I knew in London could never entice me, though they kept seeking me out as a noble known to be well-dispos'd to the true faith. Philip's claim to the English throne was absurd in its intent. If the Armada had prevailed and he had entered London, that would have been but the start of his troubles. To the scheming French I always said no. The de Veres took the side of the Red Rose in open warfare and have both paid and profited for it. We have supp'd in exile. But no de Vere has ever entered a shadowy conspiracy for foreign purposes.

Both the Queen and I had suffered from claims of illegitimacy,

She more than I, for I bore only taunts from the kitchen, while in Her youth She had been declared illegitimate by the Parliament and from the pulpit of St Paul's. The Spanish king and his embassadors referred to Her in no other way except Jezebel, daughter of David. Let us not wonder then that She was loathe to take too much joy in the issue of who would be the father of Anne's child. She refused later to entertain my suit to have the child declared illegitimate. The matter was not helped when the child was born and Cecil named it Elizabeth. But she could then feel much advantage in the decay of marital affection and added to it the unexpected gift of permission to go abroad again with Her letters of advice to the Courts of Europe, the constant dream, which had grown great-siz'd after the start of my first and near still-born tour.

It is clear that Death is coming, though not, I fear, post-haste. Rather its hired post-horses are dallying by the roadside. In these years they have been too well-fed to need to hurry every time. If time is going to linger, I shall stop here and start again. What I have so far written is not a virtuous copy, but I have taken the start and now can better measure my pace. Some things I'll strike, some insert. I'll stick like a burr to my premise, well-borrowed from *Troilus and Cressida*, and continue to provide:

> A story arm'd, but not in confidence
> Of author's pen; the tale is only suited
> In like conditions to life's document.
> Thus be warned, good reader, that my order
> Leaps o'er the vaunt and first things of the matter,
> Beginning in the middle; starting thence astray,
> It must then be digested in this way.
> Like, or find fault; do as your pleasure be;
> Now good or bad, 'tis the path that best suits me.

Time's order does not reign within our ears. Stories are but cups; time provides the spoon. I will take my cup and spoon from anyone. My business is with the liquid pearl and tear within.

First Anne and First Elizabeth have now been literatured. Ahead the two who meant much more. I'm spending too much ink on Burghley, but he was my very false father and merits my reply. How he whin'd to the Queen when I'd complain about him. It is still within me! Here is what I have to do. I'll try Castle Hedingham again, not yet quite destroy'd. My enemies accused me of burning it down to spite Anne, which was not true. There is my father at the boar-hunt in France long before I was born but as bright as the day he told me of it, and behind him the Aubreys, Ralphs, Williams and Johns, stretching back to Aubrey de Vere, baron of the Conquest, who was rewarded with the lands of Wulfwine in 1066. The long and painful dalliance with dark Anne, which I could not break – that must be faced full. The time in the Tower. The happy marriage with Elizabeth, of which I must not say too much because I have betray'd her already enough and will not do that, too. My sons. My daughters, less. How I fled England late at night, and the stages of my Grand Tour in the following year, 1575. My military expeditions. The campaigns against the Northern earls and in the Low Countries. Glory against the Spanish on the *Edward Bonaventure*. The public theatre at Shoreditch and environs and the private theatre at Hackney. My writing and my men and my boys. My changing faith and the plots against the Throne. The sale of lands, and my investments in Greenland and China. How favour slipped away quietly and closed the door one fine year. There is sufficient to show if I live a year, which I shall not do. Let me not forget to include a word on the perfidy of servants.

No. Once more I've whittled my list to my advantage. There must be provision in my art to unwhittle such caution. I'll carry each and every dead fleece of denunciation to the telling. How my boys were pirates of the road. Dreadful Arundel's false charge of buggery and why I really ran that boy through with my sword. Then how the frost of straitened means at last fell fully on the ground so that I could no longer support those who have supported me so well, till here I am, almost without servants and held from a distance by a loving wife, who watches the sorry spectacle from afar in the company of my best friend.

Almost all will be told. There will be no pedigree given to falsehood. I shuffle my honour with my necessity so that every colour will show clearly, independent of line and time. My tears turn dry, the ink still flows. With luck I'll see it through and countervail the knaves. With luck I'll be gone before the sorry tale is finished, and so it will not matter at all.

I see a simple chambermaid when I was in Sicily. I'd slept late, luxuriating in my returned good health, and was still finishing my grooming when she came to tidy the rooms. A lovely jug of flowers purple, blue and white had wilted sadly through the night. She laid them out on the slate tiles like soldiers on parade and picked off all the bruised and wilted petals. Then she gathered them, held them upside down outside the window and poured water over them. There was ice in her bucket, so evidently the castle possessed a straw ice-barn. She changed the water in the jug and added to it some honey from a phial. She took a small sheathed knife from her waist and cut off a portion of the stems. She took a drink from the bucket and, again holding the flowers at the window, she spat a fine mist over them so all the leaves and petals looked set in fairy pearls as the morning sun glinted on the bouquet and her young burnished skin. And finally, she unrolled a kerchief in which a spider's web had been carefully cut and laid flat. This my queen of curds and cream draped over the bouquet with a delicate but sure sweeping motion of her fingers, as though throwing a shawl around her lean shoulders, and the heads of the blossoms were invisibly held upright again.

I marvelled at the speed and the craft with which she worked. I did not know those flowers. Were they rare mountain blooms to be worthy of such work? I would have thrown them out, yet their weary new-webbed beauty outdistanced the easy charm they'd had when fresh. Was it the pleasure of resurrection she enjoyed? Here, my task, too. The clear call of a cornet, I recall, floated through the pale Sicilian morning sky. How I wish I were there now, and young and in her arms once more. I should have had more caution, but I didn't, and I'm glad.

Let us start with the buggery.

In the year of Our Lord 1567, some months after I had begun my seventeenth year on 22 April, three notable things happened to me, which were all interwebbed. Eleven-year-old Anne, pampered over her shoes by her father, who was having some difficulty spending all his money and so had given a trail of fawning servants to his little daughter, conceived a ferocious adoration for me. I treated her like a sweet but annoying pet, I treated her like a sister, I pleaded with her own sister to distract her, but the greater my indifference to her, the greater was her attachment to me. That was my first and still my truest lesson in the ways of all women at some stage, save my wife Elizabeth.

With Anne's adoration came my first spies, for Pondus at first had other plans. Perhaps it was even my fury at his goblins and bugs behind the curtains that finally drew me to the arms of his twig-legged darling. No, there was more to it than that. I was an orphan in his well-fitted mansions and very lonely. Such family as I had in those years was my friend Mouse.

With the adoration and the spying came the necessary murder. His name was Thom Bricknell, and he was an apprentice cook assigned to the blood puddings and sweetmeats, the odours of which tainted him. I sniffed him out in the still July air and motioned Mouse out of the chamber. An old wrought-iron fencing sword was hanging above the mantle. I took it down and waved it through the air like a sword. It made a wondrous swish, and the curtain began to stir uneasily. With my rapier I pulled the curtain to the side and faced Thom. He was arm'd with a kitchen knife and a face in which pure fear struggled with entire cowardice. But then his fatal mistake was to counter me too boldly with offers of glad news. If I would but spare him, he would share with me information about my father and my mother from the most privy files of Hatfield. The words were scarcely past his profane lips when the next phrase was frozen for ever. I leapt forward and pierced him short, quick and home. Rage moved in me like a mighty tide.

The charges that later Leicester and Arundel whispered against me were nothing but their own one common bond: little boys. They were, it seems, in competition to be chief rogue for Queen Mary, though it would be nearly fifteen years before Walsingham had full details of their deeds. Arundel's summit of achievement was his booklet against his villain-friend, which appeared first in French translation as *La Vie Abominable du Comte de Leycester* and then crossed the Channel more quickly than a Venus pigeon to be published in English as *A Copy of a Letter by a Master of Art of Cambridge*. That may have been a clumsy attempt to point authorship at me, because the first title was *Master of Art of Oxford*, but that was caught in time and changed. The episode showed me that the way was clear at Court to tell the truth about Leicester, and indeed he eventually made me a most excellent Claudius in *Hamlet*. As his speeches unfolded at its first Court showing, one could hear the knowing hisses rustle along the gallery benches: *It's Leicester, it's Leicester*.

There was inequality in their common ambition between Leicester and Arundel. Both Robert and Charles were nobles, of course, but Leicester was an Earl and Charles was but a younger son with no title and limited means; Leicester was handsome, though his evil eyes frightened women, while Arundel was both clay-brain'd and ugly.

The custom of choirboys had been in England for at least three centuries but fell into the realm of moral turpitude only in our time. Beautiful downy boys had long been culled from the common people in the villages and trained by elderly church musicians to sing the sweet old church melodies. Such boys were treated as keystones of the service and often lived with each other in considerable amity and luxury, lovingly waited on by austere monks, who taught them to play instruments, to sing, and to read and write Latin in a flowing hand. The boys would begin in the monasteries when they were about nine and rarely lasted past their fourteenth birthdays, by which time their voices had begun to break and squeak. From there they would usually pass to good guilds and professions or would be monks, musicians or teachers.

From the times of my father John an additional stopping station was added as many of the boys were apprenticed to theatre troupes, thereby opening the doors to having women's parts on the stage for the first time. For the best of these changeling-lads could outshine any real woman at her own game, as we proved on more than one occasion by planting one of them at a high dinner table, where he would invariably be fully accepted by the women as well as the men. Like the most alert little dog of the Court, the boys would watch and react to the tiniest facial gesture. Whilst from time to time a woman would play among us, as another joke, I never saw a woman play as well as the best of the boys until I came to see the extraordinary and well-trained actresses of Venice.

When I was a young man too often the beautiful boy player had become a mere item of trade. An aristocrat who wished to enjoy a boy would underwrite his apprenticeship to an actor, thereby serving several needs. The actor had a servant, the play had a woman and the noble, under guise of training the boy to play, had his pleasure. Leicester brought this practice to the very hem of fashion, and, when the boys were later scattered into the countryside as schoolteachers and choirmasters, he spread buggery throughout our land.

I recognize no impediment to love but also know that to love is not merely to co-join, and that it is tragic to trammel up an unripe youth. Thus did Leicester become toad-spotted and capable of anything, and thus were many young lives wantonly broken. It was only natural that Arundel and Leicester would transfer their cold-eyed unnatural lust to me in their rumours and denunciations.

The inquiry was composed of three marvellous good neighbours, all indebted to the Cecils, who duly decided that the cook had thrown himself upon my rapier after I'd discovered him in dishonest business. They did not call me to testify, though I had just begun my legal studies at Gray's Inn and was keen to have my word. Burghley sat with me in the corner during the proceedings and grasped and tugged me by the arm whenever I started. It was difficult to credit the masque they were enacting. Two false witnesses said they were in the chamber and saw Thom menace me with his rapier – imagine that, spotty Thom from the kitchen with his rapier! – and then hurl himself upon me, trying to grab my weapon. A more improbable story I never heard. Though I did not care about the law, I had my interest, because conviction in the slaying would have barred me from Gray's Inn and their dramatic revels, and the state would after all have been obliged to reckon me some punishment. Burghley had an interest, too, though I did not know it at that time. A verdict against me could well have brought the Court into the management of Burghley's orphan heirs, which would have benefited me in spite of any punishment I had to receive. Had I testified, the incident might well have rebounded on Burghley. But I did not see all the possibilities and was not resolute.

Bricknell reached for his knife and must have ripped apart his shirt as he did it, because one of the pictures I remember most vividly was his terrified quarter-moon smile hanging above his great defenceless belly. He was like a young dog caught in the pantry, which, despairing of the chance to run away, throws itself on its back and your unexpected mercy. *A rat! A rat!* I called out as I sprang forward. It was an ancient and heavy weapon, which should have had its last use long ago, for its tip was slightly bent and the edges of its bevelled blade were dull. Whether it was that or a misplaced lunge, it did not seem to me that my blade pierced deeply. I withdrew and sheathed it in his body one more time, and that, too, must have failed me. I could not remember how many times I struck him until I heard the satisfying tinkle of the lead window behind him. His every effort had been to hang on to the curtains. Later Burghley told me that I had put the blade in him eight times, and that would render me without defence in a proper hearing. I cannot speak for the eight strikes, but I do remember that his repugnant belly was gradually painted red and several places gave little spurts as he was hanging there. I do not know whether the body fell or was cut down in the end, nor do I remember if he made a noise, though I do recall his mouth opening and closing rhythmically like a perch on the pier. I knealt down and wept, not at the knave I'd killed, who was a born devil, but to what my life had arrived. *Wherefore was I born?* I asked myself then, and not for the last time, knowing that I was more than I seemed but fated to be much less than I was born to be.

## ∽ 13 ∽

My father managed to regain at least the favour if not the wealth
from Harry that had been lost in the time of Henry. After he had
assumed the Earldom and ceased to be John Bulbeck, he served
Henry VIII in the suppression of the first Northern Rebellion in
1536. He served Him so well and so bravely that he became a
favourite of both his King and his men. His double skill led him
to an awkward position as Lord Lieutenant to the Privy Council.
When I was a lad at Hatfield I found and copied from the library
a letter from Sir Thomas to Cecil in which the sixteenth Earl is
praised at his calling:

> I do assure you I think no man in England either in Queen Mary's
> time or any other could do so much and so readily with threatenings,
> imprisonments and pains as my Lord doth here with the love that
> the gentlemen and the whole country bear to him. Whether it is
> caused by the antiquity of his ancestors or his own gentleness or the
> dexterity of those he keeps about him, or rather all of these together,
> I think you could not wish it to be done better.

I treasure that letter as evidence of what no one in Colchester or
at Court ever needed to be told. Often it is said of someone,
*Antonio is a good man*, and that is always a warning. Which is not
to say that good men do not exist and are sometimes even seen.
What happened in his short term was that imprisonment was
always the chosen instrument over pain. There were copious
confessions but always terse and true. The realm was defended;
reason reigned. The public good was always held, which was one
of my father's few and firmest instructions to me: *Your king must
stand for the public good, and if that public good becomes too private,
withdraw with dignity and await another king.* My father did draw back
after some months, when decorum permitted, and served his

48

Essex for many years in strengthening the county's defences along the coast. It was England's weak heel when he started, her firm line when he ended. But the Star Chamber was evidently disgruntled that he'd left them, he told me. They ordered him to round up more heretics in Essex for burning. There were somehow, it appeared, fewer heretics to be found in faithful Essex than anywhere in England, at which they sent in their own heretic hunters, who swiftly excommunicated four thousand, and he was ordered by the Council to attend the burnings of the seventeen high heretics in Essex. That periodic witness, he held, was the sole toil and trouble of his Earldom.

My father remained a faithful subject and was one of the twelve chief mourners at the funeral of Henry VIII. He held back, however, from the coronation of Edward VI, because, he said, he did not like the smell of that new Court with its Council of Regents ruling over young Edward. He did not come forward to perform the office of Lord Great Chamberlain but said he would be content to perform its lowest office, to serve the King with water before the Coronation dinner as well as after. Yet he named me after Edward, which kept him away from trouble on the point. I am the first de Vere ever to carry that name. It was his way. Though my father never said so, it seems to me now, in my own circumstances, that he might also have judged that it was meet to effect economies at last and make the point of the parlous financial situation in which the cruel caprice of Henry VII had placed our line.

All the strife of later years, I hold, was sown in Edward's reign. The Protectors wanted to rush the Reformation along, but villainous liberality can always be expected to have its secret garden. They brought in the Book of Common Prayer and caused Catholic rebellion. They said they would brake the absolutism of Henry's time, and yet the destruction of the relics and sales of the chantries continued apace. The Scots were defeated, and yet they were allowed to continue and even strengthen their alliance with France. Somerset fell and Dudley became the reigning Protector, which meant one less head and still more damage. Catholics were expelled from Parliament, and an ignominious treaty was signed with France. Protestantism was supreme, and still the accession of the Catholic Mary seemed inevitable.

It was the dawn of queens in England. My father in June 1553 was one of the twenty-six peers who signed the Letters Patent settling the Crown on Lady Jane Grey, but after a month he saw her infirmity of mind, switched and was one of the first to declare openly for Queen Mary. He officiated as Lord Great Chamberlain and was at Mary's side in Her progress through London to accept the Crown, and it was he who placed it on Her head. For all this he had to suffer belonging to the Privy Council again, though at least he was able to avoid further service in the Chamber. In Mary's Council, my father was, as a Protestant, under considerable suspicion when Dudley began to plot once more. But his worries did not end when Elizabeth came to the Throne. It was not then my father's faith that Dudley worried about but the affection of the young Queen for him. Religion was the pretext. It was the same for me. In Elizabeth's Court I would be suspected of being always-wind-obeying in my faith but Catholic in the silence of my heart, which I was and am, and my father was, and I strongly suspect the Queen was, too. He came early to Elizabeth's cause, but it was not from selfish calculation or on matters of dogma. He saw that there was heavenly stuff in Her, the daughter of predecessors who knew how to deserve their kingdom.

The old order thought they had him horse-broken to their way when they summoned him very shortly after Elizabeth's Accession to preside at the trial of Lord Wentworth for the surrender of Calais, for it was he who had refus'd my father his daughter's hand. But he would not change his fair and outward character. Wentworth was acquitted and became my father's close friend and one of my guardian-trustees, a task, alas, he succeeded at no better than he did at Calais.

The Earl my father had his finest hour when he led four thousand men across the channel and fought victoriously in the front ranks at Boulogne in 1544. Though he was not the battle's great commander, there was agreement that he had been the king of honour on that field. When the peace was concluded, he was well received at the Summer Court in Paris and toured throughout the French realm for ten months. He told me that his heart would always look first to England, but that he could never forget that he had been happiest in that year in France. He went as far south as Roussillon, where he admired the wine and the exceptional independence of the people's spirit, being consanguineous with Spain, France and the old Moorish realm. Their tongues could switch at a whirligig rate, and some of the languages were gabble no one had ever heard. Soon he was able to drink with any of them in their own language and learnt many interesting things from them about Roman religion and Mediterranean life and how they'd learnt to keep Paris gently at bay. It was, he thought, like the merry little town of Sedburgh in Yorkshire on the borders of Westmorland, where my father had often promised to take me, a trip that was prevented by death. There they were customary tenants, quiet and industrious people who knew how to drink merrily and who'd had no need to keep courts these many years. My father lov'd such towns and shires and states of mind.

He spent two months living like a monk and picking blood plums in a monastery in the Dordogne region, which, he said, was very pregnant with Englishmen, clerics who'd fled from Henry's wreckers. He'd heard no word of such a little England-in-exile. The yellow'd monastery was a low, moated grange and yet built with the turrets of a castle, though it could not have laughed a siege of cats. After morning prayers he would pick plums with the monks until in the late afternoon they went with their pack of bonny little white dogs into the woods to root out black truffles, highly prized in France, though their reputation is as a tuber for chastity. Near-darkness was necessary to their task, lest their best troves be discovered. Then there would be a fine repast with much plum wine, plum liquor, plum sauce and, always, plum pudding. In the evening philosophy, religion and lost England would be hotly discussed. Such a warm kingdom, he held, should be an ever-fixed mark in all our lives, so that even if fate does not portion us to live thus, we may all the same measure our lives with sidewards glances to it. And now at last I am in peaceful Hackney, too, though plagued and not at peace.

## ∾ 14 ∾

Here is the brightest memory of my childhood. 'Tis but a tale oft-told to me by my father, but I requested it so often that I can set it down with considerable precision, which will only be to make public sport of what was public sport, though the telling of it now wants his laughing face. It was his last appointment before returning home. The Court had come to the forests behind Le Havre, as once each year they always did to hunt the boar, and my father was invited. He did not have to try to be eager, but he saw at once that there would be impediments. We English hunt in cloth and leather, while the French do it in feathered hats and gold-braided coats, with their women watching. Silent scouts have found the boars before the day and placed fences on all the paths save one on the morning of the hunt so that the beasts, when aroused, have only one way to run. The horns then sound.

The hounds are loosed not to discover the boar but merely to madden it, and, setting it roaring down the fatal path, a hurricano of dust and snapping twigs overwhelms the sound of dogs and the frightened birds, with their strange screams prophesying death. The French boar is smaller than his English cousin, but in compensation his gnarled yellow tusks are longer and sharper. The damp snout skims the surface like a fast-pitched ball, your fate rushes to you like a wall. But the Gallic way is not quite fair. Attendants crouch at the sides and thrust knife-edged poles in the path of the speeding earthquake so that he often trips and his forepaws are bloodied. At the moment of the coup three long poles shoot across the path and are grabbed by firm hands on the other side, so that the huntsman seated on his horse has a moment of perfect safety to do his work. A long, sharp and heavy blade between the shoulders finishes the frantic and confused beast as it snorts and tosses its head against the three poles. While the killing takes place a dozen noble women sitting on folding chairs on a raised platform nearby stage their own drama as they fall about with soft moans and passionate flute trills. They are caught in artful poses by their waiting Pages.

My father watched all this with great-ey'd interest. It was not a hunt but a theatrical pageant in imitation of the hunt. He expected the huntsman to sing a song or bow, but the reality exceeded expectation. The hunter took each fainting damsel in his arms and restored her to life with sweet nothings in her ear. The restorative process lasted nearly half an hour, longer than the hunt itself, and then four huntsmen from other fields returned with their boars, attendants and lookers-on to a feast spread on the grass on rich carpets. The huntsmen changed their dusty costumes in a striped tent and emerged in silken jackets and starched collars on which a too-red swath in semblance of blood was displayed.

It was to be my father's boar on the next morning before the Duke of Normandy. He was travelling without hunting attire, and besides he was not inclined to play their sug'red game. And so it was that on the pale grey morn he came to the hunt in his bedroom attire, wearing a very good dressing-gown but clearly nothing else but a dressing-gown, a fool's nightcap of soft wool and leather slippers with little boars' heads at the toes. More than that, he went a-field without his horse. The men and women were astonished. Only the Duke himself met my father with his usual subtle-witted smile. *He would not have shown himself to be less surpris'd if there were bird droppings flowing down my face.* The main jollity of his disguise was not his bedroom attire but his weapon, a thin dancing rapier whose blade wiggled like a grass snake in the hand. In fact it was a fine-hon'd steel death weapon made for murthering at the dance, which he'd bought in Paris to show at Court.

My father took his place at the point where the path from which the boar would emerge came out of the forest. He gestured to the men to lay down their long poles, but there was a quick conspiracy among the fearful French who had no desire to see a brave English Earl self-slaughtered while their guest. The Duke himself came down from the platform and motioned to the pole-bearers to stay.

He'd barely had time to say, *Good Earl, we cannot so change true rules for odd inventions*, when his Pages hustled him back to the platform in overlusty fashion.

They had set the boar to fly. Even from afar it could be determined that it was a deadly beast. Suddenly screams arose from everywhere. The boar had swerved into the underbrush to gore one of the boys by whom it was first pole-slashed. All abandoned their stations, and the closest ones came screeching from the woods. *Exeunt pursued by a boar*, my father used to say. At which, in fear of their own lives, the ladies behind my father now screamed in genuine distress and could not be quietened by the boys or the noblemen on the platform. They rushed to the stairs, thought better of it and threw themselves sobbing into a cluster, at which the platform began to sway and crack.

The while my father stood ready in his dressing-gown with his dancing rapier poised at the ready, a scarecrow on the field of God. When the beast showed, it was gigantic even for England, land of boars, and scythe-tusk'd. My father had time only to see its bristled hair chafed with sweat, the dark spot that the rapier must pierce if he would live. The thrust was cleanly and quickly put. The boar, very like a whale on ground, skidded to eternity but sent my father flying backwards with the force of the final impact. *It was a close thing. The ground was very dry. I was nearly sand-blinded at the key moment.*

For admiration at his feat, my father at first harvested snow. The spectators were on the ground together, having slid from the tilted platform like so many apples from a tray. The men were out of their element, except the Duke himself, and even he was mightily annoy'd. The women were most metamorphiz'd back to babes and cried pathetically. The scene waited for the wonder of the other returning huntsmen, who first saw the havoc of bodies and fear'd some bloody slaughter, then saw the dreamer still in bedclothes and the largest boar they'd ever spied. He told them he had killed a pig, a common skill for schoolboys in his land. *The ladies took no sweet nothings in their ears that morning, but the news did not tarry on its way to Paris and beat me to London as well.* The boar was carried to the King.

I had a father once called John and would sooner forget my fingers than lose my rights of memory to the kingdom we briefly shared.

I vaguely recall that I much tried but could not pry a single secret from my father's childhood. From my grandfather descend, besides my father, his grandsons Francis and Horace, commonly conceded the two most stalwart soldiers of our time. Of all the other five centuries of de Veres, by contrast, I heard enough as a boy to keep Hollenshed busy for months. I'll set down only some of them briefly, in my immature preferences. No forebear could exceed for me in romantic glory the thirteenth Earl, a seaward exile who swooped and stang every Yorkist port for more than a decade after certain victory for the Lancastrians became total defeat at misty Barnet. And then the final victory and return at Bosworth Field when Oxford brought the Crown to Richmond, our same Henry VII of blessed memory. That ancestor stood as godfather to Prince Hal in the Parish Church at Greenwich. The ninth Earl was slain by a boar in 1392, and John, the twelfth Earl, and his eldest son were beheaded by grumbling and suspicious Edward IV, both fates to chill and excite a young boy. The seventh Earl, fighting at Gascony with the Prince of Wales, had my favourite speech: *England will never pay my ransom. I shall either conquer or die.* The French fell before him, terrified of the barbed arrows of the English archers.

The de Veres were always in church or in battle, and either way they stopped to drink. Under the fat Conqueror the first Aubrey shouldered the task of establishing the new Norman vineyards. He laid them out with vines imported from the valley of Gaillon, already beset with the rot of taxation, at Hedingham, at Kensington, a gigantic vineyard at Belchamp Walter in Essex, and in Suffolk at Lavenham. The Hedingham vineyard lay to the west of our castle. When I was a boy wild vines that still bore red grapes grew there. I would work with my friend Geoffrey, the son of a first steward, in our own barn, so-called because it was rotting and abandoned wholly to us. With smooth round Viking mortar balls we ground the grapes, allowed them to ferment and strained the juice each summer through cloth into some light green-metal bottles from the glass house at Wealden, which we had borrowed from the kitchen. We would tie their corks down with stout string and leave them until next season. We learnt that though the grapes were slightly sour, they produced a *vin potable* provided only that the full contents of the opened bottle were drunk straightaway. Overnight the wine would be a mess of vinegar.

Once a year in September two tipsy lads would drink the wine that William quaff'd and play we were the valiant victors. Geoffrey always said that it was not his part to be the King, but I held steadfastly to Aubrey, without whom the Conquest would not have succeeded and who married the noble Beatrice, a rare beauty with but one defect, a huge misshapen foot. Yet he'd declared, my father said, a love of her that was *of hand, of foot, of lip, of eye, of brow*.

For me, the Veres, faithful and fighting, served only as a model for the inward greatness to which I should aspire but which would not be laid before me as a tithe from the past. I was also taught that, long before the crossing, our ancestors worked in a mill in the Contentin and owned no land. By virtue and good fortune the Veres were ennobled and the land where once they'd worked took their name. My father scorned the pretence that the family traced its way back to Charlemagne and Caesar. The Veres, he said, went on the pathway of nobility for eight centuries, which is enough, and never let their feet slip from it, though their lands were taken from them more than once. When Aubrey came in 1066, he discovered still-simple Veres who had already been settled among the Saxons for a hundred-plus years and took them gladly into the family trust. What has happ'd now to the proud chain? Is this the moment where chance has chosen to nurse or end it? I cannot say that I was pushed, nor that I fell myself. Simply, that it has occurred. Things at the worst will cease or else climb upward to what they were before for the children of my children's children.

˙That is the natural order. The story of our line seems to be that we are too high-born to be propertied for long. I'll die intestate. If words were wealth . . . , but they are not.

In my passing wisdom today I see myself in the ghost of the ninth Earl, where before I saw nothing except the glory of his death in the hunt. For his bravery and success in battle in Scotland he was created Duke of Ireland and held more honours and titles than any nobleman had ever gathered in England. But he grew insolent and dismissed his wife, Philippa, which set her uncle, the Duke of Gloucester, upon him with five thousand men. He was defeated where the Isis and the Thames meet. Forced to flee Gloucester and Bolingbroke, he threw down his sword and gauntlets so that he could swim the Thames. His tragedy was that he left behind letters from the King in a leather bag in his war carriage so the bellicose dukes came to know in detail the plans of the King, which were to flee with Oxford and surrender England's last holdings on the French coast to the French King that he might enlist the French to put down his rebellious lords. He was one of many convicted by the Merciless Parliament which the lords forced the King to convene. The sentence was banishment and loss of all his lands except, needless to add, those that were entailed. He ended, the family story has it, poor and bitter in exile. Question: how did such a bitter beggar come to the hunt? Was he killed, or did he walk to his death? I am too weak and 'tis too far for a demented fool to wander into the forest, with no retinue, no sword, nor even a proper dressing-gown.

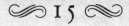

## 15

My father ceased his hermit habits when Elizabeth came to the Throne. No other earl was shown greater favour than he. The magnificent priory on Candlewick Street that Her father Henry had given to my father's father was lit with candles once more after years of dim glumness. What I loved best of all were the annual processions from Castle Hedingham to Oxford House. My father was always preceded by fourscore livried gentlemen of Essex county, all of whom wore chains of gold around their necks. Behind him would ride fivescore yeomen with the blue boar embroidered on their left shoulders. When I was very young I had to ride behind with the women and baggage, but when I was seven I had my own saddle and little palfrey, Scoggins, and rode proudly behind my father. I was watched after closely in my early years and always fed new skills, which I mastered well enough to be sent up to St John's at Cambridge when I was still in my ninth year, the youngest student ever admitted to the university. St John's was the chosen charity for virtue's cause on the part of my father's close friend Cecil. He spent much money and time there, walking up and down in his robes with the masters, who'd chuckle respectfully at all his witticisms and profundities. His project was to give a sudden push to his little academe and make it the best college at Cambridge, which it was far from being when he began.

The nobility sent their sons to St John's primarily to learn to eat at table and play tennis. The newly crowned Queen's preferment for education and social graces had caught many of our fine families quite unawares. I found it all rather odd and not terribly delicious or even beneficial at St John's, though I concede that part of the problem lay in the fact that my head then came up only to the shoulders of my fellow students. Much had to follow from my immaturity. Though I had all the skills from my private training in the Great Court at Castle Hedingham, I did not once sign on the tennis court at St John's in my three years there, because the length of my arms and legs would have given easy victory to inferior opponents.

There were other problems with the tutors at St John's. They frequently themselves made childish errors and wanted instruction. I asked my father to have me transferred to a better college, at which Cecil arranged to have me stay at St John's but be supervised again by Thomas Smith, who was at Queen's teaching quietly before he transferred once more to become my private tutor. After the Protestant reascendancy, he first took his place at Court and then was sent to be Vice-Chancellor at Cambridge. He was what I gained from Cambridge and if they had kept him with me I'd not have needed the place at all. As my father loved France, so Smith loved Italy.

What I missed at Cambridge was the sort of warm feeling that was enjoyed there by so many of the city wits with whom I later made the plays. My time and needs were simply out of joint for college friendship. It was there that I first met Gabriel Harvey, who'd show me warmth too condescending. In the end I'd have to cut him: *Come, elder brother, you are too young in your argument.* So I sat, a little boy at university, and for three years I read the many books and boxes of documents that the other students and their tutors were too busy to read. Of this fact there was considerable proof in the number of books, particularly from France, whose spines I would discover had not even been cracked, and the number of boxes that still sadly wore the seals with which they had been sent to the university. In spite of this deplorable state of neglection the librarian, who did not welcome visitors and wished to sit upon all his treasures like a hen, would not allow me to take the books to my rooms or even home between terms.

It was difficult for me there because I lunged between the insistent damp of my rooms, warmed though they were by fires, and the cold dustiness of the reading room. The wine cellar of St John's, at least, was excellent. The food was less certain. On ordinary evenings we were frequently presented with roasts we had met before, the spices of which were to cover the body's last steps into a nether world. Mystery meat we called it in the dining hall, because it was impossible to identify its animal source. But on those days when Cecil sat among the tutors at high table the food was crisp and succulent, and the endless trifles would be replaced by Cecil's obsession, a delicate bread pudding rich in cream and egg with fine, light colour and balance of saffron and nutmeg. For the midday meal, if the weather was good, I would ordinarily absent myself from the hall and have a quick meal of bread and cheese wrapped in cambric, which was brought to me on the riverbank by my boy, Peter, who was ten years older than I.

From the time I was an infant I'd favoured clothing exclusively of black satin and velvet, but Cambridge demanded brighter colours to wear underneath the black gowns, some lined with sheets of wool. Altogether a strange town, somewhat like an island port because indeed shallow-keeled boats had once been able to make it to the sea from there and now it was filled with shallow-keeled tutors and students who pretended – and often it was more than pretence – that they did not love books. I have to say that I was glad enough to leave there, and happy, too, to bring my graduation scroll *honoris causa* back to Castle Hedingham, though it brought more joy to my father and Cecil than to me. The custom has changed now, but in those days the sons of noble families received their degrees as of right for simple attendance, nor could there be especial satisfaction in the honours awarded by men who themselves smelled of false Latin, French and history.

My more true compliment came two months after I'd returned home when my tutor, the Dean of Litchfield, resigned his commission with the honest words that he found he had little more to teach me. That was when the decision was made to place me under the tutelage of my uncle to read ancient Roman poetics and statehood. I migrated to take a master of art degree at Oxford but this time was not required to reside at the university. It is an oddity of our family's history that, with estates scattered across the East, West and South of England, we have never held land in Oxfordshire, neither do our family records show any connection with the university's formation from the congregation of young scholars who came to the town's monastery and later to Balliol College after the twelfth century.

When it came time for my degree to be presented, Cecil decided to present himself with an honorary degree as well and to invest the occasion with the full extravagancy of a Royal visit. I was installed at Oxford for several weeks with my friend Rutland while the proceedings were being rehearsed. The plan was to restage with variations the Cambridge ceremony that She had attended two years before. I was assigned to do recitations, though I would far rather have participated in the drama. I recited from *The XV Books of Ovidius Naso*, which I had recently completed with my Uncle Arthur. It was indeed a metamorphosis of the great poet, for I'd dusted off Chaucer's English and marched Ovid in my mind through our fens and fields; in the end, I'll confess, more me than either Ovid or Chaucer but in places not too bad for all that.

The Queen declared me the English Ovid. Such praise had been my exact ambition, but strangely that ambition flew out of my fourteen-year-old head the instant She said it. The solemnity and humour of the occasion had, besides, by then been bent by the circumstances of the play, which had been interrupted by catastrophe. The play was an enactment of Chaucer's *Knight's Tale*, but the academic dramatist Richard Edwards of Oxford had larded in bits of every known tale of Palamon-Hercules and Arcite, so that in addition to love for Emilia, Hercules shows lust, more mad than manly, for his men Hylas, Iolaus and Eurystheus. The excesses of Palamon and his madness were attractive to me, and news of them in rehearsal had excited all the town. The crowd, all of whom had letters of free entrance by previous arrangement, rushed into the theatre so quickly after the trumpet blasts that one would have thought that the players had already craftily endeavoured to commence without them. The younger entrants thronged up the tight old corkscrew stair that led to the balcony. Under their weight, they say, the staircase began to sway wildly and emit sharp cracking sounds. In the Royal box we heard it first as a kind of landslide blanketing over screams, and then we saw a brick wall slowly bulge until it burst with flailing youth and flying wood.

At the inquest afterwards it was shown that there had been only slapdash preparation for the festivities, that the stairs were ancient and ill-repaired, and the mortar in the wall had been mixed with a surfeit of straw. In addition someone had made the decision to sell tickets in the town. For that six men went to prison, and for that a student and two tradesmen were crushed to death like poultry and ripe cherries in a press.

The Queen sent in Her physician, but even with that there were only three doctors in the town to minister to forty wounded and many limbs to be set, five to be sawed off.

We at first all retired to the Great Hall to drink ginger beer. What was my surprise when I was informed that my recitation was to be moved forward from Tuesday and start in an hour. As I began to read the translation, workingmen were still clearing away debris and it cost considerable effort to shift the audience's natural restraint to captivation. In truth I should say that most eyes were not on me but on the steely jaw of the Queen, whose entire being said that there would be no halt in the ceremonies, except that, when the play proceeded on the next day, there was unexpected and genuine weeping among the students for their fellow student Clark as Arcite died on stage.

Burghley's influence, which was strong while my father lived, became of course all-powerful after his death, which was how I became a student of the law at Gray's Inn a few months after the Oxford ceremony. I had little enthusiasm for the enterprise, but my guardian said that legal study would dignify my place at Court. I'd seen several of their theatricals.

# ❦ 16 ❦

I have not made an entry in this chronicle for three days. Jane the tinker's wife tells me that I was so sleepy that I could not be called to life, and that the doctor, the Bishop of Hackney, my wife and Henry all paid last visits to look at me, after which I simply sat up and called for food as if nothing had happened. It is well that I've been taking care to put away each double-sided sheet as soon as it is filled or my project might have furnished my life with one last scandal. I'll continue to beat the drum of this the life that I have lived to frighten dumb sleep to death. True, fever and pain begin to run loose within me again. It is only fear that I'll not be able to come back again so easily that holds me awake. I do not fear to die. I want to live.

## ❦ 17 ❦

There were many surprises for me on entering Gray's Inn. As Earl it was not necessary for me to proceed along the usual path from grammar school or university to an Inn of Chancery, such as Barnard's or Staple's, before the Inns of Court, but no one had informed me that once through the arch all distinction and rank are cast down except for the twenty senior benchers who must take time off from their work as barristers to teach the law and enforce some discipline on the pensioners. This beauteous enforced freedom, however, had within the Inn its own dangerous laws against gentility. They called their festive law 'perfect wrong', and the master of the annual Revels, which I was in 1568 and 1569, was the Lord of Misrule. Here was my first well-appointed theatre, and in remembrance of those good times my most convivial play, *Twelfth Night*, was shown at a mixed revel in the Middle Temple hall not that many years ago.

The Inns, larger and more prosperous than either provincial university, are properly spoken of as a secret city within the city. The students, pensioners, practisers, pleaders and judges cluster together in some fourteen societies with just two common aims, private revelry and a seasonless golden harvest from the ever-ripe public. While it would hardly have been fitting for me to attend to the windy side of law and present myself to wear a wig at a Call Party, I willingly took in enough of the language of the law to save myself at least the legal fees in the process of acquiring debts and losing lands over the years. By the age of seventeen I could often compete successfully in the discourse and rhetoric, though after some time I wearied of that.

My delight and energy were given to Gray's Inn's other curriculum, which was dramatic hospitality. Though all four Inns were supposed neither to claim nor to concede priority over one another in any way, there were of course certain differences. The Inner Temple and Gray's Inn were especially close to one another in their greater commitment to painted pomp and triumphant Revels, and Gray's Inn enjoyed particular favour at Court, where we were frequently invited to restage our Revels. The Queen visited us three times in my years. That was my only true school and the seedbed of all my later efforts. The library of Gray's Inn was the richest I have ever used. Though too many of the books were posturing treatises on theology, there were in all eight thousand volumes on every imaginable subject, all carefully numbered and restitched and glued whenever necessary. At first I was determined to read them all, but at the fortieth it became clear that my knowledge by this method would be too ill-ordered a heap of learned rubbish, and so I switched to following out the further tributaries of things I already knew. Before I left the Inn I'd read more than seven hundred of its books, and there was rarely anything I needed to know as a playwright that could not be discovered at Gray's Inn. As for the lawyers themselves, they appear to have limited love for the word and to content themselves with two-score useful books.

There was no comparison between the feasts of St John's and Gray's Inn, or even, owing to Her natural parsimony, with Court banquets. Four times a year, once in each term, a Grand Day feast was held in the Great Hall, and besides that, each year had no fewer than two Revels, and there were smaller Readers' Feasts as well. On Grand Days all the senior judges of the city and distinguished visitors from Court dined with the twenty benchers on a platform from which they looked down on the barristers and junior students. During ordinary feasts extra commons and wine were served to the lower tables, but the Lord of Misrule was expected to provide a Roman feast for all.

The first of my two Revel feasts was the best. Word had reached me that a baby whale had been taken from its mother's belly and brought back preserved half-alive in a net to Southend from the North Sea. I sent Robin Christmas to the docks with my stamped letter to make a bid. It was not a trifle. Unfortunately the beast died two days before the feast, which did not matter to the meal, since there was no intention to eat it, but mattered much to the nose, since it was to be carried through the hall in triumphal procession on poles by ten serving-men. This delicate need was satisfied by filling the Great Hall with aromatic incense burners that our forefathers employed. Small animals that had been cooked and stuffed with great care back into their skins, sugared duck and salted deer, peppered pheasant and piglet painted with mustard, rode astride the child monster's beribboned back. Trumpets led the way, and pigs' bladders brought up the rear. The spectacle repeated on a smaller scale the whale of the marriage banquet of Charles the Bold and Margaret of York a century before, about which I had read in the library.

The Queen was there and enraptured. That was how it happened that, when Burghley complained bitterly of the cost of what I had done, She gladly took a portion of the expense and proffered more again for the next year's revel. That marked the first of a quarter-century's careful support for all manner and shape of pageants and plays. Even if most of what I did has vanished and flown like smoke out at the chimney, sweet smoke of rhetoric, my fires, have they not warmed England and made her stir?

## ❦ 18 ❦

In 1568 Mary Stuart made her move to grab the Throne. She also made the matter almost a friendship feud for me by moving to arrange a marriage with my cousin Thomas, Duke of Norfolk. It was a clever ploy, because, though no single Howard was a person of great substance, the sum of their shadows made them one of the most powerful families in the land, and he was head of the clan. He was foolish in the beginning to let himself be caught up with Mary; he was foolish in the end to let himself be led off so meekly when everything was discovered; and there was not much wisdom in between. Yet I loved him. He'd already buried three wives and had the air of an unlucky cherub. Perhaps Thomas was merely befuddled to wish a Catholic Queen of England for his next bride. He did not know himself to think that he might be either a king or a ceremonious courtier beside such a Queen.

The match was his own idea, though I daresay he did not realize how much warm reception of the notion hung from the legacies of his three rich wives. For that he could be forgiven much, including, temporarily, his Protestantism. Soon after She became Queen, Elizabeth had sent Norfolk to fight against the Scots and their French allies as several of his ancestors, most notably his grandfather, had done before him. The Queen then later set the tangled train of actions in motion by appointing Norfolk to head the commission to inquire into the relations between the Scottish Queen and Her subjects. Somewhere in the course of his commission Thomas became converted not to the cause or faith of Mary but to the woman herself. I myself had frequent occasion to observe my sweet cousin's taste for syrups. Little that he did made sense, and yet one had to love his naïve smile and his easy self-mockery. I loved him for his lightness. He was fourteen years older than I, and yet I often felt the parent towards him.

Mary consented to the marriage after Maitland indicated that the Scottish nobility would favour the union. But having declared that he would marry Her, Thomas's wit went halt and he refused to take up arms against Elizabeth, for which loyalty he was repaid by prompt arrest in September, no, October 1569.

After Norfolk's imprisonment, a military sortie was mounted under the command of another great friend, Thomas Radcliffe, Earl of Sussex. Mary had been spirited away to Coventry in disguise, and four thousand Scottish troops went across the border to face Sussex's men. Because of Court intrigue by Leicester, however, Thomas was sent out with insufficient troops and cavalry to face the rebel earls. It was only a synchronization of fortuitous circumstances that prevented a much more serious rebellion. That Thomas and my future son-in-law's father, Stanley, then Lord Strange, later the Earl of Derby, were imprisoned, which threw the Earls of Northumberland and Westmorland into confusion, did not help the Catholic cause. What was worse still was that the expected uprising of the people was too small and too slow, even though pamphlets calling them out had been distributed to every city, town and village. The monasteries had been closed too long, and life had managed to proceed along in much the same way it always had without the excessive exactions and unwelcome domestic advice of the monks. Besides, whilst the Scots can scarcely be said to love the English, they'd seen our Queen and loved Her, whereas Mary still had sea-water on Her from Her crossing into Northern exile and had not bothered to take the time to let the people see Her and learn to love Her. Money makes a good soldier, but it does not follow from this that you can have good soldiers with money alone. The soldiers of the rebel earls were a mongrel lot and, sensing the anxieties and restlessness of their generals, they broke ranks as soon as the troops of Sussex came into view. And so what might have been a desperate battle for Thomas became instead little more than chasing frightened cattle through the fields.

My misfortune at this time was that I was in the midst of one of my dark eclipses. They have not come often, but there have been few years of my life when they have not come at all. It will usually begin with an early waking at the hour of the wolf when the sky has lightened ever so slightly to show a false texture of grey slate with still no certain sign that the sun will ever rise. Then do I think idly of all my past and present, with no pleasure and very little interest either. When the sun comes up my heart takes no notice of its rays, while my imagination races ahead to the scores of possible wheres and hows of my future death. I am disgusted with life and yet fortunately too lethargic to raise my hand to end it. If this indolence of the spirit were a long one, my body could waste away until I could see and caress certain usually hidden bones.

As the Scottish rebellion took shape I was in such a situation. Rutland was preparing to go to battle under Sussex and made a detour especially to go with me. When he found me staring at the floor he knew what it was, for he had grown up with me as a brother and knew my dull-ey'd melancholy at a glance. His friendly nonchalance brought me back to life more quickly than all the mock jollity and despair with which I was usually entertained. Though I did not respond to him as he spoke to me, I could feel clearly that I was emerging from the dark wood of despair. I stretched my eyes until I saw him and everything doubled and thus all was imaged up as insubstantial. It was then not long before my soul became expansive. I awoke like the maiden in a fairy-tale, and soon my talk and thoughts began to run. These initial moments I came to savour and to fear, for it was at these conjunctions of my spiritual forces that I felt myself elevated like a magician with power over everything, and many of my most foolish amorous indiscretions and ill-starred financial investments in maturity too frequently began in these rare moods.

My mood was, however, well-suited to this military moment. It was at last perceived that the rebellion, even though it had been caught in time, still held real danger for the realm. I sought permission from Cecil to join Sussex and Rutland, and it was given, though only after five months, when the campaign to remove the last remaining enclaves of the earls was underway. I joined Sussex in the preparations for a stealthy forced march at night to take Hume Castle. We had to wait a fortnight until the moon was not in the sky. We took our troops nearly thirty miles, with all our wheels well-greased and our weapons and gear wrapped in cloth. Waggons had been sent ahead to forest stopping points with grain and water.

The excellent stratagem worked flawlessly. The castle was asleep when our first archers crept close enough to let fly the first sallies of flaming arrows, and it was immediately evident from the smoke that some of the arrows had found good targets. Light cannon were trained on all the crenellations and archery slits by the postern tower, enabling us to have free access to the base of the wall at that one station. The only danger to the little party that I led to the wall were the chunks of stone that rained down on us as a result of our bombardment, but we had shields and helmets. A mineshaft was dug at the tower corner to the depth of two men, and a large barrel of rash gunpowder was placed in it. The walls recoiled from the fearsome blast, and, though they held, the application of our one heavy cannon began to create jagged windows in the loosened walls through which terrified people running about could be glimpsed. While the heavy cannon did its work on the postern tower, the light cannon began to fire in the same way on the tower closest to it. At that rate it would not have taken two full days to breach the castle's security. The procedure of attack was perfect, and no baronial fortress today, save those few on mountain peaks and islands, can hope to stand against such attacks. As it happened, Sussex had with him sufficient powder for only a day, which Lord Hume did not know. The combined effect of surprise and an onslaught that was on the verge of breaking down the walls after only the one day led to a white cloth being draped from a battlement before the sun had set.

In the meeting that followed on the drawbridge Sussex was attended by Rutland and me. He quickly granted Lord Hume safe passage from his castle with all those he wished to take with him, provided only that they pledged a sacred vow not to take up arms again. The Queen's pleasure, which had been conveyed to Sussex, was not for further arrests. The final dispersal of the possibility of further rebellion was what She desired and what She received when Castle Hume surrendered. If the chance of Hume's early surrender did not permit me to engage in battle, the success of our powdered mineshaft caused the surrender, and my stone bruises were the finest medals of the engagement. I was annoyed at the treaty by Hume's dour fourteen-year-old boy, just back from France where he went regularly to study, whilst I was still forbidden to set foot outside our over-constrain'd isle. I liked him more many years later, when he wrote his song 'The Triumph of the Lord', celebrating our victory o'er the Spanish. I wrote my only hymn then, too.

When we'd returned to London, Sussex was free in his praise of me, which I was sure would smooth my way overseas, but I was wrong. Plato, that most abominable of all philosophers of every time, cautioned against both poets and travel to foreign lands if the state would rest secure. My Queen loved poets but seemed to find it useful to hold back foreign travel for certain of Her most devoted subjects. In part that was, I'm sure, because She herself could never have the freedom to enjoy the foreign lands about which Her tutors Grindal and Ascham had taught her so well. In part as well, it must be said, the praise of Sussex could sometimes fail to serve, for he was always mistrusted by the Court.

There was no greater noble in our time than Sussex. Younger slightly than my father, still he was his ancient friend. With my father he signed the letters patent to settle the Crown on Lady Jane and then with him switched his favour to Queen Mary. He half-conquered querulous Ireland, and only half because, as in Scotland, Elizabeth and Her ministers were too stingy in their support to see their own interest. He knew exactly what the problems were and how to solve them all, but the trickle of supply was so meagre that in the end he had to give up and apply to come home, for which he was unjustly much distrusted. He had made England's power felt throughout Ireland for the first time, and we shall see if any of his successors will be able to ride in peace beyond the Pale on that island. For his partial triumph against grave odds, Sussex had to sit through an inquiry like a suspected traitor.

He was staunch in his opposition to the Queen's engagement to Leicester, and, though his enemies grouped together against him at the start of the Scottish campaign, the thoroughness of his surprise raids throughout Dumfries removed any doubts about him. His post as Lord of the North had been meant to be a dull backwater.

The Earl of Sussex was equally brilliant as soldier, courtier and diplomat. He was a patron of the arts, not least drama, and had he lived a few more years he would have given great support to my endeavours. I freely grant my family affection for the man, which was buttressed at least a little by his connection with the Wriothesley family. But surely it is impossible that I would not have loved him even without that. We have lived to see England be united and a force upon the seas. Still how much greater we would have been had the Queen been inclined to list to that one wise man at Court rather than to Burghley, Leicester, Hatton and Essex, the self-glorious ones. I always praised him alone at Court, even though I saw too well that my weighty words did not count for much on the Court's airy scales of justice and favour.

# ❧ 19 ❧

Plague, plague! I am cursed with a not-quite-false plague that proceeds too softly, and so I am double-plagued with my past as well. A proper plague would have consumed me like an invisible bonfire many weeks ago. How am I suffering? Of proud and bitter heart. Of heart sick with thought. Of thoughts turned into words, which alter nothing.

My only relief comes not from my stubborn pen trying to make my sorrow simple. My five senses are not up to that task. My sole relief belongs to crushed cucumbers. The milk is first extracted and then it is refined like spirits to make a soup. The coolness of this old English balm soothes my face even when it is at its worst. If we cannot be cured, how often we are satisfied with some splashing solace. Odd drops of cucumber, I see, have gone into the ink-well and perhaps into my prose as well.

## 20

After the campaign in Scotland I had my only pastoral period and played the Lord in my various Essex properties. It caused me pain, because the times were different from when my father performed those duties and was known as The Good Earl. The majority of disputes that were referred to me by the local justices involved either women, deer or little wooden bridges over streams between properties o'er which no one had proper domain or responsibility. The disputes of passion, I found, could usually be calmed with a show of patient good humour. Deer-poaching was a much more straightforward affair. Either the poachers made off with their booty undetected or, if they were seen by good and trustworthy men, I would confirm their arrest and committal to trial. No deer were safe from some of them, whether wild or fallow or even doe with foal. They would regularly come into the Great Parks of castles and manors, knowing the beasts to be tame there. The usual punishment was three months in prison followed by a good behaviour bond for seven years, but the bond was not more than the profit of a night's mischief, and the same men came back again and again years after I decided not to participate in the farce. Rumour reached me that the rudest of them marked my own lands for particular revenge, and poaching was always heavy at Tilbury Park, because the deer were particularly fat and the land was mine. The joke was that the revenge poaching carried on by tradition long after all my Essex lands had passed from my hands. I was amazed in discussion with some of my actors years later to be assured by all the men that scarcely any common lad in England can grow up without poaching deer at least once. *Surely you can deny that*, I said to stolid young William.

The most fierce vexation was always a bridge. When I was a boy I saw my father participate as a juror at Stansted Bridge with the Lord Bishop of London and the Warden of New College, Oxford. Ford Bridge, Ox Bridge, Dry Bridge, Low Bridge, Angry Bridge, No Man's Bridge, it was almost always the same old song: rights of passage and duties of repair. There was even one suit by two villages in which I was both arbitrator and unwilling participant, since it happened that I owned the land on both sides of the brook.

One sort of situation only did I attend to with great gravity. With some regularity there would come before me common orphans with rights to a meadow or a cottage. Friends of the family could always be counted upon to be clamb'ring round them to be appointed their guardians. Always it meant that the orphans would be robb'd by the demi-devils we call guardians. An arrangement that had been done by a gullible or bribable magistrate while I was fighting on the heath had to be unravelled and completely redone when I returned and found out about it. The orphan, William Taylefor of Walthamstow, had been well-provided. Three properties had been willed to him, and by divine coincidence three lower worthies of the town, two brothers who were brickmakers and a friend of theirs named Dickison, a carpenter, had been appointed his guardians. None of the properties was entailed, all of them produced income and yet one was already being put up for mortgage when I came on the scene. I had them called to Blackmoe for an explanation before me and the magistrate. We called them in separately, and each gave a different version of their intent. One of the brothers Collard said there was a better house for investment, while the other spoke of the general benefit to be had from having the means to hire more brickmakers as the days of beams and plaster houses were clearly numbered. The new man wants a solid house like his masters, the old crook said with pompous assurance. The Christian carpenter told me with an unctuous smile that young Will's inheritance was over-happy and that the good citizens of Walthamstow were of a mind to share some of his good fortune with other needy children of the town. They were then all called back from the rear chamber into which I'd had them led after giving their statements of intent, letting them all flap together in their own words for half an hour. Upon their return the three fell over themselves in their haste to withdraw their proposal of disposal, while the magistrate watched glumly with his head hanging like over-ripened corn and was no less unhappy than the scoundrels themselves. I suggested that they take good care to see that their charge was raised well and placed in some profitable apprenticeship in the years before his patrimony came due, and to that end I laid upon them a massive bond for men of their station of £40 in order to make sure that they would render the boy's accounts without cobin. The bond was the exact value of the three properties. I was not The Good Earl for them.

The kingdom holds the law, and our fine laws are greas'd and smooth'd to have matters roll down the path to perfect wrong. A Lord or judge of wit and good intent may set some single matter right for the moment, but that is all. There is no redress against the polished and strange machinations of a Leicester, who with his right hand would dolefully refuse the wardship of a genuine and needy relation, Sir Arthur Bassett's son, while his left hand tugged mightily, if unsuccessfully, to prise the more profitable children of the late Duke of Rutland out of Burghley's hands. There was, of course, consolation given him to keep the peace among the powerful, while the wards enjoyed their temporary bliss. Leicester's main ward had been little King Edward. The only retribution that he had was what he could not hear, the banter with which his death was celebrated on the streets and in the taverns:

> Here lies the worthy warrior
> That never bloodied sword.
> Here lies the loyal courtier
> That never kept his word.
> Here lies the boy king's protector
> Who toss'd his ward to fate.
> Here lies the poisonous Earl of Leicester
> Whom heaven and earth both hate.

Finally I grew bored upholding a justice for my common people that I myself still could not enjoy. I stay'd a few more months in the country, brooding and reading. All invitations were turned away. I did correspond at length with my former teacher Dr. Dee, who was full of new theories of passages to wealth confirmed in the stars, and, though I was chary of his wild schemes, some careless part of me was determined to believe him all the same, that peculiar mad facility to believe that let me trust my money to good Fenton even though I well knew that he was a man who found schemes being plotted against him behind every breeze but gold nowhere.

I might have lived awhile longer playing the honest country Lord if my nose had not got in great indignation from the contumelious taunts from below with which my enemies contrived to surround me. The worst of the local villagers was a salt-petre-man from Dedham named Thomas Wixsted, who'd come to my town to insult me, at first subtly by passing near me on occasion without a nod or a bow and dressed out in a faint sneer, later with open words, which reached the local justices. I stayed their hand for several years, because I wanted to determine by whom he was employed. At last it came out when in his cups he was heard by several of my men to declare that the Earl of Oxford was not worthy to wipe his Lord of Warwick's shoes, and that the Earl of Oxford had been so worthy to lose his head as the Duke of Norfolk. With that he'd gone too far, and I sent instructions at last that he should be sentenced to the stocks in Colchester on market day with his left ear lobe nailed to the pillory. I made a point of passing by so that I could nod and raise my hat to him.

Wixsted had his own grudge as well as Warwick's cause to pursue, since the de Veres had from my father's time claimed exemption in all their lands and manors from saltpetre searches, and, as the demand for gunpowder was growing rapidly, saltpetre had become of late in very short supply. Even worse than Warwick's saltpetre-man were several men of Colchester who supposedly belonged to me. They went about tarring Leicester and Warwick so openly with the truth as to cause a public disorder and draw me into disrepute for not keeping my men in order. They surely were in double pay.

Here was the problem. After the revolt of the Northern Earls and the famous Ridolfi plot, thoughts of faction, secrecy and revolt were in people's minds and on their lips for many years. They understood less of what was transpiring than they thought, but their ill-considered passion for public quarrels raced ahead and they all eagerly took sides in matters that concerned them as much as Venus in the sky. It seems that every country man from nothing to do had conceived a passion to be a politician. The lords who are happy to blow upon these pointless passions and warm the coals to flame do not see how they themselves will be one day consumed by the fierce blaze of riot. *We'll follow Cade! We'll follow Cade!* the people cry in *Henry VI*.

## 21

That was how the Court seemed by comparison fanned with the air of paradise, and how I threw myself into its dances and witty coils with all the skills that I possessed. In that year, 1571, the Queen had eyes only for me, and I was at ease in my assumption that with my Northern exploit and recent triumph at the tilts my way would now be free to visit foreign courts at last. I reckoned wrongly and soon was suffering a ceaseless itch to escape even as I wed Anne that December. My first attempt to flee was stopped, and my successful dash for freedom in 1574, as you already know, was for various unpleasant reasons shorter than I'd intended, as for that matter was the tour of 1575 and 1576, for which I'd finally received official authorization.

When first I landed at Calais and rode through Normandy I was surprised at how like England it was, though there were matters of some difference that were quickly evident. Here, after all, was the land from which my family had come. The churches, the castles and the manor houses, the stone town houses and the country farms of wood and plaster were all first cousins to what I knew, and yet I did not know this land. Even their French had some sounds and words in it I'd never heard before. Time moved more smoothly here, the cows were fatter, the people were happy and conscious of their special fortune.

On my way to Touques to meet the Duke of Normandy we stopped at a small inn where we supp'd on cider and veal. It was raining, and the calf was slaughtered in the same room where the table was spread for dinner before a stone hearth in which the beams from an old *dépendance* were being burned. While the meat was being hung to roast above the fire a young girl mopped the red-tiled floor until it sparkled from the flames of the hearth. As we waited for the meat, which was being basted with a pear and apple syrup, to cook, the innkeeper and his wife gave me sea-fresh oysters and cider and chatted with me as though I were their neighbour. I admired their gleaming *armoire*, which seemed too grand for their modest inn, and was told that every bride of Normandy comes to her marriage with such a cupboard, symbol of their land's prosperity.

The only difference when we arrived at Touques the following day was in fact that the *armoires* were upstairs. It was still raining heavily, but the rain was soft and pleasant. They say that it rains only twice each year, from Christmas 'til Summer solstice, and from the end of wanton Summer 'til the New Year. Here, too, the beast was slaughtered in the same hall in which we dined. While we watched the calf being turned on its spit, we munched another local harvest from the sea, this time tiny grey prawns, each no larger than a collar button, which were toss'd live into a hot pan and eaten whole. The Duke and his Duchess, as much at their ease as the innkeeper, asked me questions about how we live in England. From some of their questions on fine points such as the growing number of members of the Puritan creed I surmis'd that they knew rather more of us than we bother to learn of them, though they had never crossed the Channel. Their explanation was that the Normans had crossed the Channel once, whereas the English have repaid the visit many times since then, and so it is necessary for the people of Normandy to watch England as they watch the sky.

They lived in a manor house not too far from the castle, which in most seasons was too cold and damp for happy habitation, but they took me there as to a sacred shrine, for from that castle William had mustered his forces for the crossing. Perhaps it was the simpler ducal life they led, but I came to form the view that there was no long bridge between the poorest and the nobility in this prosperous kingdom, and that Normandy was indeed very like a pastoral poem. Their cream was thicker than our butter, and I never tasted better apples. Though those two years were to see me through elaborate feasts and revels in four lands and another island, the simple meals and conversations of Normandy, which proceeded with the calm of a cow and the wit of a quiet fox, did not recede before them.

From Touques we went overland to Rouen where another sort of surprise met me. As I passed through the elaborate gates of the city that would have been capital I beheld my first grand city of Europe and was pierced by the feeling that my own land was rustic. The city's lace-in-stone combined lightness with solidity. A thousand stories were being played out on the streets. But I did not even stay the day there because now I was in a frenzy to see Paris. I took my men and went there at a gallop. It was dark when we arrived, and we had to camp the night in the meadows outside the city, which, by comparison with Rouen, seemed the next morning unexpectedly devoid of splendours. That was but the coquetry of a woman too beautiful to need to paint herself. The city I saw that June seemed an endless fair, and still seemed so when I revisited her during the next wet and windy March. The fennel on the street stalls was plaited like a woman's hair. The liquorice was carved into life-sized ravens from which you bought a delicious black hunk. Many of the young women dressed half in calico, half in silk, as though readying themselves for whichever door opened for them in life. After all, the King himself sometimes and all the nobility always yielded to the temptation to shop in these streets themselves. Everyone in Paris makes magnificent occasion of the littlest thing. The back garden of every house returns you instantly to the depths of the country. Though in places Paris smells as vile as London, in no other way are they the same. I watched their night-time dances, now passionate, now soft and pure, and thought of our own poor mechanical morris dancing and the crude dances and devices by which our people mock the marriage vows or the breaking of the maidenhead.

The contrast was even harsher when I was presented at Court. At the castle I first saw ballet performed, a dance with such delicacy and discipline that I would weep with deep frustration thinking of it years later whenever players sawed their way roughly through my plays. The excellent musicians played sweet music that yet called forth the heart's deep sores. It was healthful music and yet music fit to die to, polished silver music and yet aerial music of the spheres.

This excellence in the French Court whether in Paris or in the country, for it shuttled like a gypsy camp, was presided over by the Italian Queen Mother, Catherine de Medici. No longer young, perhaps never beautiful, Catherine was still the most gracious hostess imaginable. Her nose was knobby and her cheeks sat high, but such petty defects were swirled away in the midst of Her energy and the divine circus She controlled with smiles, raised fingers and nods. It was strange to recall that most gracious Queen, with whom I talked for many an hour, when it became known to us, only many years after the fact, that She had been the chief author behind her son, a foolish little man, in plotting the Massacre of St Bartholomew!

Oddly enough, I found that the food one could buy on the streets of Paris, often already cooked in little clay pots which needed only some fresh warming by the fire, was often superior to the fare served at Court, where there were too many sweet and salt meat courses turned cold on their way from the distant kitchens and intended anyway to be more tasty to the sight. Here was the source spring of what I had done at Gray's Inn from the books. A cooked hawk redressed in its feathered skin grasped a hare, also reclad in its fur coat. A bear's paw, which was a muff of charred cubes of bear-meat steeped in honey, clasped a long, golden honeycomb. Every sort of roasted or boiled meat or meat-pie imaginable was served up on poles and platters large as military shields, until, at a certain point of satiety, the guests at the feast table toss'd pieces to the artisans and tradesmen who had been permitted to witness the feast from benches by the walls, and finally they in turn toss'd pieces to the servants, who sometimes brought pieces to their friends in the city to let them taste of the Royal table from afar. In my Parisian feasts I ate as little of the viands as I could and savoured the red wines which were, and still are, the softest and most poetic wines I've ever drunk.

The table would speak in French and Italian, and there were

those who wanted to practise their English with me. The women were beautiful in their way but somehow almost dressed to lie in state. *Les belles pralines* my table neighbour called them, meaning tarts too beauteous and elaborate to taste.

The real delight was in the theatre of Her feasts. I speak not of the various circus surprises such as the giant meat-pie out of which performing musicians arose or the episode of sparrows that flew from artfully folded damask napkins, nor even the toothpicks at the end so flavoured and perfumed that one wanted to chew them up rather than clean one's teeth with them. These comic rites serve merely to remind us of our Roman ancestors. The glory of Queen Catherine's entertainments was what took place between the wall benches and the feast tables. The singers, the rhetoricians, the instruments and the dancers were of fabled perfection. Often the feast would stop of itself to listen and watch. No monarch could have wished them thus into their proficiencies. Their skill was rather the fruit of generations of instruction and devotion to their crafts. *It is hard work to be a Parisian*, one of the musicians told me when I questioned him. Only their plays and players I thought were not strong.

I saw in Paris what had to be done in London, but I also saw the impossibility of duplicating their finer feats. After thirty years of work on the stage and on the page I'll say only that the richness of England has become somewhat better ordered. The kingdoms and city-states of Europe now ask for our players to tour in English, and it has become fashionable, I'm told, to learn our language to hear them. But I also know that the plough-iron has not gone deep, and a hastily sown shallow crop is easily blown away when the weather changes.

Paris was not a good city to choose to hide in, though I was not really hiding and had frankly not thought that the Queen would send Her guard after me. I'd stayed too long at the French Court. A messenger from England with a letter for the King requested my immediate return. It was all done with courteous office, and there was no suggestion that I should leave like a courtier in custody, though the four armed horsemen who came with the messenger left no room for doubt that such a possibility was not to be excluded if I decided to resist their urgent invitation. My vexation was almost unsupportable, but I had found friends at Court. I was sooth'd by them and left with my men and Her guard the next morning, carrying a scroll from the King with greetings and an entreaty to return their gracious visitor as soon as possible. It turned out that my whereabouts had been known at all times, but the indecision as to what to do about me had fortunately lasted several weeks.

The Queen was very angry, but I affected indifference, though I was angry, too. I told Her bluntly that a kingdom from which men are not free to travel must be a kingdom where wise men will not wish to stay. She ordered me from Her sight, and I reminded Her that we were then agreed. Then six days later Burghley, who was trying hard to placate his daughter, brought news that the Queen had reconsidered and was pleased with reports of how well-met I'd been whilst I was travelling abroad. She had a notion, he said, to send me abroad as embassador at large for certain purposes together with Edward Seymour, styled Lord Beauchamp notwithstanding claims as to his legitimacy. Her interest in him was by way of now softening Her extreme displeasure with the Seymour clan which arose from the secret marriage in 1560 of Edward's father, who had himself been son of the Protector to King Edward, to Lady Catherine Grey, sister to Lady Jane and therefore too close to questions of the right to rule as far as the Queen was concerned. The irritation all the same remained in some degree until Her death, for I am told that when it was suggested that the Crown might be passed to my friend Edward, She shouted: *I shall not have my Kingdom pass to a descendant of rascals!* The real problem with the Seymours, I gathered from what once She told me, began with Thomas the grandfather, who'd made advances to Her whilst he was Protector but then married Catherine Ashley, as a result of which She much resented Thomas and much envied Catherine.

But the Seymours had remained loyal and innoxious if quietly Catholic in spite of their trials, and I suspect that the Queen was simply disinclined to be an agent of any declaration of illegitimacy.

I judged Edward, younger than I and an amusing and docile fellow, to be an acceptable travelling companion. I was also given young Ralph Hopton, son of the Lieutenant of the Tower, but, though he was just a boy, I feared him as a spy and had him carefully watched and kept him always away from me. An audience was arranged at which the Queen conveyed Her needs, which seemed as small as they were contrived. Four sealed scrolls were to be delivered by me in Strasbourg, Paris, Budapest and Frankfort, and I was to be prepared by Burghley to parley on the matters contained in them before replies were sent to Her. After that we treated the length of our sojourn and the other places to which we might go. The Queen forbade Spain, Milan and Rome for fear that English Protestants might be imprisoned there, or worse. I craved to have our trip end in Constantinople, but to that She replied that Turkey must also still be considered a dangerous realm where anything could happen, and that our trip to Hungary was precisely to such neutral ground where I could hob-nob with Turks to my heart's content and pass one of Her scrolls to the Turkish Governor there for transmission to the Sultan. It would please Her to subsidize part of the cost of the trip, about which we would be informed by the Treasurer. Here I interjected that, though I was grateful for the Queen's largess, it should be understood that I was comfortable travelling only with my own men.

*Do you know then, Edward, who are your own men? I envy you. I've had several who I was sure were my own, and they were not.* At this She lowered Her head and looked at me archly.

Here young Edward made bold to ask how he should worship when in Catholic countries.

*To God, Lord Beauchamp, to God!* She said with a wry smile.

My father-in-law counted on the Royal sanction to mollify me somewhat, but I swarmed with resentments 'gainst him and his daughter and so gave fair quiet warning that there might be private things said in public if he and Anne presumed to come to the pier. He did not relish my advice but knew enough to take it. It was a gusting January morning when we set sail from Wivenhoe. I wore two capes and several scarves which stretched out in the wind like flags. My dancing soul was celebrating a long-awaited joy, the sweeter because it had been sipped briefly once before.

## 22

Only my best men had been chosen for the journey, and since there were just six such men, it was necessary to bolster the number, which I did with Savoy players and musicians. It served a double purpose, because I was happy for their company and wished them to have instruction by example as we travelled. It turned out as well that many of the players could play at servant better than my men. In any event, I took as little company as I could. It was a far better departure to set sail in the morning with the Royal insignia flying and warships, one on either side, to give us safe passage. I'd left six months before at three in the morning on a small sloop that reeked of fish and had all its lanterns extinguished. We found soon after landing that it was not really necessary to have a man gallop ahead to announce our arrival because word travelled by itself and in the narrow streets of many villages people were already lining the way to watch us as we approached. I'll confess that we paraded like turkey cocks with outspread feathers. Even timid Edward had begun to smile and wave to the crowds.

I called once more at Touques, and then I stayed four weeks at Rouen where I wondered at a city in which every building, however modest, had either some dignity or beauty, and also at their industry and craft with furniture. The Rouen artisans and joiners made back stools and folding chairs far lighter in both weight and style than is our custom here in England, with tablet arches carved in low relief, and their upholsterers made fine down seat-cushions for them from crimson or blue gold tissue. Their hinged arm supports have a pleasingly flamboyant appearance, and the simple straight legs and crosspieces have much grace. There are no dreadful knobs and bulbs such as mar all our furniture. This furniture once made is waxed to a golden hue that is the secret of the city. I purchased one of the folding chairs and carried it with me for the sixteen months that my tour lasted. It was not too long before I discovered that these chairs were of Italian design, but I do hold that, like many of my stories and myself, they improved by travel, for I never saw better ones in Italy. If I linger now on the folding chair, that is only because by chance it was not taken by the pirates and thus has remained with me and is the sole solid piece left to me from ten thousand fast-fading moments of that mirth and pleasure of my youth on tour. For twenty years I have used this chair in Hackney and written from it, until I think now that I could not write without it. It is the seat of all my artistry and self-knowledge. And wants repair.

In Paris I was embraced by King Henry and the Queen Mother Catherine once again as though I were an old friend. I was introduced to King Henry as though we'd never met by Valentine Dale, our Embassador, in the Castle of Madrill, located very near Paris in the woods and lakes of Bois de Boulogne. Dale and the King both took an interest in me and furnished me with passports and letters I might later require for my journey to Italy. Added to those I carried from the Queen, I possess'd more documents than I had time to use. I then blushed to myself to recall how I had once implored Elizabeth to let me join a revolution against the King of France, and She had softly rebuked me for my desire, telling me: *I cannot wish that a man of such note among my people should find himself on the side of one who is fighting against his own king.* Now I think that I was right in my youthful ardour. First impressions need not be less weighty than careful reconsiderations.

The Massacre of St Bartholomew's Day, which had upset me so, the more so because wretched Burghley had withheld true information about it as was his wont, scarce three years in the past, that slaughter that filled Amsterdam, London and Lübeck with so many fine French craftsmen and steeled legions of pre-viously uncertain Protestants against the power of Rome, that persecution which had been begun under Henry II, was now strangely eased by his widow after the self-administered blow to France. Young Henry bemoaned the loss of his silk industry to other countries and half-seriously suggested that now He would like to call His Huguenots back, but that alas they had gone too far, even to Africa. Thus after the storm an unexpected air of religious tolerance reigned in the Court, the prevailing politic of which was to unite the country's fourteen provinces in peace and order, neither of which, according to the King, was in great supply anywhere in the kingdom.

I witnessed a painfully awkward Court dance in which fourteen of the ladies-in-waiting, too large and too little trained, performed a ballet of all the provinces in amity. From all I heard it was a most wishful fable as well as a feeble dance. Had I been a lady of the Court I think I would have feigned any illness to avoid competition with the regular dancers. These women dancers were particularly enchanting. They were very lean and yet still juicy with charm. Their beauty flicker'd between boyhood and full womanhood. Without exception they were as tiny as elves. Behind it all was the taste of Henry III, who could love a woman but only if she appeared to be a boy, and a boy if he could flawlessly counterfeit a woman. Thus in France the Court and the bedroom played out what was our custom only on the stage. The dancers lived in garrets on the Isle St Louis near the centre of the city, as a result of which it had become known among wits as l'Isle des Hermaphrodites.

I danced a nimble Galliard in a duet with the most fetching of the elves which made the muscles of my calves tremble with the effort. After we had taken many bows King Henry gallantly motioned the two of us to a side waiting-room, and it was only as I removed her last linens that I was sure she was not a boy, for her voice and laughter had deeper register than any man's. I was pleased to see as she embraced me that the dance which had so strained me had at least not been without some effort for her as well, for her chest and sides glistened with sweet-smelling sweat like a horse after the races. She loved as she danced, intensely and with the natural abandon of a bath one takes unnoticed in a secluded mountain rock pool, though I suspected that her natural ways were practised like everything else about her. Perhaps I was being rewarded for being able to keep up with her.

As for the Queen Mother, She accepted the errant ways of young Henry with noble calm. *My mother taught me*, she told me openly, *that, as I am not a beauty myself, it will suffice to surround myself in life with beautiful hubbub and be content to be the queen bee at the centre of the flower.* She took the Court on progress with King Henry throughout the length and breadth of France, an army without guns or spears, visiting deep Catholic Lorraine as well as still secretly Huguenot Chateaubriant and forcing enemies to sup and jest together. The Royal master chef, Guillaume Verger, was a poet at his trade. He commanded his *sous-chefs* like generals in the field, and, when the Court travelled, thousands of horses raced back and forth between Paris to fetch the food supplies. Catherine had begun the tours with her second son, Charles IX, when he and I were youngsters. In fairness our Queen's task was harder, and I saw the preparation for only one French progress and heard of others by repute, but it seemed to me that the French progresses had more chance of success because the King came to them not as a guest to be entertained but as a beneficent and healing Monarch. What matter that He was a very queer fellow?

King Henry's ambiguity extended far beyond boys and girls. In conversation, too, no subject was allowed to be itself. I quickly picked up the custom but saw less point in it than in the simpler graceful eloquence of our creed of Euphuism. Whereas Euphuism aspired to a certain elevation of the soul through fastidious delicacy together with elegant, extravagant diction, King Henry's Ambiguism was a game designed merely to license licence. Every word had its secret pair word that held its true meaning, the logical deduction of which was that in the end nothing could mean anything or anything, nothing. It was another language which sounded exactly like but was not at all French. No verbal potter could hope to work with such colliquate clay.

Things fared better with the food. The Royal meals were served under inlaid covers and guarded on their way from the kitchen by two officers of the Court, to watch the food and each other. That was one service I brought back to the Queen. But it was not like other food in other ways as well. In addition to the life scenes with animals that marked the banquets in the French Court, there was another entirely different order of repast for the Royal platform itself where the guests were served nothing but foods that represented themselves as something else. The sweet courses were always notable. A marzipan cake would be decorated as a mouldy circle of Dutch cheese. Stewed apricots and glazed white sugar icing were griddle-fried eggs surrounded by strips of cooked ham which were really pressed sweetened bean paste artfully sculpted and painted. The only firm realities were the several actual hermaphroditic servants who were at least allowed to remain what they had become by Nature's whim. There were many depths unsounded in young King Henry an all this silliness, and it was only fitting, was it not, that I should playfully dress him up as someone else?

## 23

I left Paris in April after nearly three sunny months (though in the main the weather was bleak) with the Court in which I had performed well for them and learnt many things, but it was time to pass on and perform my errands. We swung Eastward towards Alsace, where I was to transmit one of my parchments to Johannes Sturmius, by repute the finest intellect in Europe and a leader of Protestant resistance to Rome.

We passed smoothly along the Marne, where we feasted by the river-bank and some of the boys caught a large hamper of fish, almost one each time they cast their lines, which was convenient when we reached Nancy in the night, since my man who'd ridden ahead had been able to raise no suitable quarters for our entourage at such short notice save rooms at the university, where both the beds and the food were rather spare. I was even pleased at the mishap, because I thought it meant that we were out of Burghley's grasp. When we arrived we were able to cook our fish at the hearth, and the catch was sufficient for all. Scholars from the university came to talk with us, but I was tired and gave that task to Edward, who was anyway most eager to learn about the religious struggles in Germany. Nancy is a city of many gates, but when I visited it, there was not too much of note inside those gates. It could have been any one of a number of English towns. On the next day Strasbourg as well turned out to have many buildings in the English manner, except that the roofs were pitched much higher to throw off the snow, and there tended to be more windows, sometimes as many as eight on each storey.

In one respect Alsace might be a fancy of King Henry himself, for most of its inhabitants speak what they tell me is a dialect of German and yet have French hearts. It is set in the trough of the Rhine River between the scarp of the low Vosges Mountains and the Black Forest to the East. The plain of Alsace and Lorraine is rich, and the province is the natural road between France and Germany, which is also its main problem, for it is surrounded by strife as England is by water.

I was rather cross with the journey we had made, because Sturmius was not as imposing as his reputation. As I spoke no German I'd assumed that we should speak in French. He spoke good enough French, but it had regular Germanic phrases set in it like a string of pearls. Even worse, he would throw all his verbs to the end of every sentence. His English consisted of perhaps fifty words, which he threw together in the most surprising combinations, always ending with the proclamation: *Ve live in a vild vorld*. Soon we switched to Latin by mutual consent. He was accustomed to speak for a long time with both arms outspread. Sturmius made speeches on any pretext, which always ended with the need to oppose Rome by military means. The view was one I'd held and dropped and held and dropped yet again, and so I simply nodded as he spoke. During one morning I scarcely had to speak at all. A few odd phrases every once in a while would suffice to start to fill his sails with his own wind if his discourse started to slow, and he would race on again for another hour. He had no sense of humour and seemed to sense it. The fault was remedied by over-frequent satirical anecdotes from his own teacher, the Humanist reformer Ulrich von Hutten, of whom I'd never heard but learnt three times that he was a pupil of the illustrious Luther. By listening carefully for the name von Hutten and watching his owlish face I would know when to smile or laugh as the need might be. Whatever humour there might have been in the remarks when they were fresh had perished in the transport to Latin.

For social entertainment Sturmius took us up into the works of Strasbourg's famous clock, which we had seen and heard on entering the city. We stood on narrow scaffolds while he explained the intricate workings, which involved a great train of wheels, since the clock, besides the time of day, tells you the day itself and the settings of the moon and all the planets, while little men move across a shelf-like stage and a cock comes out to crow. It was to be sure quite clever, though I am bound to say that I was bored by the time I had witnessed my second hour parade. Edward was of course in glee. Among all the Germans there seems to be a certain preoccupation with clocks and precision that is perhaps not altogether congenial to my spirit. They all carry their own small clocks in watch-cases fixed to their clothes or even on their wrists and seem mechanically forced by them to lean forward and hurry on their tasks. After its clocks Strasbourg can boast its invention of the printing press.

To Sturmius our Queen had for many years been paying a salary of £40 a year to be Her agent *in partibus Germaniae*. The university of which he was the Rector had, he informed me again more than once, two thousand students, among them speakers of every language in Europe. On the wise plans of Sturmius, I'd been inform'd by the Queen, a new system for schools and the universities would soon be modelled in England.

However bored I was with Sturmius, I noted that he seemed sufficiently pleased with my attention and surprised by my Latin. He pressed us to stay longer, but I explained that the Queen's errands required us to press on to Frankfort. Elizabeth's message gave him every encouragement in his religious struggle but no stronger commitments than that. Nearly a decade later, in 1584, Sturmius, who was by then in extreme distress, sought aid from England and requested that I be placed in command of an English contingent in the Rhineland. It was a nice notion, but there never was any hope for it, even though the Queen did have armed forces on the continent that could have been sent to his aid. Faced with any serious problem, Her decision was always to hesitate, the more so in this instance as Prince William of Orange had recently been murdered with a musket at close hand by a fanatical Catholic. It was not certain whether he'd acted alone or as an agent, and chaos seemed near in Holland, so that was the good pretext to hold back the voluntary troops. She could plead so wisely in excuse of anything when it suited.

Frankfort was the place at which my third parchment had to

be delivered. The city had many Roman traces. It was now a place of banks and merchandize, and England's goods from many places such as Poland, Moscovy and Transylvania, were first held there before we received them. The purpose of the mission was to announce a change in order and place of payment. It suited the Queen and Lord Treasurer henceforth to receive their goods and make their payments in London because, they said, some shipments were being lost after they had been paid for at the docks of the River Main. Another reason, not given, was doubtless that it simply seemed better to delay payments. The presence of Her highest-ranking Earl was to help smooth over any possible disagreement. The bankers and the merchants trusted me about as much as a stewed prune, but there was really not much that they could do, as it would have hurt the city considerably to have such a lucrative trade route shifted. I hinted as much as though by chance when they suggested that an additional transport levy would be in order in view of the added distance. A compensation for their loss was to be a large order of new cannons.

While England meanly held back its pennies, I, having sold many properties to finance my tour, was already sensing that I should need to sell some more. In a money-lending shop in the city's old Jewish quarter I found a man who guaranteed a letter to London and its reply back in my hands within a week. More than that, any gold I wished to receive could be safely sent to any place I cared to receive it, secured by the money-lender's own gold held against release by my seal at one of the city's banks. At a certain cost. Much as I did not wish to take up ties again with Burghley, I wrote to him by this means, asking that funds be sent to me for my collection in Venice, against which I would place five estates. He did, which surprised me, and I lost these properties as well in the following year, which did not surprise me.

After Frankfort we went to Vienna where we were invited to be the guests of Charles and Elizabeth of Austria through the good offices of King Henry. Austria was to be the stopping place before I delivered the last parchment in Hungary. Along the way to Vienna we observed many industrious and domestic towns.

The people dressed roughly all the week but then paraded back and forth in finery on the main street on Sundays, nodding and smiling as they passed one another for the fifth time. As we had not one person in our retinue who spoke German and encountered no one who spoke French, English or Italian, we made the journey to Vienna as barking mutes except when we happened to find a priest or parson who spoke Latin. I learned a few phrases of German, sufficient to order their strong beer and find us beds. I was pleased to hear the echoes of Old English still ringing in the German tongue, and it seemed to me it would not take long to learn to speak it if I cared. But the harsh explosive sounds of German had little appeal for me. Until I heard a young girl cradling her kitten and speaking to it in a doorway I was not even sure that the language possessed any warmth at all.

Vienna was an old and independent city, but its Court was in total thrall to Paris, which made its style a kind of living death. The naïve young Queen was over-quick to point out how everything was done as in the Court of Henry. They'd in fact gone too far by half, for most of the windows of the Grand Hall had been hung with allegorical carpets and the resulting dark had the solemnity of a grand funeral. The courtiers all tried to speak French, but did not do it very well and mumbled to each other in German whene'er they were certain no one was looking. The lack of light in the Court was hazardous. The candles did not always give sufficient warning of the pale brown little roaches that often came to test the food before you tasted.

## 24

However unfamiliar the road from Frankfort to Vienna may have been, the path to Buda and Pest was clearly no-man's-land. It had not been that long before that the Turks had nearly taken Vienna, and martial scouts galloped about. Our fears of gentle thieves and the other kind proved baseless. We were clearly safer than we'd been on the road from Paris, where we'd experienced soft extortions at many an inn, and where men on horseback had sometimes eyed us with clear intent but had noted well the arms and guns that we were carrying. In Hungary, though the men look'd well-attired exotic savages with scimitars, there was nothing of the kind. We carried a note written in Hungarian that produced warm and modestly priced accommodation at the three inns where we stopped and friendliness wherever it was shown.

All Hungary is divided into three parts. Before I was born the nation had suffered internal division, which led to an attack by the Turkish Sultan. Hungary's king fell in battle, and Turkey occupied the most fertile portion of the kingdom. Transylvania became an independent principality ruled by the Hungarians, though obedient to the Turks, which was also most prosperous, and the rest of the country fell under the dominion of the Prince of Habsburg. These western and northern regions were held in an iron-glov'd grip and harshly squeezed for the betterment of Habsburg.

My errand was to bring my message to the governing Sultan of Buda and Pest, which are twin capitals bifurcated by the River Danube. Whatever their religious persuasion, all the wise men of my time, except Johannes Sturmius, seemed to fear that the internecine strife among the Christians of Europe would lead inexorably to conquest by the Turks. The so-called terrible Turks in Hungary seemed to me, by contrast, the most affable and courteous of men. That they have personalities that are as stubborn as they are strong no sane person who has met them can doubt for a moment. It is from this flinty and obdurate character that they possess the largest and most far-flung empire on earth. But they are also highly refined and seem inclined to share the riches of empire with their subjects, who are prosperous and contented, unlike their countrymen who live under Habsburg rule. The Turks had reached their pinnacle of glory under the late Sultan Solyman and, though in recent times Turkey had suffered a serious naval defeat in the Gulf of Corinth by a coalition headed by the Spanish, at the time of which I write their frontiers extended from Persia to Morocco, the Black Sea was a Turkish lake, and their corsairs still challenged every boat that dared to sail on the Mediterranean Sea.

Sultan Abd Ul of Buda and Pest was a sallow but most worldly man, who knew some languages of which I'd never even heard. We often conversed until late into the night, beginning in English and French and ending with Italian after midnight, when he sipped a black juice of the strangest kind, which gave his conversation much stimulation. I tried it but did not like it. Before that he would sip berry juice and, in contravention of his faith, provided me with thin but sumptuous wines from the far-off mountains of Georgia, land of the golden fleece, while he softly recounted tales of Turkey and her empire. His assurance was that, while there had been some difficulties in the past in restraining certain rapacious generals and admirals, the new Sultan and his advisers now intended to confine the Turkish dominion to the lands of the Muslims. Hungary was an exception, he said, because the languages were cousins to each other, and once the Hungarians had lived close to the Turks and the Khazars and so held many customs in common with them. I had indeed noticed that the Hungarians and the Turks seemed able to make themselves understood to one another.

From my folding chair in Hackney it is clear in retrospect that I was a credulous listener, since the Turks mounted a ferocious attack on Vienna once more eight years later, and there can be little doubt that, if they had succeeded, the Turkish dominion would have stretched within my lifetime to Scotland, Sweden and Finland, another land towards which my diplomatic friend seemed to hold a warm cousinly interest. But then I am a credulous person. I know that of myself, yet cannot cure it. Since I have trusted too greatly in everyone all my life, why should I not have trusted a most friendly Turkish sultan, especially when he put aside his berry juice and toasted the peace and good fortune of England with wine and Turkish verse? Neither of us, loyal to our rulers, ever knew what the message to Constantinople was, for it was counter-seal'd. I had to smile, thinking of how casually it had travelled to him, when he assured me that the Queen's secret message was already on its way to his ruler with five hundred of his most trusted troops.

What amazed me most about Budapest was the almost perfect order with which the tributary province was arranged. It is true that a heavy exaction was demanded and fully received from every harvest and every merchant's transaction, but the land was so rich that a sufficiency remained for everyone. Sultan Abd Ul would, however, often dolefully complain to me that he wished he were free to take less from his part of Hungary, since he could see how free Transylvania was prospering even more and had the means to establish colleges and bring scholars and inventors to them from other countries, which in turn was making their trade wealth leap forward in bounds. Be that as it may, every inhabitant knew his place and its privileges as well as precisely where they ended. Palace feasts are given in different halls at the same time, and the room in which you sit is who you are. The women cannot sit with the men. All halls had musicians playing from small interior balconies. Some had only two, while the Great Hall had ten. As all the rooms played in unison the palace itself sang out. The music was most sweet but not like ours. It combined the most dextrous zither playing I had ever witnessed with long-stringed twangs from curious instruments.

It is understood, too, in Hungary what foods your station permits you to eat. Silver and china dishes are reserved for the best dining-castles in the Palace. Pewter is used by the lesser nobility, the guild members, and doctors and scholars. The peasant eats from wooden plates, which could be most beautifully carved, and on every feast day, and there were many of them, he has a right to boil a calf in soup for himself and his family.

Moderation was everywhere. Though the religion was Muslim, little Christian churches in good repair performed their services throughout the countryside. Though drinking is forbidden by their scripture, there is no shortage of taverns for those of other faiths. The Jews are not sequestered in a special quarter but live peacefully everywhere, though it seemed to me that their main business is imports and exports. Turkish women wear veils, which does not prevent them from casting their beauty by their eyes, but Hungarian Christian and Jewish women go veil-less. The roads are the best-pav'd I have seen anywhere and spread out evenly, shaded by rows of poplars from Budapest like spokes from a wheel. Again I blush to say it now, but I shall say it: the Hungary I saw then, though divided and held largely in foreign hands, was in many ways what I dearly wished Britain to be again. I recognized the thought as unworthy of a Vere and pushed it away.

It was the end of an exceptionally warm May, and Sultan Abd Ul had decided to mark our departure with an outdoors feast. It was cooked in huge iron pots and had for its centre-piece a whole ox turned on a giant spit that looked very like a war machine intended to subdue a castle. Inside the animal were successively nested a calf, a turkey, a capon and a hare, and the nested animals were lashed with butter, groats and herbs. It was a spectacle worthy of Paris, and the food was hot as well. Looking at the people who milled round us as we ate I had cause to wish I were a painter rather than a poet. There were among them not only Hungarians from all its regions, with bright rugs wrapped around and over them, but also Serbs, Croats, Montenegrans and gypsies, the proudest and grandest gypsies I'd ever seen.

Our departure for Venice was, however, not going to take place as planned. The week before the Sultan had warmly offered me his harem, or more precisely, he had offered me my choice of the brace of strumpets that attended his four wives. I am told that the savage seal hunters of Greenland offer frozen guests their wives themselves. The Sultan gave me only one *caveto*, to avoid the tallest girl, which was not very easy to do as she was also the most beautiful, with musky skin, an eagle's nose and hair that glisten'd like polished black granite. The harem was the most serene place I'd ever been. All the rooms were tiled, and all the ceilings were as tall as private cathedrals. Fountains splashed and gaudy African birds twittered in potted trees. I was disrobed and led into a room with a shallow pool for bathing, where two of the girls soaped and sponged me like a babe. All the while the tall girl looked at me with a half-smile on her face. I wondered whether she knew that I'd been cautioned against her. None of the girls was educated, and so we had no language in common, but everyone understood that a beckoning gesture would be enough. I was about to reach out for a plump but lovely girl – there were no unattractive ones in that harem save Abd Ul's oldest wife – when the tall wanton quietly drew aside her blouse to reveal her breasts, and at the sight I instantly motioned to her. The ambiguous smile didn't leave her lips as the solemn eunuch led her by the hand towards me. That was a difficult hey-day.

Abd Ul blamed himself with a pained smile for not having warned me more specifically. The girl had given me the pox, but it was only a mild illness, which he had had himself, and could be quickly cured, he said. The purity of the harem is a myth if the man who keeps it is himself defiled. Now I saw a new room of the harem-hothouse, a deep sweating tub just like the ones we have in England for the same purpose, but this one was made of brown marble. I soaked in it every day for hours until I was the colour of braised crab or lobster, while the sorrowful Sultan crouched by the edge of the sweating tub in a luxurious towel from Bursa, the ancient capital of Turkey. The steam swirled round his hairless body as if he were a wizard. At first he told tales as he always did, until suddenly he spoke quite differently.

*Dear friend, I am guilty before you. It was chance that led us to meet*

*far from our beloved lands as we have. It was chance alone that let me fail
you as a friend, and yet I shall not forgive myself for it. But if chance lets
us meet at some future time, know that I shall not fail you again. If we
meet in Constantinople, you will be accorded the welcome due to a Sultan,
and if fate brings us to meet in London, perhaps you will be a Sultan, and
I shall be your brother.*

I held my hand up to his lips from the seething water to quieten
him. I knew of what he spoke, but I would not accept foreign
shelter merely to evade the private storms of my life. The subject
was not raised again, though the whisper of temptation continued
to be heard. Abd Ul set about curing me as if he were my physician.
For days on end he continued to neglect his duties to sit with me
by the tub, and then to ride through plains of purple wheat with
me until I sweated coldly and shivered, which was cured by
another long steep in the tub. I felt that I was melting away in
the steam.

The pox had first become apparent on the day of the departure
feast. My urinals seared me with pain whenever they functioned.
There was nothing I could do but raise my face to the ceiling in
silent screams. The alternating baths and gallops through the
countryside gradually began to have effect. The only food that
the Sultan allowed me for ten days were rare blood oranges
brought to Hungary from Morocco. They were served most
deliciously, floating as slices in perfumed flower-blossom water.
I ate them more than willingly at first, but they were placed before
me without respite on huge shallow brass trays and it soon was
clear to me that the oranges were not intended as food so much
as bitter-sweet medicine. I was served by Vashti, my suddenly
much chastened wench, who, I gathered from the Sultan's vague
response, was no longer in the harem and now wore the veil. *I
loved her once and have harmed her, but she was only Persian*, he said. She
made me drink all the flower-water, which I was most reluctant to
do, for it led to much more silent screaming. As I drank the liquid
she would place her fingers on my arm and gaze at me with
concern and sympathy. As my hands had been placed in gloves,
it was Vashti who would scratch my face when I itched. We had

no language in which to do it and so we forgave each other with a smile.

The last modestly extravagant purchase of my life, after Elizabeth and I retired to King's Place, was a young Moroccan blood-orange tree that I ordered through a bribe to Andrew, the Queen's gardener, who'd long been first apprentice to Burghley's famed John Gerard. If it had been John himself he would have given me the tree for nothing. For whatever reason Hackney is one of the few places in England where the orange tree grows in profusion. My tree ten years on is getting tall and full, though in a good year it is luck if there are four oranges on it; our English climate does not favour the exotic. Thus do I maintain a memorable aroma of a time of my life and the sad eyes and touch of beautiful Vashti.

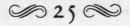 

## 25

I was not cured when we set out for Venice, but at least the searing agony had given way to simple pain. After majestic Lake Balaton, the well-paved roads gradually turned into horseways, but they were well-trodden and caused no difficulties. When we left Hungary, it was the exchange of one babble for another as we passed into the Southern reaches of the realm of the Emperor of Russia. The people had clear advantage in being so far from Moscovy, for they did not have the dark and baggy ill-fitted clothing or the dour looks of the Russians who visited our Court a decade later, when the Queen declined the Emperor Ivan's offer of marriage, proposing instead that they put off any notion of union and maintain instead welcome haven for each other in the event that there should be a misfortune in either kingdom. Their local prince did not from all we could gather demand much of them.

At every house and village along the way where we stopped for water we were met with gifts of delicious salted bread that had been sculpted into animal shapes and a pleasing powerful liquor made from fermented rye and plum. In exchange, as soon became clear, a daughter or young woman would freely select a scarf or cap to commemorate our visit. It took some time before Edward and I learned to dress ourselves in less fine raiment before making such a halt.

The only sizeable city we encountered before we passed into Italy was Laibach or Ljubljana, a twin-named city of mixed Germanic and Russian tradition. It has a lovely old castle and in some other state of health would have made a good stopping place, but I felt strangely more comfortable riding than resting, and so I urged us on. Edward, who'd been irritating me somewhat by overpraying for my health, wanted to tarry in Laibach because it was a Catholic place, but I pointed out that Italy, just ahead, would have more churches than he had prayers.

We came to Italy at Monfalcone on the Adriatic Sea and proceeded to San Dona before going on to Venice the next morning. The milk-white flow of passion's wound had fortunately ceased by then, although I was still a bit afflicted with pain. I'd read every book at Cambridge that touched on Venice and its history from the time the first exiles took refuge in its swamps until the height of its proud independence. We learnt that all the wooden bridges could bear horses and so we proceeded along the *calli* and over the pontoon bridge at the Grand Canal until we reached the Palace. I needed directions from no one, because all my reading came to life. There were the groupings of buildings, still each on its little islet, as described by Cassiodorus, like the nests of sea-birds afloat upon the waters. There, by the Riva degli Schiavoni, where now there were one-storeyed houses with laundry hanging on their roofs, was the place where once Petrarch's house had stood between two flanking towers of the sort that sprouted everywhere in a city long used to keeping watch for pirates and armies. There was the splendid old Ca' d'Oro in the Lombard style, with its Roman light and Byzantine shadow in the balconies and windows, and its roundels of porphyry. Our horses were tied at the giant elder near the Procuratie Vecchie and fitted out with bells, by law in Venice that people not be surprised and trampled by them as they come around corners on the narrow *fondamenta*. When I was there many wished to ban all but the Prince's horses from the city. I do not know how that argument has resolved itself. Certainly the number and size of some of the black galleys going up and down the canals were sufficient to every apparent need of the city, though I myself thought most of the gundoliers were base and dangerous-looking fellows.

It was untimely in the extreme to be taken away at once and by my own hand from this city so new and so familiar of my dreams. But after we'd been received and had presented our letters at Court, I asked advice of the Court physician about my ailment. He sniffed a glass bowl of my urine and held it up to the light before advising me: *Hie you to Padua, good Lord. There is there a famous physician knows every cure to strange sores and evil flows.* I had to stay awhile in Venice because my money had not arrived on time, but then I left and set off angrily for Padua, intending to return to the most admirable of all cities forthwith. The two cities are less than a day's distance from each other. In fact, it would be many months 'ere I saw Venice again, and on that visit, too, my stay would be too short. This was my Venice, and that was nearly the cruellest joke of my journey.

Padua had been one of my intended destinations, and yet the god Circumstance ruled here, too, that I would not see much more of one of Italy's oldest cities than I had of Venice. A letter from my Pondus expressed grave concern because, he heard, English gentlemen had been killed in Padua. In fact, it was two noble gentlemen of Polonia who'd been killed. The Italians, for whatever reason, call all foreigners *Gentiluomini Inglesi*. It is not, I fear, a compliment.

We were received with full ceremony by both of Padua's Venetian Governors in the Palazzo della Ragione. But Fra Giovanni, who was to be my all-curing physician, had left the city to attend the Governor of Verona, Venice's other subject city. We were not free to leave Padua until we had been properly fêted in the huge and columnless Great Hall the next day, when salt or spice in the soup made me jig furiously in my bedroom through the night. It was not long to Verona, but there was no Fra Giovanni there either. He had indeed gone to attend the Governor of Verona, who had fallen ill in Bologna. Though Bologna had become a Papal state it was not reckoned to be a dangerous one for Englishmen. Once found my priestly physician offered me cure after Confession. I accepted his invitation quickly. His examination involved prolonged staring into my eyes while exhaling his strong breath over my face, and his prescription was an equally noxious mixture of ground herbs and roots. Whether it was indeed his cure or simply that the disease had run its course, I never had any more trouble of that sort, though I doubt if I would now even notice such a petty pox against my current affliction.

Cleansed or purged, it was now possible to begin to savour the Italy that I had been seeing with little enthusiasm until now. The unhealthy traveller sees only one monument. Bologna impressed us all the same as somewhat dreary in comparison with Padua and Verona, which themselves had a tendency to run after Venice. As it was one of the cities of the young man Dante, I reread the *Purgatorio* while we were in Bologna, finding it, too, as tedious as I'd remembered it, though I sympathized with his displeasure at incessant changes of manner of government. We dipped down to Florence and Siena, spending about three weeks in each city and participating in all their tournaments and ceremonies. There are no better cities in all of Italy.

It goes without saying that the past of Siena is more interesting if less pleasant than its present-day vassalage to Florence and the de' Medici rule, which is itself only on patent from King Philip. Spain does not yet rule Italy, but she controls her and is poised to rule at any time. Thus Siena takes pride in an independence that it knows has been tried and is false. The city has been the alchemist of freedom, and all of its failed and partially successful ideas still live in the minds of its hopeful people even if there is base metal in the crucible. Their tradition of faction has always insured instability, as the people of the majority, the people of the middle faction, and the people of the minority have endlessly combined and broken with each other in a determined struggle for supremacy. At one point the nobility was swept entirely away from government, then restored to a share in rulership, which was again removed after the death of the Sienese Pope in the last century. All one can say is that the city has for hundreds of years been mostly in the hands of ignorant, obdurate and tempestuous men interspersed with Summer seasons of magnificent prosperity before the disorder begins again. None the less the arts flourish best of all in Siena, aided perhaps by a long suspension of building in the city during the centuries of demagoguery, which has left the town unspoilt by vulgar novelty. The ordinary people carve wood and fine tiles and dishes better than it is done anywhere else in their country. Their wall art with its great vivacity and colour belongs mostly to their past, but there are now many poets, writers and historians. The poets are hindered, as are ours sometimes, because they cling too much to the old Latin rhythms. I found the historians the most engrossing and frequently would engage in disputes with them far into the night. Sometimes we would scarcely have fought our way up to the times of Pandulpho the Magnificent before the first rays of dawn illumined the murals. In everything they do the Sienese gaze steadfastly into the navel of their state. I was surpris'd to observe that Siena was overfilled with Englishmen. Some come to stand in awe before the ancient buildings and works of art, other younger travellers to admire their endless experiments in government, oblivious to the fact that all have ended badly. I avoided these countrymen with grace whenever I could. They use whatever Italian they have with an unctuous smug smile and fail to note how their affection for the Italians is often not reciprocated, even in Siena, which is the most courteous of Italian cities.

Florence is nothing if not patrician. Here I felt most at home in enjoyment of the seams and fall of their garments, the tool'd leather bindings of their many books, the care and exactness with which they speak. It is true that their artistic glories belong to the past, but to that past, after all, belong both Dante and Boccaccio, as well, I must admit, as Machiavel, though it would appear that he exercizes far less influence in the city of his birth than he does in England's Court. I tried once more to admire Dante while I lived in Florence, but to no greater avail. Though he may be a great poet, there is a certain something, a lack of concordance between our spirits, for which neither of us may be faulted. Whenever the conversation turned to Dante, as frequently it did, I'd deftly counter with my deep enthusiasm for Boccaccio. My hosts often wondered at the length to which I could recite his tales, and I did not expect the strong volley of our Chaucer with which the compliment was returned. One learned young Medici even astonished me by reciting my dear uncle Thomas's 'Ditty Representing the Image of Death', which I later gave to the gravedigger to misquote in my play. The Florentines have much wealth and long lineage to pride themselves upon, but their city had once long ago been decimated by the plague, and this misfortune has stamped a grave disposition upon its posterity, though they maintain the noble Roman tradition of carousing as well.

## ᘒᕉ 26 ᕉᘒ

My tinker's wife has brought me a tale from the city, of a young man and his betrothed, who suddenly was stricken with the plague on the day before the marriage, which was moved forward to that evening so that she could be married moaning at his side in an empty church and with the priest at a great distance from them. As the words uniting them were spoken, the bride fell down dead at her husband's feet, and he fled in grief and horror from the church. I wondered what suicidal priest would have encouraged such nuptials, and who would have been the witnesses to this tragic tale in the empty church, and which church precisely had it been? But she did not know, of course. Such double-tender tales and plays are what the people want. Once I could do that sort of thing rather well, but now I haven't the taste for it. It is curious how enthusiastically the event was related to me, as though it were an amusing anecdote that had nothing to do with me at all. It is only the quickness of the story that really takes my fancy. I shall not mind the slow pace if I recover on some swift wing of good fortune, but if the slow coach is all the same to come, as I suspect, then I shall meet death not with fear but with scorn.

I'd left a handful of my players behind in Venice to study their
playing and was glad that those who'd come with me were equally
able to profit in Florence because the players there were very
practis'd. Edward and I were living at the edge of a beautiful plain
called Valdarno in a courtier's estate. From a nearby hillside
Valdarno's gardens looked like an intricate green bedcover. All
the best people of Florence, except the Duke himself, lived there.
Our men were housed in the poor quarter of the city and came
to us each morning. Among the delights of our estate was a
miniature house built on the slopes behind the estate. An intricate
maze of hedges and flower-beds led to the house, the walls of
which were painted with naked women and satyrs. It had only a
leather bed and glasses and bottles of Tuscan wine within it. But
I had just regained my full health and so I smiled ruefully and
shook my head.

An autumnal migration of the nobility was just beginning as
the weather turned crisp. It was explained that every year at this
time first families and their entourages from everywhere in Italy
left their affairs in the hands of their prefects and sailed to Sicily
for a rustic rest in the sunshine. Sicily is ruled by the King of
Naples, but there is an unwritten treaty between all the city-states
that no animosities will be allowed to arise between any state or
family during this period of traditional rest. There is something
droll, I should add here, about this tradition, because the Sicilians
themselves maintain a sacred and ferocious tradition of family
feud, which may be not only between different families, but also
between branches of the same family, and though sometimes the
good offices of the *parolanti* could avert fatalities, that was not the
most common outcome. Sicilian habits, however, never were
allowed to come closer than idle recountings to the high-born

Autumnal visitors. Even the pirates understood that it was a dangerous time of year to ply their trade from September through November, as this was the time when all the shipping channels were most carefully patrolled.

As I had to go North again to pick up my men in Venice and was anyway keen to have a proper look at the Tuscan towns I'd been forced to dash through with such minimal ceremony, it was agreed that we should proceed to the North for three weeks and then be met by an excellent cargo ship belonging to my Florentine host, which would bear us directly to Palermo in just a few days. The intention was to visit four cities, but the hospitality in the first was so great that I did not even in the end have time to get to Venice and had to send word ahead to the players to await my return there in two months.

## ∞ 28 ∞

And so we set off to Mantua, the scene of my youth's first green dramatic passion, *Romeus and Juliet*, that overripe romance that well we used many years later, John and I. I knew that place of old by the tales of my music master. The sojourn to Mantua was a petty prince's progress. I held only fifteen men with me, but they were all fit and pleasant. In Florence we had taken on some additional lackeys, too, brighter than the servants of many travelling lords. It was a matter of, say, two dozen men and boys; I forget precisely how many.

Happily it is the habit in Italy for a Lord on progress to hire his post-horses and carriages like any English townsman, which suited us well in Florence, for plenty of carriages were available. The tedious difficulty in Venice had been that six equipages stood waiting and tied firmly already to foreign hire, bound most for Milan, and it had cost dearly to get any at all. I sent my second-favourite servant, Deny, to hire the carriages in Florence. He had no Italian, but his French was fine and he was called Deny the Frenchman. We'd been surpris'd how the French tongue was deep into Italy comprehended.

The custom was this. A double hire fee was taken in Genoa or Venice, but after this honey fee the way back would be free, and half the carriages returned empty from Florence and Rome. For the Englishman, the Frenchman and the Spaniard invariably elected to spend another season in Italy. The traffic was steady in one direction only. 'Twas not hard work to have the drivers well-brib'd with several ducats. We thus quickly had five fine and level carriages, which was much better than our departure from Venice, where we'd had only a single heavily overloaded baggage carriage to follow behind us. These carriages met us before dawn, and all our goods were swiftly loaded by our men as though they were desperate to save the bags from road-way thieves. There was some delay while Deny's Angela wept and swore whore's oaths of love and grief for him, but I tossed her a coin and he was freed the very instant with a monkey grin.

I showed my ring at the gate and our twenty wheels and ten horses swept out of Florence. Edward's coach was behind mine, with our agents split between us, and after that the vassals in two carriages with some spare trunks and, lastly, the baggage train itself. The leather panels were well-oiled, the seats were soft, the road-way was well-paved. I breathed deeply and imagined I could smell the passengers before me. One could hear our gentle Italian knaves debating as they drove us how they would finally report their delay, broken axles or horses' health. They also speculated how best to trim my purse, as though I was the nose between their eyes and nowhere to be seen, until I turned and shouted up to them through the slot a simple question, *Che é la citta piu elegante dell' Italia?* This Italian wondrously defus'd their knavery, and I do smile even now to remember how many black-brow'd or worried looks came from them after that. We'd had exactly the same thing out of Venice.

Our procession stopped in four villages and questions were put about the craftsmen at each, but there was little to purchase save polished barrels with silver hoops, and so we rushed past the rest to reach Mantua by dinner.

Little Mantua wrenched awe from me immediately I came within its walls. I'd been pushed to go there by the Medicis and quickly came to love it as much as any city in Italy. We spent almost all our time there until we had to report to Genoa. The Etruscan walls of the city hold thirty thousand men and will not soon be taken, I think. The city is really two landed islands slightly above an almost sea of marshes, and these are webbed together by bridges. The walls are too cunningly effected. If your enemy can never take you, neither can you easily move out to drive him from where he is established. The defect that torments this town is its poisonous moisture. It is a fine town that never ceases its coughing. But the Mantuans, like the scholars of wet Cambridge, evidently forgive her her malicious air.

As we entered, a full-dressed battalion stood on either side. In truth I did not expect so much. At dinner we learned that the Duke had been expecting Pope Gregory as well that day, but he had sent a messenger with word that he could not be timely parted as he'd promis'd. For myself I am scarcely Catholic enough that I missed His Holiness and was content to have the mellow trumpets of his intended greeting corps for ourselves instead.

The town was full of that rare Italian master Giulio Romano. Her cathedral itself rises from the highest ground and is executed, badly, in mockery Roman'd style, but the interior has been done according to Romano's plans after his death by his disciples. The old ducal palace, certainly one of the finest in Europe that I myself saw, has likewise new and wondrous apartments by Romano and his men. I thought of the best bed-rooms and the very first houses of my island and felt some sorrow for England. We have rich rooms but they are dark and heavy, all luxury with little lightness. In Mantua the Dukes have trusted their artists with the matter of their lives as much as any martial master. Even Romano's own little house on Via Poma was an artist's locket. Pure surprise came later at the Palazzo Te, the Duke's summer house in that same city. Again Romano, frescos worthy of Apollo's own Temple wherein the Titans fall backwards towards the eye before cascading rocks and the thunderbolts of Jove. The man knew neither river-banks nor frame in his artistry. He was painter and architect and sculptor and poet and scientist at once and everywhere. Never have I seen women and cherubs closer to lust. He was Raphael's student and had been set up in his place in Mantua by the great Castiglione; there he enjoyed the protection of a prince who shared his every move and aspiration, and so his art flower'd until Pope Clement frown'd on his licentious lines. Sooner or later that is the fate of every artist. I put his painting hand in *The Rape of Lucrece*.

The Duke Gian Francesco was pleased enough to have me in his Court. I spoke Italian to him, he English'd me, a little clownishly perhaps, but I showed nothing of it. We served each other warm and noble gossip, attended by his slender Duchess. The wine was served in toy decanters floating in chilled water. They pride themselves on their cloudy, fruity wine, but apart from the Friuli it is not as good as the French wine. The Pages were comely young women dressed as Roman soldiers in loose tunics. Mine almost gave me her breast with each serve. As we ate, again with forks as in most of the Courts in Italy, a chorus of eight lutes played shepherds' tunes. As eager courtiers of a less important city the Mantuans had mastered the new eating device better and more universally than I had seen elsewhere.

Suddenly I was sad because I saw that Castle Hedingham would have, should have, could have been the hub of just such a fair city, and I'd have played Romano to my father John. Silly dream. Time and circumstance ran counter. I paid courtly respects to the Duchess, whose breasts and cheeks had long gone dry, but she was yet a striking Italian lioness severely draped in silk and silver. Her eyes were that still I thought I could see my velvet cap and thin moustache in the liquid within the crystal. The straw colour of her eyes said it was Autumn but that fierce fires still burned in the haystalks o' the field. With neither leave nor leisure to love the lady, I saved my words and listened to her still, passionate talk of Giulio Romano. 'Twas well for her husband the Duke that Romano was already in his deep pit.

Mantua caused my mind to speed, and I bethought myself of still other possibilities. Happy a land or a city where art is on every wall, in every fold of cloth, within every eye and heart. Here once lived Virgil, lately Romano, and now every art and scholarship. There is even an archival castle. Cough on, happy Mantua. I shall convince Her, I told myself then, that it is the least expensive charging staff, emboss'd in mere silver, for any gentle nation after swords and brave soldiers. 'Tis not a lowly servant or trusty fief, but rather the powerful heavenly cherub, whereby one knows a well-ordered people, dangerous if they are roused. Who knows what to expect from a nation whose art may grow so great? Only let the embassadors see such a vigorous Court in London, and they will counsel caution to their Kings.

It was at last time for Milan, Spanish fortress of Italy. The trunks were packed, the men were counted, horses fed, lovable silly Edward was drawn again from church where he had repaired for just one more Confession. The Seymours are parched of England's Church and thirsty for noble Roman ways, which is fine, but they are nowhere to be had in Italy's Church, hourly coining its plots. As we left the city, the morning winds pushed thick cloud into the sky and, though they were summer showers, they gave us six lashes when the rain was delivered. Twice we had to stop because we could not see the road, and once a back carriage went rutting out of the road, and it took an hour for all the men to harness and draw it up.

I was amused while waiting by Robert Rose's merry tale of Thomas's dusty seduction in Mantua. That Page, more given to fornications than any other of my lads, had marked the comeliest maidservant of a Lady-in-waiting to Isabella. The Lady herself was of no alluring beauty, but Thomas pretended that he was bringing her a message of attention from Lord Seymour. The maidservant appointed herself foreign secretary in matters of high passion and willingly went to conspire with clever Thomas. He gave his intended Maria a small lace pouch of balsumum and pine needles. Shaped like a long strawberry, the parcel was to place in her generous bosom. Thomas was practised in unlacing neck-manacles, and Maria herself was not bound by her namesake and in fact was well-heated by the prospect of their several mutual passions. But when he placed his other hand within her linen bodice correctly to position the fragrant lace pouch from below, he found that he'd unloos'd a wind of leaves and gnats and cobwebs. The maid remembered herself and grasped her neck. For the women of Mantua, as Robert explained, hire their warmth to nurture the Oriental silkworms wherefrom the city's famous silks come.

Thomas was too eager a lover to let his passion be so dusted, and so he switched to her skirts and lesser heart. She fought him like a tigress, but it was not her honour she defended. When he laid bare his treasure, it was more dust and pods, of which one was broken and a-birthing on the floor. That day he had nothing from Maria but bites and scratches. For my part, though, I hatched two of my favourite *Midsummer*'s lines from Robert's merry tale:

> To have my love to bed, and to arise,
> And pluck the wings from painted butterflies.

The road and rain improved. The carriage sway'd like a cradle. When Robert woke me, we were in Milan.

## ❦ 29 ❧

Milan was very nearly a grave mistake. To go there was contrary to the Queen's desire, and one could scarcely argue that such a visit was not dangerous as far as I was concerned. Edward's declared Catholic sympathies made his family one of them. My suspected sympathies might have been tested. There were Spaniards who would have liked to see Elizabeth's highest Earl given slight cramps upon the rack. Eternal enmity is often particularly reserved for those who are your not-quite friends and allies, from frustration that your real enemies are out of reach and to cause them pain from a distance. None the less, I was determined by the perversity of my nature at least to sample Spain in Milan as I had sampled Turkey in Budapest. I'd taken a monk's robe with me from the wardrobe of the players in Florence, paid the coachmen a ducat for their silence and thus rolled through the gates of Milan a holy father.

Milan I found a pell-mell of activity and bustle. Upon entry we were immediately at cross-purposes with a coach that had wished our procession to cede way to it. Our lead driver waved his fist and shouted maternal allegations at the facing coachman, who did not reciprocate strongly enough. A slender beauty in a black dress, which blossomed out like a lily with much snow-white lace upon the black, jumped out into the dusty street and took up the exchange with our coachman. They knew no differences of rank, sex or age as they railed against one another. Our driver sounded firm-set but then shrugged his shoulders and pointed to the row of carriages behind him almost apologetically, whereupon the fiery lady gave a grimace smile and turned upon her own timid coachman, ordering him to pull their coach to the side. The tempest had passed as quickly as it commenced.

The twin powers of merchandize and the clergy were everywhere in evidence and not in any conflict. On the contrary many priests walked by with large unchurchly articles of silver and brass, and almost all the merchants could be seen to cross themselves endlessly as they bargained. The Spaniards of all sorts stood out immediately to the eye because they walked more soberly, with solemn bearing and their heads often tilted slightly backwards. Even the servants knew that they were the rulers.

For three days I accompanied Edward as his good friar who had lived concealed as a schoolteacher for many years in England and now was subjecting himself to a ban of silence whilst the true faith was suppressed in our native land. From Edward I learnt that those monks whom we encountered accepted me for what I seemed, though they spoke of me as manifestly eccentric and too-long removed from the direction of an order. I felt like an ambulatory ear and did not like much of what I heard. Charming and conspiratorial in London, the Spaniards at the Duke's palace in Milan were stiff-borne and cold-eyed. They were the vaward [vanguard A.F.] of Spanish Italy and their table talk, half Italian, half Spanish, consisted more often than not of positioning who among them would rule which cities when their hired Italian dukes and princes were at last turned out. As for the Pope and Rome, he was their great ally to be sure, but only of convenience, and sooner or later Madrid, or perhaps Barcelona, would have to be the New Rome. When the conversation was not politic, it would be religious and theoric. Everyone was always too intent upon his purpose ever to be in good humour.

It is my nature's inclination to spy at people by day and books by candlelight; when I spied a lieutenant of the Court from a distance talking intently with one of our coachmen, I knew that it was time to cease my games. After speaking with Edward, I took the best horse and rode straight out of the city unmolested. My disguise was my real appearance. Edward and I met by prearrangement the next day and drove directly to Genoa.

Genoa the Superb was yet another of the long'd-for cities that I scarcely saw. We rode through the Apennines behind the city and swept straight down to the docks without calling at the Palace of the Doges. Our boat, which was not even due to meet us until the morrow, had fortunately already docked. Though the Corsican Captain refused to depart early because he was due to take on other passengers, we rested peacefully and comfortably enough on board the boat until we set sail on the morning after the next day. Genoa, silver-bright in the early morning, did, in fact, finally look quite grand set against the hills as we sailed away. Coming into the city down its foothills, it had appeared clumsy in some places and mean in others.

Waiting to depart had given me the idle time to rest and scribble down some notes on my hard-favour'd Grand Tour to date, and it is thanks to those sheets that my memory appears, falsely, so famous for those days. Well, too, they were happy days an their sundry difficulties, and it has been uplifting to me in this hot, dry valley not far removed from death to remember them. I'd been abroad for nearly a year and it was the first period in my life when I'd not written a single poem.

I don't know what I was thinking of when I plunged into dangerous Milan for no particular purpose except my insatiable energy and curiosity. I paid the suspect coachman slightly less than we'd agreed upon and suggested that he might ask the missing portion from his lords of Milan, whom he also served. He look'd at me with scornful narrow eyes and then, after a careful pause, he took the money quickly and turn'd his back. Since I was well content with the success of my adventure, it was hard to fault that trip to Spain by conjuration, complete even with a proud Moorish general. My only real regret was that I'd had to shave to play the friar and would still look a bristly boy when we arrived at Palermo.

## ~ 30 ~

The sea was calm, the wind was steady. The hard part of the trip was the necessity to stay on board when the *Gentiana* put off part of its cargo of Swiss herbs near Rome. Gregory XIII was a friend of neither England nor art. He wanted to convert the world, to which end he rushed about showing himself to it like a player. But failing that, he was more than ready to have armies do what he could not. I climbed the mast to see if I could catch a glimpse of the city, but I was not even certain if I saw smoke in the far distance. I could only take comfort in the fact that there were few in Rome who knew its history and its poets as I did. There was a similar short stop in Naples, and then the weather reverted to the second Summer I'd had that year.

As the ropes were thrown out on our arrival at a pier protruding from a little tongue of land in the old harbour of Palermo a small welcoming party assembled, and we knew most of them. There was even Othman the Moor, whom I had seen less than a week before in Milan. In truth, the inhabitants of hostile and rival cities and countries here consorted happily with one another. It was the traditional character of the island. From Norman times all sects of Christians, the Muslim and the Jew have lived there without strife. The visitors stood barefooted in the water at the end of the pier, wearing mock-Roman cotton costumes. In these same costumes I later saw they would, men and women, slowly walk into the harbour up to their necks and swim exactly fifty artfully slow strokes in parallel with the shore before walking from the water. Though I can swim, I did not have the practis'd strokes that had been learnt by my Italian friends, and so I declined their invitation to swim with them. Edward splashed earnestly and happily like a puppy thrown overboard, yet when he left the water exhausted, he would almost invariably be at the same spot at which he'd entered it. When the swimmers came out of the water, their togas sculpted their bodies in high relief. The men looked like disembarking heroes from Homer. The more beautiful of the women were wanton ambling nymphs, with long, dishevelled hair and stiffened nipples. They plac'd their hands upon their hips as they talked to better dry their costumes and show their breasts. It was not always easy to recognize the same subdu'd noblewoman from Siena or Florence. Modesty it would appear had been left behind at home.

At first I was disinclined to frolic with them, but after several weeks I had Summer lovers. They did not seem to care that I was married. An English traveller named Buck had brought the news to Florence in September that my wife had had a daughter named Elizabeth in July. There is naught of that Winter's second Summer in *The Winter's Tale* save the constant confusion of station and person that often reigned in Sicily. For that play I simply reversed the myth of Protesilaus and Laodamia to demonstrate how our thinking of a thing may often surpass the thing itself, a problem that is, alas, too well-known to me. Another of my plays, *Much Ado About Nothing*, better conveys the froth, foam and rumour of that Sicilian Summer.

When I had been in Sicily three weeks, there was a universal tournament in which courtiers contended for the honour of their princes, and princes and dukes fought for the glory of their cities or their kings. I was the only Englishman in attendance and the only Earl, though there were, beside the several-score Italian nobles, a flock of Spaniards, a handful of French, three Turks, a German and a Swede. All the combatants assembled at the ancient square of the city, the Quatro Cantoni, and march'd along the harbour under banners that had been prepared by the Prince of Naples, who walked under two flags, Naples and Spain. There were throngs along our route. I'd known little of Palermo beyond what Thucydides tells us, that it was first the possession of Phoenicians and then of the Greeks, and of course I knew of the Norman conquest of the reigning Saracens in later centuries, but I was unprepared for its size, expecting a sleepy provincial capital.

No city I'd yet visited in Italy, except Venice, was as large. The procession ended finally at the Palazzo Chiaramonte, the finest in the city, before which the contests would be held. Palermo's buildings, in keeping with its character, are a mixture of Saracen, Latin and Greek styles, and the tournament could have been in the twelfth century.

The first event was the wrestling, at which I had to be at a disadvantage for my slight size. But the sky was a blue of heaven's own tint, the resplendent lawns and gardens seemed to return the sun's rays, and I felt huge and competent beyond all thinking. The very clouds then were but my breath. By frenzy and change of pace I won each grapple until I toss'd my friend the burly Moor, whose fierce frown of war changed to surprise as he lay on his back. The races were easy, but then I lost the javelin contest to the Swede, and rage sounded within my skyish pride. With a shout, I named my own contest in three languages, which was a challenge to all who dared to joust with me with any weapon. I fought seven contests over three hours and won them all, mainly by storm, though not without skill. The hardest was the last, a fence by dagger with a sinister Spaniard. There would be no easy contest decided by a nick or a dropped sword or shield here. He was fast but reckless, and so I gradually let him take the offensive as we hacked away at each other, calculating all my readiness to leap aside faster than he could lunge. It happened as I hoped, and I knealt by him on both knees with lightning speed, my left hand pressing him to the ground while my dagger hand was poised above him. He muttered something in Spanish, which I could not understand, but the cheering and the sound of the bell-tower told me I had won. It was just as well, since it was becoming clear that he was combining public sport and private villainy. The dagger is a vile tool.

In my triumph a laurel wreath was placed upon my head and the Prince broke the symbolic staff of his office, a thin black rod embossed with silver rings, and handed both halves to me. I had conquered Italy.

Now I was fought over and passed from hand to hand as guest

at the exalted country houses of dozens of ancient kings. They had quaint ancient and deeply recondite poetic names such as Ziza, La Favara and Mimnerno. The grandest of them had been built by two kings, William the Good and William the Bad. 'Tis pity I never used that. As for Edward, he'd retired to a monastery and spent most of his time in the Royal chapel and San Giovanni degli Eremiti, both Christian churches wearing Saracen cloaks. As I was becoming fond of Edward and worried about so much worship in one so young, I was secretly glad that our travels had chanced to throw him into such a confusing ecumenical pot. Our blissful island life stretched out endlessly before us. At Christmas we had a feast in weather worthy of Palestine before a manger on the Palazzo lawn between tall palms. Ordinarily most of the visitors would have returned to their Northern homes after Christmas, but the frost to the North was strong that year and the majority preferred to remain in the balm of Sicilian weather.

In all these weeks I still moved through Palermo as a fearless warrior and knew there was nothing I couldn't accomplish. But my high spirits went into full eclipse as I stood on the coarse and hot black sand and ash of Mount Etna, Jebel to the Saracens, and stared at its fiery and bubbling anger. Ten men and twenty servants had ridden across the island to see Syracuse, Messina and the giant mountain of fire. Standing swathed in sulphur fumes, I suddenly shrank and was smaller than a man. There was the sulphurous pit, burning, scalding, beckoning. An o'erpowering urge seized me and whispered inside my ear to go forward and hurl myself early and at last into the teeth of time and razure of oblivion. I remember little after that except that I was being manhandled back to the horses, which were being held at the edge of the green slopes a quarter of a mile below. My hands were tied behind me as my horse was led along, with the servants and Edward tending me. Later Edward told me that he had heard me mutter to myself: *I shall hurl myself into Etna*, and then I had toss'd off my riding cloak and run forward, but he'd been able to overtake me and grab my arm. He said that for a long time I twisted and gnash'd my teeth as I was led along. All I recall is the poisonous reek of sulphur in my clothing and my passion to be freed.

Everyone agreed that some are subject to be maddened by the sulphurous fumes of Etna, and that a full cure was to be had simply by never returning to the cursed mountain. It was of no great matter. But I well knew that the lunatic, the lover and the poet are subject to strange calls. And I was ashamed on that ideal island, where yesterday I'd been the hero.

There was a ship loading bananas, date palms, lemons, olives, figs and almonds to be carried to Venice, and I determined it was time to quit Sicily. The Captain complained that there was no room for so many men on his floating fruit-dish, but he didn't protest too much, as I was prepared to pay him more than he would have had for the extra crates of cargo, and I think as well that he knew my reputation on the island. We had an unbroken though choppy voyage to Venice. The men passed the time playing cards and eating fruit. And when their bowels were too full of fruit, they would suddenly burst out over the railing. By the last day the men had laid aside their cards and in great good humour were betting on each other. Part of the trouble with our glorious Queen and Her Father, I think, was that, like so many of our richest countrymen, they always ate beef for breakfast. I think it makes the bowels and the character strange.

## 31

My second stay in Venice was destined to be only a little longer than the first. My repute had swelled proudly on word from Palermo, but I was by then disinclined to enjoy it. I would announce my illness and tell all my conversants that I would speak to them on this or that when my solemnity had passed. Rumour at once of course held that I suffer'd in love on Sicily, and that drove young women to try to heal my spirit and make me feel love again. In consequence I took considerable refuge in galleys and acquainted myself with all the hundred canals of the city, frequently stopping to bargain for foods and trinkets I did not really want or need.

Sir Richard Shelley once again had sent me one of his gentlemen to offer me a furnish'd house to cost me nothing while I was in Venice. I had double reason to refuse this time. The first time was because I had reason to suspect he was an agent of Burghley's. I'd sent my father-in-law a letter in which, to protect myself, I'd said the opposite of everything I felt: that I adored Germany, never wanted to see Italy again and had seen enough of Spain in Italy to be able to guess the worst. It was always painful to write to Pondus. There are people with whom any morsel of truth carelessly given will be used to entangle you in some way. Because I knew from childhood that my illnesses always made him happy, since it meant I was more controlled, in my letter I extended the illness that I'd first still had in Venice as a cause to have me yet remain in these most unsatisfactory places. Then one afternoon Brian, one of the players I'd left behind, met me in the early evening at our landing on the Grand Canal and warned me that a messenger from England had been searching for me throughout the city all day long. He did not know what news the messenger brought or even by whom he had been sent. It was obvious that a message could be only from the Queen or Burghley, though in fact it turned out to be much worse than that.

Instructions were given to bring a horse straightaway and to instruct sweet long-suffering Edward to come with all the men in a calm and secret way to nearby Ferrara that very evening. I had not finish'd breakfast the next morning when the smiling messenger appeared with his report, which also gave me the strongest possible surmise that there had to be an agent among my men, else how would he have known to come to Ferrara?

Thus it was back to Venice, not to stay but to board a ship as soon as possible for France and then to England. I'd decided to ignore any order to return from the Court, but this was wicked slander, which, grown restless with the litany of my bastardy and buggery, now needed to make me a cuckold. Or else, it might be true. Either way, it would be necessary to return.

We sailed on a boat to Marseilles, and I was even glad for the long voyage, which gave me sufficient time to calm down somewhat. I left Edward among the early Christian heretics of Southern France whom my father had loved so much and proceeded over land to Paris and Calais. If I'd left my store of purchases with Edward's train I'd not have lost them all.

While we were still within sight of the coast an encrusted and flagless boat three times our length bore down on us, and the wretches easily attached us with their lines. Their boarding was absurdity itself. There was not one weapon on board save my own sword, which I therefore did not even bother to draw as they had muskets, besides which they were all scullions, even for pirates. Both boats stank like fish-galleys. It was not an heraldic encounter. What put the sea-cap on it all was that these were pirates of our good allies the Dutch.

When the pirates saw that we carried not only no arms, but also little cargo, they were mightily vexed, until their linguist, in searching the papers of my red-faced messenger, discovered that they had at least caught an English earl. We were taken to the harbour of a modest town, the name of which I never learnt, and I was waited on with elaborate deference by the rogues for ten days while they sent for my ransom. They were, though, paid out scot and lot, because early one morning three fully-arm'd Dutch frigates sailed into the harbour, and I was passed over to custody of the Dutch troops by the pirates as effortlessly as they had taken me. Five hours later I was in England.

But the Dutch pirates all the same managed to steal almost all my goods before they were arrested, including most of my gifts intended for the Queen. They could not be found before we were freed to go to England.

When I landed to meet Pondus and his daughter with her head hung low, I experienced an almost overwhelming desire to kill for the second time in my life. I did not push them off the pier as instinct bade me, though I did stay away from Anne for five years from that time. I made one effort in April to attend Court and carried the Queen's train at ceremony, but my heart was not in it, and I began to spend more and more of my time in my apartments at the Savoy with the players and at Blackfriars Convent with my writers.

## 32

It's time now to write of that woman, my Dark Lady, Anne
Vavasour. She was a child when we first were lovers. Anne was
a tall Yorkshire girl from near Saxton. They are not for all men,
but for some the Yorkshire woman has a special force, and I, alas,
am one of those. There were echoes, I think, of my first wench
at Earl's Colne, who was also a Yorkshire girl. I did not love
Anne most of all, but I shall not deny that she brought seasonal
passions and the greatest rages of the heart I ever experienced.
More, as this was the time I was worst troubled with the other
Anne, there was all the same freedom in that lightning-cross'd
love.

Her father was Henry Vavasour, head of the Vavasour clan of
Yorkshire, famous for the boldness of its soldiers and the beauty
of its women. The Vavasours are even more famous, of course,
for being the first among open Romanists left within the realm.
King Harry, I am told, traded passions with the most beautiful of Anne's aunts, and the Vavasours alone in all of England
were allowed to keep their parish chapel and two priests and a
sexton when Henry dissolved the Church properties. It was this
special situation that served to double the natural marginality
of the Vavasours, that which gave them their sadness and their
strength.

For the Vavasours derive naturally from the *valvassores majores*,
which is to say, they were tenants-in-chief of many of the higher
noble families but not quite themselves noble. Their standing
would waver. Under Henry II they loomed above most of the
lower knighthood and seemed about to become minor barons,
but somewhere along the way in the next two centuries they
descended, until it could be reckoned precisely that it took five
vavasours to be worth one knight. They kept their land and

their great dignity as they were pressed from below by swelling numbers of lower and mediate sub-vassals of substance. Somehow it happened among us that there was never suitable place for those of middle rank as there is in other countries. They never knew whom they should marry. The middle has taken its revenge upon us later, in these days.

Henry Vavasour was tall like his daughter and had the same sadness and dignity, which, in his case, made him look a Spanish grandee. They were country cousins, though far-removed, of the Veres and the Howards, and so they stopped regularly at Castle Hedingham on their way to Court. We knew them well.

Anne's mother was the daughter of Sir Henry Knyvett of Norfolk. The Knyvetts and the Vavasours mingled friendship and then blood in Henry's Court, though afterwards the Vavasours stuck to the pure solitude of their chapel while the Knyvett clan crept and flew in and out of service around Elizabeth. The very name Knyvett is a razor to my wounded heart after all my suffering from them. They have the same overhigh pride as the Vavasours, but they are also sharp and passing empty. The Knyvetts made a myth of how I'd ravished innocent Anne and set her on her woeful way. Let's grant, by now, that it does need some explanation to account for the heavy harvest of lovers and husbands she reaps.

I swear her virgin's faith had fled from her a year before I laid an eye on her that Summer at Hampton Court. She was thirteen but already a woman. Anne may be both wounded and wayward, but she has settled now, whereas in the years I knew her she grew backwards, starting as a solemn young beauty and moving towards unripeness. She told me later that during the previous Summer she had frequently evaded her nurse, who could manufacture large sleep from small beer, and so she often ran free and rolled with the older boys in the field. *That is our Yorkshire custom,* she said simply, as though it were a matter of most common knowledge. *I knew in an instant what your eyes were saying when they glanced at me, and that's why I took you by the arm and made you show me the hawk that flies a pitch so high that it vanishes from sight. And*

*when the hawk was gorged, so were we. You remember that, don't you? Or
do you remember only your moment of victory?* That was how she talked
even then, all sauce and strange sorrowful smile. She told me that
she'd had nothing but boys the previous Summer. It was dull
and she had calculated that the matter would probably be more
interesting with a proper man. *Besides, I'd never copulated with a
lynx-eyed cousin.* There was never anything maiden-hearted about
Anne. Yet there was at the same time always an improbable tender
grace in her face, as though she were in perpetual mourning for
life. When I asked why she was so sad, she'd act surpris'd and say
she was, on the contrary, very merry and would live to be a
grandam, for a light heart lives long. Then she would cut me with
her wit, as deftly when she was my child-lover as later when she
was the most notable of the Court ladies. She was maddening and
always mysterious. Her eyes and mouth worked at cross-purposes
and even changed roles in the instant.

Long after her name was freckled and I had fought with her
Uncle Thomas, I had to endure the insult of a challenge from her
nephew Thomas, armed with sword and sting though still hairless.
The knavish Knyvetts, not the Vavasours, stood behind that, I'll
wager. It should not have been possible, but the young lad's
currish snarl hurt me, that's all there's to it, and hurts me still,
though I have lately greater wounds to nurse. His lewd letter, I
know it still by heart nearly twenty years later, began:

> If thy body were as warped as thy spirit is dishonourable, then my
> family would be yet unspotted and thyself remained with all thy
> baseness unknown.

He called me out, but I could not contemplate butchering the
boy, however great the temptation. I'd fought for honour with
the elder Thomas Knyvett, after all, and was made lame by
fortune's spite. I've never heard nor read of a duel fought twice
o'er a single insult, however foul, much less by an Earl against a
lad who ranked himself a gentleman a trifle early. Dimly I do
remember how that Thomas's glib and oily grandfather, a
Thomas, too, they were all Thomases, hover'd round my Father

for favours and would speak only in Latin, which made the servants giggle and my Uncle snort: *Vir illustrissime, quod pristine, humilitatis et clementie gratia in varius honoru progressibus*. Such babble, my Uncle would say, shows that noble Latin is at last in its death throes in our time, and he was right. It is now the language chiefly used among us by over-educated fools. I've long since destroyed my own wooden Latin poems.

I suppose I was ready to be trapped by love that Summer, which was the worst of times with the other Anne. She was my enemy and guilty busily preparing to be my wife. That year, 1571, I stayed away from home and gave my talent to Court, where I excelled. At the Tourney in May I conquered all except Sir Henry Lee, Anne's future husband, a paltry knight but then still contesting the tilts with the Queen's special protection. I dressed in our colours, the Lancastrian rose, as The Red Knight, but there was more than that in my red mood then. I was feeling the red glow of fire, scorn, anger and proud disdain. Delves, Stafford and Bedingfield were my closest challengers, and, of these, Delves almost unseated me as he went down. He'd taken the same cautions as I in careful choice of horse and wood for the lance. We'd both given weeks to practice. My advantage was that I risked leaning further forward at the last moment so that the point of my lance touched his armour first. An easy topple, but also my sweetest, was Thomas Cecil. Only now may I take particular pleasure in my defeat that May of Knyvett, who showed his vulgarity when he would not give me the obligatory bow of reconcilement as he arose angrily from the dust.

Though Anne Cecil was actually seven years older than Anne Vavasour, I saw my future wife as monstrous for her childish shallowness. Well, what sort of daughter would William and Mildred have had? It is stale and hoar to say, but true all the same: attend to the girl's mother carefully. Later, of course, I saw Anne Vavasour herself as also monstrous in her own way. Oh yes, there was one other monster in my way: myself. I say no more than truth. I was unkind to Anne and even, if I press it hard, to Anne. At least I lashed myself smartly over the first fault in many a play.

When Posthumus is faithless and discards Imogen in *Cymbeline*, it is I. When Leontes condemns Hermione in *The Winter's Tale*, it is I. And when Bertram coldly rejects Helena in *All's Well*, that is I again. I was not kind to her, and hers is a troubling face that sometimes still comes to me at night weeping. If tears could help thee, know you have some of mine at last. There are times and words in my life I would pluck back if the play belonged to me.

Anne Vavasour and I joined together just five times that most memorable August. She moved me, and herself sighed passionately and flailed like soft flame in a windswept field, yet seemed suddenly unmoved and cold afterwards. It is not meet to say much more than that, save that her high place at Court and the shadow of shame that fell on her afterwards both had cause and merit.

Her casual openness about her stray'd virginity was match'd by the way she would not mince the matter of cousins in each other's arms. I was a cool drink from an unexpected well for her, nothing more, nothing less. Yet how could that be, by witness of how she acted? She told me that she would have many men in her life and outlive them all. Perhaps she would love one man most of all, but that would be decided by herself looking back by some fireside far into the future. It was quite an amazing bit of foolish prating for a thirteen-year-old. At the time I put it aside in favour of the fervour of her passion. It was a Yorkshire custom, she said, to speak plainly. Some lasses were practised to wait until the ebb of their monthly changes so as to be able to deliver a fresh virginity to each new lover. Did I not prefer her candour and her natural love-juices? I did, though I was never fully at ease with either.

As it happened, I had, besides Anne Vavasour, another great distraction, which turned into frenzy that Summer. The matter touched a closer cousin, Norfolk. I loved Norfolk. Thomas was an older brother to me.

Norfolk was fortunate at first – though he did not see it that way – to be second to Leicester in the first round of Elizabeth's fancy. But Thomas suffer'd from over-marriage, and the Queen finally would not brook the suspicion that he was about to set out again and take the hand of the Queen of Scots. He had too much the look of kingly ambition about him. She let him learn the smell of prison for a year, but that spell merely hardened his resentment. He was scarce out of confinement when Ridolfi drew him into his plot.

Roberto Ridolfi was a Florentine banker who spent much time in England. For several years I saw him often hovering by Burghley's elbow. On my second trip in Italy I saw him again, for he had been in Brussels when the plot was discovered and so lost nothing but his crimson livery left behind in Britain. He had become a Senator in Florence, but his dress, once so bright in London, was now as severe as it was elegant. He looked in perpetual puzzlement over the great past that had slipp'd past.

Roberto's machinations came unstuck because he retailed his wares everywhere and became like a pedlar of pots and pans, whose approach could be heard all over Europe. He had the support of Thomas, but was too foolish to see that he did not need the support of Mary before the fact. She possessed the discretion of a parrot, was quiet as a bagpipe. Nor did he have to run like a busybody with all his plans to Brussels, Paris, Rome and Madrid. As if Burghley did not have spies in all those places, too. When Ridolfi's servant, Baillie, was seized with letters at Dover, it only confirmed what had been long known at Court. Ridolfi was using the secretly Roman Bishop of Ross to bring together all the discontented Roman Catholics in the land. Have a conspiracy of two, and you have reasonable odds of one traitor. Have a conspiracy with a crowd of strangers, and what chance is there?

I stood to the side, because I felt there was everywhere sound affection for the Queen, while Mary was a toothless tigress without the Spanish, and, if they conquered, Philip's mouth would have been both the Parliament and the Throne of England. So I remained loyal to Elizabeth, but would have been loyal too to Thomas, though for all my love for him, I would have been less than perfectly happy had he become king.

When the plot was dismantled, Thomas sat in the Tower. His

men Madder and Berny were taken, too. It was a time not for velvet or careful friendliness but to be a great and loyal friend. Between man and woman, man and man, there is no higher station in life than to be an unfeigned friend. I have been extremely fortunate in my life, for I have had three such friends. Of these one was beheaded, and I remained true to him to the end.

I laid my plan to pluck Thomas from the Tower. It was a fine plot, composed of a lusty fire set by the kitchen one evening; some civic aid rendered by a company of players belonging to the Earl of Oxford, which would be just passing by; a forged order to move the prisoners temporarily to safer quarters, that to be delivered in a royal carriage that I trusted Deny would obtain on loan without too much trouble. The Tower stairs would have been far too narrow to storm. We'd got only as far as the delivery of the dry hay for the horses stacked near the kitchen when word reached me that all was known. It thus was necessary to take refuge in the London house of Lady York, widow of the Master of the Mint and a great friend of the de Veres, because the ship that was to have taken Thomas and me to Flanders had not been yet arranged when all of this came about.

The newly elevated Baron Burghley found out that I was hiding at Walbrook, of course, but did not report it to the Queen. I learnt this when my wife paid an unexpected visit. It was Anne who'd sent word to me that my plan had been discovered, probably done on her father's instruction. Anne's absurd intention was to go abroad with me. She'd told her father as much before she came to me, which had greatly alarmed all the Cecils. The child clutched a pretentious Latin poem from her sister warning that she must neither detain me nor go abroad with me or else risk losing her love:

Sin male cessando retines vel trans mare mittas tu mala to peior tu mihi nulla soror

A Latin poem written by her sister was Burghley's idea of clever dissembling. In fact it was the very signature of his heavy-handed work.

Anne wished to know from me if she should heed her sister's counsel. I told her that I feared she must. Mouse trembled with indecision and said that she would consider what to do and come to me on the morrow. That same day my servant Robert Rose came to me with my clerk's list of all my debts engrossed in a very large sheet of parchment and promised for payment as leasehold against my remaining lands in the event that I did not return to England. That idea, too, belonged to my ever-cautious father-in-law. Granted, there were debtors who wished to hold me even more than the Queen, and they would have preferred to seal off my way if I had tarried.

Everything was ready shortly after midnight, and I set off in a party of three. I was riding Scilt, my most fiery-footed steed, and so I soon left my two men far behind. I rode as swift as thought, as shadow, as dream. I reached Essex and Wivenhoe before dark and with only one brief stop to rest Scilt and let him drink. I rested in a safe house while my men pushed ahead in order to prepare the ship. Shortly after dark the next day I dressed as a yeoman and galloped to the landing, where Burghley was waiting for me. I didn't have to leave. The Queen had decided not to arrest me. My wife was distraught in London and I must go to her immediately. There was still hope for Norfolk, and I must know that he was doing everything within his power to gain the pardon.

I returned directly to London again the next day and I was safe, though Rolfe the scrivener fared badly for having forged the Queen's hand. Of course Burghley did not keep his most important dangling promise. I argued for Norfolk's life with all the passion I possessed. After much hesitation, which always was Her favoured form of execution, Thomas was beheaded in January. She stayed the execution at midnight, and yet somehow Thomas saw Nowell his confessor and was beheaded on Tower Hill in the morning. *It was a dreadful error*, She said. I was silent.

That deed was an important turning on the broad road of my life. My ride to Wivenhoe from Lady York's was but an exact rehearsal of the same ride I rode freely and would take two years later when at last I did break loose to France. But on that second ride I was accompanied by the shade of Thomas, who smiled languidly at me with his loose and bobbing head, as he always did, while we raced down a long lane of trees. I was breathless as I galloped and shouted to him, while he spoke softly and evenly and every word could be clearly heard.

*Why did you want to be king?* I asked.

*Why should I have wished to be subject when I could be free?* he parried. *Have you yourself not dreamed yourself king?*

*Ah yes,* I said, *but when I close my eyes and yet do not yield to sleep I am free. If my fancies do not perform well enough I can send them off again to redress and relearn their lines. Look at you, Thomas. Your grainy yellow hair flops perfectly to the side as though you are surprised at your own words. You are quite wrong, dear friend. A king is never free, though any of his subjects may be if he is a poet.* Then an ominous owl shrieked above us, Thomas and his horse disappeared, and I started up in my saddle and galloped onwards to the rhythm of a bad poem. The branches of the trees held severed hands.

Just think, if I had freed Thomas and Pondus had not been at the landing, 'twould have meant a life of involuntary exile as long-lived as any envy or slander. There might have been plays and poems in perfect French or Italian, but neither the audience nor the language would have been my own and some essential salt would always have been lacking. Thank you again for your timely intercession, old fat-fate, oh thank you very much. Without you I don't know what I would have done with my life!

So the Earl returned and was at London again, living for months in false hope of freedom for Thomas, giving some needed patronage to some writers who would have had none at all without me, even trying to be a husband to Anne. One particular passion burnt in me over those few months: to know the perfidious servant who was a double agent for Burghley. The news did not come quickly to me, but I worked patiently through my most trusted devious men, Wilkins, Hannam and Deny, and at last we succeeded in determining that the spy was Amis, who reported to Burghley once a week. He was a sneaky little fellow with a cleft chin, who boasted he was ruthless but always looked to the side when you spoke with him. It was not worth my while to soil my sword with scoundrel blood a second time, and so I arranged to have him recruited to spy on old Giles Fletscher, who, it had been arranged, was being sent as Embassador to Moscovy, in part to protect the Golding trading interests, in part, I jested at Court, as punishment by the Queen for the treacly verses he'd composed and read at my wedding. Amis grew two inches at the thought that he was now in the service of Her Majesty, and so he was shipped away. He returned rich and as grandly insignificant as ever.

So it was, you see, a care-laden Summer and Autumn that year, and I had scarcely any further thoughts of my trysts with the young Miss Anne Vavasour. Thomas and Anne were put out in a special meadow of my mind. The Queen made great effort to win me back that year and thought that She'd succeeded. My wife was very jealous. It was the first time that I took charge of a Royal entertainment. The spectacle, a Shrovetide device of pagan hue, was held at Warwick Castle in August and was so successful that the Queen motioned for Pan's courtship of the nymph to continue even though a golden August shower began to pour down. In fact, it made it merrier, as colours began to stream down the nymph's face. All the ladies trill'd with laughter and laughed even louder when they saw what was happening to each other's faces. The loudest laughter of all was the Queen's under her canopy.

I'd practised hard and long with the dancing maids, until the speed and delicacy of their turns was dazzling. Their dance lasted an hour, and at the end the dancers circled around the famous dancing horse of Banks, which was dressed as an elephant. The dancers in a circle bowed to the beast, which returned their bow and broke wind on cue just before the pigs' bladders and pipes led the spectators away to the banquet tables. That horse was an eighth wonder of the world. He performed perfectly through rehearsal after rehearsal. On the day, too, the good steed played his part, setting off the pigs' bladders, which in turn provoked a deep-throated roll of Summer thunder. Nature herself had joined the spectacle on cue.

Warwick marked the last time that I recited my Latin poems. More and more I heard only the twittering of English in hedges and tree-tops by then. The centuries were too long to carry the echo of living Latin any more.

My lustre in the eyes of the Queen was, however, being slightly dull'd by the schemes loosed against me by the Sheep. She called him *le Mouton*, and it was indeed the manner in which he scavenged more than any wolf. Allow me to present Christopher Hatton, the Queen's most devoted and amiable guard. He stood above all Gentlemen Pensioners, who were her ceremonial guard. They did not guard the Queen but attended to her like the truest of lazy drones, close to the throne and content with their lives to pay obeisance and steal just a little bit of honey. In 1572 he was not yet knighted but had been made Captain of the Guard and had entered the Commons, where, it was quickly understood, they heard the Queen's opinions whenever he spoke. If the Sheep was a mask to cover crawling ambition, that was but a second mask. His real face beneath the mask was another sheep. His still handsome face and craggy nose were the total payment and full sum of his entire life. That's all he was: *I shall never be disloyal to my Queen.* The more often She invited him into the Privy Chamber, the more clearly She saw it Herself. Discuss Propertius with a sheep? Parry in wit with a grandiloquent simpleton? One could watch Her beam with pleasure at his dog-hearted devotion but then wince when She spoke and he fumbled Her meaning. In and out of the Privy Chamber he would go. The gossip grew worse, Her sighs grew more frequent.

The Queen began to fancy me in earnest at Warwick, which caused me sufficient trouble from two sides, because envy began to breed in the Captain of the Guard. Unsigned denunciations swarmed about me like mites in Summer. It did not take much trouble to divine the source. Anne grew furious because of one scribbled parchment. In truth, I'd have welcomed in part some intercession from the Lord Treasurer, but he saw nothing of any concern to him as the Queen roguishly pulled his daughter's husband by the collar or stroked his arm.

I'd left the Court and retired to Havering-in-the-Bowerie, which was then my Essex estate and one of the best of all I lost, to attend to various projects I was sponsoring. When I had been there only three days and was still occupied in supervising the stewards, because the building and thousand acres of grounds were much declin'd since last I'd visited Havering, it was announced that She was coming on a sudden progress to Warwick, and I was called to provide an evening's entertainment. I'd come as called, though not altogether willingly. As She was staying nearby with Leicester at Kenilworth, there was leisure to arrange a grand spectacle in peace.

I decided to end the entertainment by staging a little war and appointed Fulke Greville to lead an opposing force, assigning him £50 for two hundred men equivalent to my own. In the dry moat of the castle were swiftly assembled two facing toy castles constructed of painted material stretched tight on slender poles as though for the stage, but in depth, so that one could walk around them. Half the men were stationed around the toy castles in such armour and harnesses as could be found in the region; the other half stood on scaffolding, each with a Roman candle or other piece of fireworks, which all had been brought up from the store in London laid by for the next Accession Day. Between the mock castles were a dozen battering rams and four full military mortars brought from the Tower. When the Queen and Her retinue were seated, the rams did battle against each other with mighty thwacks and men falling all about. The various sorties of mock battle were to have been signalled by different colours of fireballs, but error or excitement prevailed in the castles until havoc and confusion reigned. It was terrific to all those who had never seen real battle, warmly satisfying to those who had. Then the mortars began to fire, and roaring terror was everywhere. I was later told that rumour of rebellion was in the royal tent, while only the Queen clapped Her hands and bounced up and down in delight. Let posterity never deny that about Elizabeth: She had the craft and vision of Her mother Anne, but Her soul and spirit belonged to a man.

The antics had gone too far, for now many of the fireworks were being shot at random and in the wrong direction. Rockets arced wildly into the river and then, if their fire was not yet exhausted, rose up again spectacularly out of the water. Some flew over the true castle and landed in the midst of the town, and the people ran into the festivities for help as four old town houses were afire. Men were being dispatched to save the town just as the crowning fireball was released prematurely to set Greville's stage castle on fire. Seeing it lob slowly into the night sky like spittle from the sun, the men quitted the castle on signal through the loose flaps at the bottom and engaged in mock combat. They would have beaten each other into submission in earnest if they had not known that their pay hung upon the undamaged return of their battle dress.

The real drama of that evening only then began, as cries of *Rescue! Rescue!* arose everywhere in the moat, for the little wooden bridge and the toll-keeper's house on it had been set on fire by one of the stray fireballs. The battle was abruptly concluded as everyone went to the riverside. The cries of the toll-keeper's wife could be heard through the crackling wood. Greville and I came together and without a word began to organize the rescue. Greville was never a friend of mine and I cut him sharply as Charles the Wrestler in *As You Like It*. But I had no complaint with him that night. One of the battering pieces was used to break away the flaming side-rails, and then a brigade of buckets and helmets full of water was passed forward to dampen the footplanks until Greville and I could hack a passage through the house's side wall with long-handled axes. The walls with windows and doors were already cascades of flame. Inside, the ceilings proved to be low even for a barn. Greville and I made our way through the terrible hell of heat up a stairway through which a stout priest would not pass in the direction of the woman's screams. There we found a rough but handsome wench in her night-gown and a whimpering man cowering in a corner like a whipped dog. The air was ale.

He'd had too many tolls that day and drunk himself senseless in celebration, to the point where he could not even defend them both against fire on a river. Greville carried the sobbing little man in his arms, while I took his wife by the hand and led them all back along the safe path through the kill-hole. When we were on the shore, she kiss'd me hard and fled into the crowd. I think of that episode often, because it was the only time in my life when I recall heat hotter than that I now feel. I have been in hell and have found hells in myself.

The next morning I was amused to learn that the Queen had graciously apportioned £25 12s. 8d. to the unfortunate couple, which was a full and fair payment for the little house that they had lost, though justice requires that one note that the toll-keeper had no means to earn his keep, and the town had the greater cost of building a new bridge. So finely practised were all the Queen's gestures. It might have ended badly if the Monarch who had danced with abandon in the square before Her people in the afternoon had been seen to preside over the burning of Warwick at night.

I returned to my work at Havering, but was followed by the heralds of the Queen: She was coming on a sudden progress to Havering the next day! This was not a normal monarch's progress but simply the romantic rush of a pamper'd beauty past Her prime, who'd have the attentions of anyone She fancied. It is sometimes convenient to be king. Of all the courtiers around Her, I was the only one who was not at Her disposal, though I fear She often mistook my natural manners and jousting for signs of more than they were.

I had only just taken quarters in the Savoy among the writers and actors, and I dispatch'd one of my men to London again at all speed to bring players back to Havering that I might entertain the Queen once more somehow. My interest was frankly also to distract Her from other purposes. She 'twas gave the assent and push'd me to the altar in December, when I'd rather have been rescued by Her whim. Now She'd rob her Treasurer of a son-in-law? But there had been December and then there was June, and our spirits, so kindred in so many ways, could now never join harmoniously.

I was then surveying Bartholomew Clerk's Latin translation of *Il Cortegiano* and writing the Latin preface for it, and so the Queen and I quarrelled amiably over Latin style and Castiglione for nearly two days. Whenever She tended to draw me aside or moved too close, one of my declaimers, player-jesters or lute players would come forward. Her vexation grew apace, though we both smiled warmly at each other. There was no strangeness in that story: the more I stood back from Her, the closer to me She drew. On the fourth and fifth days we went riding. Eliza delighted in galloping off at breakneck speed. It never took Her long to outdistance Her horse guard, and She and I would race through bushes, across marshes and down steep embankments in a mad cross-country chase to nowhere in particular. Once we hid in a gully while the desperate guards galloped by above our heads. Flushed and out of breath, She had the conspiratorial passion of a child, but the memory of languid Thomas was in that gully with me too and kept us apart.

On the sixth day the sudden progress terminated just as abruptly. She could not even grasp, I think, the reasons why She tempted me not. So Eliza left Havering with a pout: *Small joy have I in being England's queen. I had rather be a country maid.* She had too much pride to read all the small occasions I gave to know I was her courtier but potentially neither Her lover nor Her wanton paramour. There were others to perform that dance.

I worked several days more on the Latin and then for a few more days I was lost in the Psalms of David, on which good Uncle Arthur had been working. It was a pretty volume, not least because he dedicated it to me. The Psalms and the Song of Songs are to me the soul and heart of the Bible. And now I find they are all that I read when I rest from the toil on this parchment.

I am at last on notice to myself that it was quite foolish to think when beginning this table-book that I could fob off my disgrace with a tale. Still, I shall finish it unless I finish first. Some firm truths at least are being framed for me. But there must be doubt as to whether the sorrow I feel can admit society. To stand under a story and to understand it are very different things. Read on if you will, but your entertainment has nothing to do with me. *Je suis de Verre*. Imagine that you hold me in your hands. It is nothing but the shadow of a grim-grinning ghost cast off by a mirror once bright but now grown dim and sickly.

My body is a prison on fire. By this writing at least I place myself on a spectator's chair and stay a few imaginary feet from the flames. I could not have covered o'er the sorrow of this story, for the life concealed would have, like an oven stopt, burnt my heart to cinders. As it is, I have learnt to write with my awkward casualty and can now go whole days in train without stopping. For the moment, though, I'll put down the quill and go abed again. I must call Jane to tend me with cold cucumber comfort and wipe me like a child until the fever abates somewhat. I wanted to give the mirror away, but the tinker's wife told me gruffly to use it while I lived, and she would gladly have it when I was gone. I try not to look at the mirror, but my fingers tell me that warts and sores continue to sprout on all my fever spots. God have ruth on me at last.

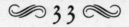 

## 33

With fresh garments and repair to my spirits I shall continue the saga of how I sparred with Gloriana, England's spotless lily. It was after the inconclusive love duel at Havering that I returned to my new Savoy apartments and the friends of Shoreditch that lately I'd acquired. If I'd been born differently, I would have been very like Nashe, Marlowe and Greene. However that supposition may be, there was greater warmth and wit in their street and stage rituals for me than in the Court. I joined in the rehearsals and street screeds, using my rights to obtain foreign books for their use from de Renialmi, the Italian who supplied Pondus with foreign books. It was he who was later licensed to open a Popish bookstore for registered customers by Archbishop Whitgift, who preferred this faithful agent to monitor the channels of interest by the learned and powerful. But Ascanius took bribes with the left as well as the right hand, and it was thanks to him that I obtained all the French and Italian writers who nourished my plays. It was while I was visiting Ascanius to obtain on credit Ariosto and several other books that he had got from Italy for me that a messenger came from the Queen, calling me to Court. Moments such as these reminded me well that I was rarely alone. It was on that memorable day that She drew me to talk of Ovid and other things. There was at least this small profit: de Renialmi was so awestruck by the attendance of the Queen's Page that he relented and let me have my pile of books on suffrance after all.

Money was then more than ever a problem, though the problems that came later made this year seem a most gentle Springtime. Early in the New Year things got out of hand when some of my boys, in their cups and vaguely aware that not all was well with their master's purse, hatched the idea of helping me out by playing Robin Hood on the road from Rochester to Gravesend. The plot as put to me, however, was at first not that. It was to be a merry pay-back to two of the men, William Fawnt and John Wotton, who'd been thick with Amis and left my service at the same time as I'd had him sent away. That was why I gladly agreed to dress as a highwayman and hide with them in a ditch near the inn at Gadd's Hill. One of my men's informers had found out that they would be on the road and planned to stop there.

It was great fun as we clambered up with black feather'd hats and screamed out: *Stand ho, boys! Murther! Robbery! Which will you choose?* What I did not know was that the lackeys were carrying overseas payment in gold to a ship at Gravesend. Fortunately they got away from us. Didn't they run back to their horses! We could smell their piss as they galloped off more like post sacks on the necks of their horses than seated riders. It was all mirth for that moment, but the joy of it did vanish when a formal complaint was made to Lord Burghley and the matter reached the Queen. It was quite a long time before I could laugh about it and send Falstaff to stop at a tavern on his way to the Boar's Head.

It could well have been a pretext to cause me grave trouble. How many, I wonder, of my servants were really foot-soldiers of misfortune? Amis was a proven case. Churchyard did work for Leicester. But surely, surely, not Deny, too! If there was a double agent among the three, I would far prefer that it were John Hannam or Dan Wilkins than Deny. He was my noble commoner, my masquing mate, the only one who could sing mass in both low and crescent note. He made me love Ronsard the robber, and I taught him to be a poet. He printed his verse under the name of John Soowthern. I've never seen anyone show so much pleasure at seeing himself in print. I put him in an elegant chapbook with one of Eliza's own poems and some of my Uncle's poems. It might have been Deny, but of all my many servants, he's been the only one to send me greetings here at King's Place. Faithful friends are hard to find and impossible to prove.

When I contemplate the secret faces of life, my spirits fall to the whole depth of my being. Die then, die, die, die, die de Vere! Most of the best are already dead. I would join them. By what licence do the least always live longer? What is the choice? If we do not live up to our promises, the gods plague us. If we do perform, we are confounded by other men. I am myself no better to others. It's fierce wretchedness that all happiness must soon enough herald. Painted love and varnish'd friendship. I, too. Should one not fling oneself in rage from the monstrous afflictions of affection? All the projects of my life have cracked, my spirit disobeys and time alone rides on in his fine carriage. If I were more a lawyer, I could delay things for ever. A wave of despair sweeps over me, as it has on odd occasion since boyhood. I feel that I am again falling backwards into the dark abyss of time. Oblivion, dark, deep and deadly, affords me some comfort. Where once in such a mood I could sit for a day unmoving in a chair, now I cradle my pain in my arms and hum it lullabys.

## 34

It was after the stop at Havering that Christopher Hatton grew too cross to bear my proximity to his Queen any more and began to bombard me with gossip and unsigned denunciations to the Lord Treasurer. Even a sheep has teeth. Each rumour from my back-friend engendered the need to write three responses in defence. The Queen sent Christopher to France to convalesce for half a year in the end, though I think it was not his denunciations that irritated Her and led to his removal from Court but what She could read in everyone's eyes as we watched them together. It was easy to loose my revenge on both of them, but 'twas an anger based, I can now see clearly, as much upon the denial to me of travel rights rather than the more obvious reason.

I was at work with Greene compiling a collection of poems we called *A Hundreth Sundrie Flowres bounde up in one small poesie*. Some sixteen of my own poems went into that turbulent running book. I was twenty-three then. I do not have the book at hand, but lines I recall will convey my stubborn mood, for all my friends advised me that I was being insanely obdurate.

> Love is a discord and a strange divorce
> Betwixt our sense and rest; by whose power,
> As mad with reason we admit that force
> Which wit or reason never may show her.

But more to the point, and how I remember myself at that age:

> Fain would I sing but fury makes me mad,
> And rage hath sworn to seek revenge on wrong.

It was an easy thing to slip in something for the Queen and Her pet sheep. The fish in a bottle that I chose to present them with was a quite long piece of prose and poetry called *The Adventures of Master F.I.* The poems were all by the hero and signed *Si fortunatis infoelix*. Fortunatis Infoelix was how Hatton sign'd his poems, which were as puff'd up and false as his codpiece, which could have doubled for a pin-cushion.

I began to write the tale after a wine-soaked lunch and was finished with it in a fortnight of forced march. That was the first prose tale I wrote and also, I think, the first original tale after the manner of Boccaccio to be written in our century.

The tale unfolds in a great English castle in the North, where a group of pampered nobles live. The story is of the cunning love between Fortunatus Infoelix and Mistress Elinor, whom the dullest fool in Court could see at once were Gloriana and Her Sheep. It was all said clearly in the ivory wide margins of every page. The poems that stood along the way like fence-posts in the prose were the Sheep's own, which had got about because Gloriana could not forgo showing them to Her trusted Maids in spite of how dreadful the verses, or whatever you might term them, were:

> Good reason yet, that to my simple skill
> I should the name of Cynthia adore

and more in that spirit. O, we did make some tiny changes so that one harmless saucy love poem ended with a new couplet:

> What followed next, guess you that know the trade
> For in this fort my Friday's feast I made.

The story was a simple one. Madame Elinor was to play the good faerie to Fortunatus in his quest for Mistress Frances. However, Elinor and Fortunatus would thus be free to use the castle's base court and her secret quarters from time to time with no suspicion. The twist in the tale was that Penelope presented herself for the stay in the country gorgeously and very bravely set forth so the mock suitor, though ever-faithful in heart to Eliza of course, let his eye stray continually to her. And She, being among friends and subjects, responded in a way certain to call Her pet to heel. She appeared at dinner one evening after Hatton had spent the afternoon with Her dressed only in Her night-gown, though Her hair was carefully arranged *alla Piedmontese* in the manner then favoured by Her, and on her forehead was affixed a small piece of paper on which was written in Her fine hand but one word: Contented. I had it from Penelope Devereux herself.

That solitary tale was the first composition in which I laid down layers of meaning. Whereas it was accepted custom at that time to have two meanings, I then and almost always after had no less than three. I'd described the romance satirically, shown myself describing it and also shown how English gentlefolk with too little to do talk and pass their daily castellated lives. I might have, in time, made more of *The Adventures of Master F.I.* had it not been stolen from me. I liked writing the *novelle* because it gave me place to show the maker's hand, but its free privacy tempted me too much and I could see it as a way of speech more dangerous than poetry. I never returned to artful prose again 'till this.

I timed the printing with Richard Smith so that the volume would be fresh in his and everyone else's hands immediately Hatton returned from his love sickness in October. I judged them both correctly. She was stung, but would give no outward sign of it. He, who could give no outward sign either, was thrown into the finest and most still staring rage I have ever witnessed. The dumb but furious beast then waited patiently more than two years to have his vengeance, when I myself was at last allowed to go abroad. *A Hundreth Sundrie Flowres* was pirated and printed again under a new title, *The Posies of George Gascoigne*. In the new edition *The Adventures of Master F.I.* was swept away, and most of my poems were debosh'd to render them barbless and inferior even to Gascoigne's own poems, which he freely toss'd in to fill up the suddenly half-empty barrel. Good old George, it was not the only task he willingly performed to become the Poet Laureate. O, far superior to both his friend Immerito and Shakespeare he was. In the first edition he'd had a translation, a schoolteacherly treatise on verse, and some poems. Some poems only because I wanted the translation.

Those night-watch constables, the critics, had been well-fed and were ready to bay with joy when the new and gelded book appeared. *A crown of bay shall that man wear*, wrote one of Gascoigne's literary friends with wondrous foresight. Where there are critics there will be some honest generosity, but, in the main, low calculation no matter where they place their mark. The thing to do is get above them and grow sturdy bark, though still you always await the axe. In this instance the Sheep was to all appearances shrewd enough, because he'd wiped away his humiliation and had the quiet satisfaction of both savaging and stealing my book from me in a circumstance where I, too, could not protest. When I at last returned to Court, he'd rushed to give me a copy of Gascoigne's pilfered book with a honey-heavy smile. He was so afraid that I might miss it. Yet something was amiss in his plan, to this day I know not what, for Elizabeth had that safe book withdrawn and destroyed. Where she had had to suffer the original in silence, perhaps the reappearance of the gelding allowed her to vent her anger at last on Her most faithful courtier.

Did Hatton all the same have the closing speech? He did not. Rather, I shaped the Sheep into Malvolio in *Pleasant Conceit* [*Twelfth Night* A.F.] so that he would have to sit beside Her and watch the story of Countess Olivia's steward, who, having faked a profession of love, is in the end snared by his own trick.

I think that play shepherded in his ambition, but the Queen never could quite turn away from his bland adoration. A steady stream of offices and lands came to him and when he died, a decade ago now it was, there were no limits to the pomp he merited. There was then a rhyme contrasting Hatton's place with the surprisingly modest shared grave of Sidney and his wife in Westminster:

> Philip and Frances have no Tomb,
> for Great Christopher takes all the Room.

It astonished me two years ago when Sir Christopher's friends came to Hackney to beseech me to revive *Tancred and Gismund*, a comical tragedy on which he'd scribbled with Noel and Wilmot. If I had time, there's a droll tale I would tell. People forget very quickly or even never understand at all. What, did they think that

King's Place was a town theatre to be leased? I have, it seems, outlived most of my enemies, and yet there is no respite. My memory exceeds my life by six months. Would that it died before me. If my best work were mine, I could hope for a memorial to outlast the Sheep's gilded tomb, but it is not, so I live out these days without hope. The writing is everything, and so much of it is both coarse and light, reading to be swept away like dry grass in a fire.

Those two years of my youth were fructive for me. At last Thomas Bedingfield, one of the most sympathetic and better-born of the Savoy scribblers who had gathered round me, finished his translation of Cardano's *De Consolatione*, a great book written a few years before I was born, for which I was much indebted in all respects to the good bookseller de Renialmi. They have a queer turn of mind, booksellers, and like to sell their pearls as diamonds when once they have tickled up a passion for their goods. I commissioned the book from Thomas and published it *cum privilegio*, the last time I could flaunt that right openly. There was much work in it for me, too, because there were infelicities in both the style and the accuracy of the translation to be corrected, and Thomas turned out to be the most fearful author who'd ever lived. He sent the manuscript to me, but then was at first ready to run or fly anywhere rather than see his name on a book. I tried to explain that there was nothing to fear from a philosophical disquisition written before he was born, of which he was only the translator, and that he had now accepted my keep and protection to do the job, which his Queen was very keen to read. That last piece of advice was unwise, for the fright in his face instantly doubled. In the end it was necessary to promise him a foreword written under my own signature, which I wrote as an apologia for the necessity to publish, and I gave him at no extra charge a long poetic homily on the subject:

> So he that takes the pain to pen the book
> > Reaps not the gifts of goodly golden muse;
> But those gain that, who on the work shall look,

And from the sour the sweet by skill doth choose;
For he that beats the bush the bird not gets,
But who sits still and holdeth fast the nets.

It is exceedingly odd that the poet, he who alone may touch the heavens, is by custom denied his just pay unless he has a patron, and how demeaning it is when a nobleman needs a patron.

Art, for whatever reason in the order of things, cannot be admitted to the practice part of life, even though the printer, binder, bookseller and player may receive their due recompense. There is proof enough that a book could pay its way. *Cardanus Comforte* was a case in point, but Thomas was right. Books are dangerous. You may live by them if you choose, but at your peril if you try to live from them. Moths must always fly by night. The theatre is at least made and seen by a minor multitude, and there is some safety there in its grand confusion. As poetry is sacred, perhaps the gods have decreed that the true poet is never paid at his true worth, lest he be merely a merchant who peddles the past. There's the rub. The price, either too high or too low, is never just.

It was in that Summer that I felt the full conviction that my fate was to labour in my vocation, and it was Cardanus of that year who not that many months ago was still the spring of some of my best-formed dramatic speeches. What stirred me when I was twenty-two still feeds me now I am fifty-two and can see Death watching me through the window-pane, a woman and a harlot, the Whore of Kilpeck. Bedingfield's Cardanus reproduced too faithfully the stiffness of the astrologer's language:

What should we account of death to be resembled to anything better than sleep. Most assured it is that such sleeps be most sweet as be most sound, for those are best where in like unto dead men we dream nothing. But if thou compare death to long travel, there is nothing that doth better or more truly prophesy the end of life than when a man dreameth that he doth travel and wander into far countries, and that he traveleth in countries unknown without hope of return.

That was but a tight bud that needed nearly thirty years to open, because all sweet flowers and fruits are slow.

At its first showing my leading player, Richard Burbage, sent Hamlet to an early grave. He was a shrewd tragedian, who'd stirred The Theatre and The Globe and the Inns with Richard and Lear, but he had one small fault on the boards: he always invented his lines as he went along, the more so if he was engaged in drinking some new wench to bed. Always he reckoned himself too grand to count the columns and learn the lines. The string snapp'd within me as he began the Prince's soliloquy:

> To be or not to be, aye there's the point,
> To die, to sleep, is that all? Aye, all.
> No, to sleep, to dream, aye many there it goes.

He thought himself important. I did not think him that important.

There he went, and in his place I yielded the part to Will Kempe, who had a passion for it and did it better than any player in the city in a passionate whisper, even though he made his madcap Hamlet disrobe on stage one night in frenzy at The Globe. This same Kempe that same year did a morris dance to Norwich from London in six days on a fat bet, and then he was gone from us. *I've lost my humour*, he told me simply when last we met. *It's time for me to wear a fine collar in some far-off colony.*

> To die: to sleep;
> No more; and by a sleep to say we end
> The heart-ache and the thousand natural shocks
> That flesh is heir to, 'tis a consummation
> Devoutly to be wished. To die, to sleep;
> To sleep, perchance to dream ...

In that finished play and the comedian Kempe's devout and skilful hands I felt the quiet pleasure of one who has been elected tailor to eternity in seeing that at last the material clings and falls just so. I die as I write, always, and these lines will have to serve me in place of pomp and vainglory:

For in that sleep of death what dreams may come,
When we have shuffled off this mortal coil,
Must give us pause ...
... something after death,
The undiscover'd country from whose bourn
No traveller returns, puzzles the will.

With *Hamlet* I knew that the lowly play had become an art again. I am all the same now ready, I think, and would enjoy the comfort and humour of a deep chat in Latin with good Cardan, who's suffered in many of the ways I have and left his achievement and also his quiet judgement amidst the monstrous crowd. His good lesson I've kept as watchman to my heart.

In the same year in which I helped Bedingfield's translation to the print shop on Fleet Street, I also wrote the first version of *The Merry Wives of Windsor*, a charming if airy thing that years later I worked up again to make Falstaff merry and tease all the newest gossip of the Court to tickle the Queen. Gloriana enjoyed best the jest about Count Frederick, Duke of Württemberg, who so coveted our Garter that She gave it to him and forgot to send word to him. We all like our own jokes best. *The Merry Wives* is how we lived wearing its best mask. To look back on't, though *Hamlet* is my finished play, it is vexing to observe how late in life I still was willing to try to play schoolmaster to a nation. We learn what we are ready to believe and only that. Once watch the common folk drunk in the pits and the gallants preening themselves in the side chairs on stage to be noticed above the poor players, themselves mumbling, shouting and drunkenly waving their arms, once watch all this and you lose desire to be a gentle pulpiter. Let them all rather, if they wish, read *Il Cortegiano*. Say then that if *The Merry Wives* is nothing but a merry frolic, still young Bertram's grandson, old Hamlet, froths and galls overmuch. It's a bitter fate from which even art cannot rescue itself to see how often for the ageing artist there is *parvum in multo*.

My *serpigo* is now almost exceeding endurance. The mind is as great to refuse this scribbling as to continue. My chest is a limekiln. The task of my life o'erteems me and provides little heart's-ease, but it does countervail the disease and keeps the harlot at bay. 'Tis pity I lost my physician, Esquire Arteslow, these several seasons past when he was charged and taken away for keeping an unlicensed schoolmaster in his house. The promise of his sceptre in his hands at night, he'd told me once, alone gave him the power to face the wails of his impatients during the days. Their ills were almost always secondary to their real complaints. There he'd be with his hands between the thighs of a fear-struck mistress or advising the restoration of a burnt wick which no power on earth could make good again, and then at eventime he would have to haul perhaps six mortal prick-songs up the narrow stairway together with his own weary soul. He was unlicensed, like his friend the schoolmaster, but in his youth had gone beyond the seas and observed many simple and true cures at the Sultan's Court in Constantinople.

Where are you now, fine Edward? If you still live in some provincial prison of the realm, I do not doubt that you minister to your fellows and your gaolers alike. Though not a gentleman, you were a gentleman. Many the time you did cure me, and when you could not cure me, you always eased me with tales of Margery Jenton, prim servant in the household of Edward Lum at West Ham, who unbeknownst to him was whore to his every house guest. Or Mistress Turner, who, whilst she dwelt as wench with Thomas Boteslye, played the whore with all my players without a single exception. There was no part she would not have. Best of all I loved the tales of Mistress Berisse, who played the whore with her own serving man, a short-legged knave named Lawrence, who was husband, lover, child, pet and toy to her, but she could only love him when he hopped upon her from great heights and hurt her so that she forgot his dwarfish ugliness. You had stories fit to take the pain from pestilence. Where are you now, fine Edward?

I'll first try to attend to sleep, this kinswoman of death, and then I'll take up again this hookwork picture of my dark love Anne. She was a relenting fool with cutting tongue, too wise by half, and a shallow, changing woman. But when she uncrossed her legs the gates of Hell were opened and I loved her for all her imperfections.

## ⚬ 35 ⚬

I shall show her to you as I first saw her at Court, a whitely wanton with a velvet brow and two glowing pitch balls stuck in her face for eyes. She came late to the dancing. All heads paused and turned, and even several of the musicians missed their beat to see her beauty in a dark brown dress all covered with fine white filigree work. The dress was clear for all to see exactly. It was the Queen's reversed as though at night in a garden with the moon catching and proclaiming metal threads in the embroidery. By unsigned decree all the ladies of the chamber had light hair, and those whose hair was not fair bathed it in a special soup of bird-lime so that being thus bolter'd with birds' droppings they needed no other yellows. On to this sea of yellow the Queen's red head shone like the sun. They say she had red baths of her own. There Anne stood, black. Her beauty had wavering lines. Her nose was a narrow mountain crag. Her chin was too narrow. She did not attempt to smile. Beneath the deep glowing arch of her hair her skin was knit into one brow of sadness.

I alone of all the Court stayed distant and whispered frothy words to ease and amuse the Ladies at my side.

*The distance is too great, fair Rosemary. Tell me, is that a black haggard will fly at anything, or is our Court merely fly-specked?* They laughed, my instant allies. It is not hard thus to play upon the sympathies of Ladies in a cluster. I looked at them with feigned surprise as they laughed. Then I put on my best appearance of sweet but slightly sullen mallycholly, as though Anne's darkness rankled my nerves and brought fresh memories of some worse hour.

The splash of laughter in our far corner broke the spell. Heads turned. I fancied that I saw a rapid cast of dark eye and displeasure from Anne Vavasour, and then the dancing resumed.

What I said was not what I thought at all. The colour of her beauty and her spirit had touched me to the quick and even now I can be sometimes rendered speechless at the mere memory of it, though I am at last truly out of love with life. Enter on time and with your part fully in your face, I'd tell the actors, and the lines will half say themselves. They'd take only the second serving of my advice, of course. But dark Anne entered a room and my life at just the fatal instant.

I wrote a short letter to her and had it delivered by an Italianish lad with glassy black hair whom I had especially dressed all in velvet for the task. I transcribe not the letter but a true echo of it:

> *Anne dear,*
>
> *You may be silent, for I once briefly shared the story of your days. I blame myself, to think one can fell beauty with a lance. My skill with words grows poor and dull against what I saw and felt last night. I see your beauty, and I see your sadness. Your faults are now as dear to me as your beauty, for they are the signature too of my own soul. Thou mak'st graces the faults that to thee resort. A sea of regret lashes at my bed and makes the tide of my love swell more. I feel a madness to pursue you and fear that madness even satisfied will not relent and give us rest.*
>
> *Beware! I love! E.O.*

Years later I do wonder how many precisely have leapt her in her dark bed. And why, so long after the blotted pact between us, has the weird love still not fully ebb'd? Granted it has helped my poetry, but it has harmed me and does still even into these my fatal hours.

I was not prepared for how Anne received my letter. I walked towards her in the long picture gallery at Court and touched her sleeve. She turned angrily at me.

> *Anne, did we not dance once in the country?*
> *Did we once dance in the country?*
> *You know we did.*
> *How needless was it then to ask the question!*

*You must not be so peevish. If thou didst know me, thou wouldst talk with me.*

*Do I not know thee? Thou art a husband of another Anne. And I, to read your letter, am a harlot, to be cured or pardoned in your poetry. They say I am a fly-speck in your eye, and also that your hauteur is proof that all the same you do fancy me, which is passing strange. That, my cousin, is something beyond a poor woman's wit. You must know that, if I am a harlot, I am all the same not for sale in all markets. I am not, for instance, for sale to husbands of other Annes!*

Her words came like gun-stone fired by the flying sparks in her eyes. She was fury itself, and yet the bevels of her face remained calm and still. The burst was clearly occasioned by an account brought to her by some comely mumble-news about my witticism on the dancing floor. Depend upon it: great loves are cast in the fire of first disdain. Those sardonic words augured more for my cause than my artful letter. I could sense that my bed-work was nearer than I'd planned. No real woman can be spurr'd to what she loathes, but her fire is never wasted on what she inwardly knows is contemptible and trivial stuff, no matter if her judgement is grossly impaired. That real woman contains within her all the books and arts it needs to nourish the entire world. The others, the larger part, merely make a list and purchase men to their best advantage, even as they are purchased. When you make a life by lists, you will be cheated, or cheat yourself, or both. In people the sums never will tally. Enough of this. I fear my old father-in-law begins to whisper homilies to me from behind some curtain in my mind.

Yet all the same it took some time to harvest my mistress. Though she was a woman, and therefore could be woo'd and won, she knew the game too well and took pleasure in the play. She was wild, and yet gentle; a wench and still a Lady; pretty and witty, and something else as well. Always, undaunted. She was wise, and she was wayward, and I wanted her. Half my lines she completed before I could get them out.

*Are you a good man, my good Earl?*
*What a question!* I replied.

162

*Without that how can a woman, with her small purse of intellect, believe that a man loves her? Methinks I read false love in your eye.*

*Then your eyes are beautiful but too dark to read such things properly.*

*I have no other but a woman's eye. I think you so, because I think you so.*

*And I am that I am.*

*Should I then fall down on my knees and thank Heaven, fasting, for a good man's love?*

*Well, be fast, though you need not fast.*

*It's said, milord, that you swallow virginities as a whale takes in sardines. Spare me from your gape. You know I am not fresh fish.*

*How needless of you to put the point! You take too much liberty even with yourself.*

There at least she laughed and I once more glimpsed safe harbour. Though practiced in winning women with my tongue, here I'd felt near defeat.

*I shall not be swallowed twice, even in a fable, and would not have my liberty bridled like a horse.*

*I have many horses, and the best of them I ride without a bridle.*

*And women?*

*None as fine as you. Without a bridle, certainly. Have you not seen me at the tilts? I ride quite well, 'tis said.*

*'Tis said, good sir, that you are both a word-monger and a flesh-monger, and I think there may be much in't. Look, your eyes are now glistening bright pools of eels.*

*My eyes, spirited lady, are but mirrors for your dark beauty. They sparkle like a fountain at what they hold and reflect. They will grow dull when you leave.*

*Then I suppose I should stay and swerve to your bed if you must pretend to love me. There is at least this: all men are April when they woo, December when they wed. As you are married, your false affection will perhaps hold me back from wintry wifery for yet another season.*

The change of wind was just as swift as that. I assured her with all the mock gusto I possessed that I was truly married, which she and all of England well knew, and then she reflected with solemnity that, yes, I was indeed married and, therefore, well-practised in declensions and copulatives.

*A man may well come to his mistress passionate and yet at base subdued and grateful enough, for it seems to me that in seeking a new lover a husband leaves open to the motley view a wedlock that was at best forced shut and has only waited for the proper key. That public peep is what makes the deceived woman rant and hate, who would willingly accept her freedom from the quiet hell of her love, too, if only it could be done in perfect secrecy from friends and neighbours. So say just we shall entwine a day, without the for and without the ever. If a week that will surprise me; if a month that may surprise the world as well.*

Her banter was the best of Euphuism that I ever heard, the more because it all had meaning and was kept sharp by the whetstone of her wit. Sometimes, I would later think, it would be better to juggle knives than toss words about with Anne. She meant to cut both herself and me, and did not much seem to care who caught the handle and who the blade. When we were good we had no interdictions and much rapid intercourse. We did chatter together, though often I could see that we had built a mansion for our love that was ruined from the start. Love, when it truly comes, often dresses out of season and later cannot be chased and will not go even from a burnt shell. Ten times in ten years I left her, but her shade always ran with me and there was nothing I could do to stamp it out, though I still cry to see how it's made this truer love I have fester from the start.

There was one condition to Anne's agreement. We must meet again, she said, as first we came together. It would be at midnight in the stables at Hampton Court. She would come dressed as a night-maid with fresh linen for the clean straw that would be laid in advance in an empty stall.

I was not eager, but it was made clear that if I would not have the stable I would not have her. The matter had further complications in the event, for when I saw her waiting at the stable door with bodice already very loosely stitched, I was taken by the hand and led by lantern through the warm breathing and shuffling of the horses towards a far stall where another lantern hung. I took the lantern from her and blew it out and placed it on the ground before beginning to untie completely her leather straps. Not a word had passed between us yet, but she was pushing me away with snorts and puffs.

Then suddenly I saw with my left eye that her twin was standing in the stall's open half door with her hands on her hips and laughing at me. There were two many Annes.

*What's happ'd here then?* the new one mocked. *Are you bat-fowling or are you coney-catching? In either case I judge you must make bold in the attempt or your quarry will fly and frighten the horses.*

In truth the horses were rising up from their sleep, and neighing filled the air. The new Anne took down the little lantern and handed it to the one with whom I'd been tussling. The flick'ring light on her face showed that she was but a servant with her hair done up to pass for her mistress in the dark. She turned her head away in confus'd amusement and tugged at her bodice to set her rude modesty straight. Anne marched her Joanna off to guard the entrance. When she came back down the dimly and distantly lit aisle, she'd shed her clothing along the way and stood naked at the stall door, a tall black statue with eddies of light passing around her.

That was one of our strange bonds. Like me, Anne liked to pass among the people and was artful in her disguises. She claimed that she breathed easier without her self, which is, of course, also the secret of all poets. It is not such an easy leap to jump out of yourself. She had a special wardrobe to the purpose, and also a musician's ear, so that she could do all the accents of our land better than any player I ever knew.

Once, or was it twice? Once, I think, she came up on the stage and played parts, but her profile and her stature were too well known, and rumour reached the Queen. I modelled Viola and Rosalind in part upon this trick of hers. One thing was hard for Anne – her hair loomed so large that her wigs made her seem either a carnival figure or immediately a lady at her pleasure. The actors themselves rarely spotted me when at first I felt the itch to play. I came as Willy Fenton, a visiting stroller from the Queen's own company, but I found it too hard to muff my lines to play with my men, and so one night in *Much Ado* I smiled with all my teeth and hissed softly as a ragged speech ended: *You have not learnt your lines*. After I dropped my mask and showed the patron, they'd share my joke and only the audience would be twice fooled. And once Anne and I came upon each other disguised in the pits with much laughing and hugging. I never went there to hear how they heard my plays – sometimes indeed it was hard to hear anything – but to study their turns and phrases. There are many fine phrases I still could use if time were suddenly to refill my sails, but, then, a full wind can do but little for a half-capsized craft, can it?

My blood runs to recall that second tryst with Anne. I've gone to six full sheets of parchment today without a respite and if I were more mad, I could almost imagine myself better. My humour overcomes my *serpigo*. Anne did play her part in my damnation, but the play, that was my own creation. 'Tis a grave mistake to judge our lives in retrospect: look at what you have done only from the side and thus spare yourself regret 'till later, which will come soon enough anyway. I see the food has grown cold and dun on the tray. To sleep now and to hope that the spirit of those days will carry me through the night and another day.

## ❦ 36 ❧

She drew me down to the fresh hay, chiding me for my timidity. She did not have it in mind, she said, to be ravaged by a snail. Her cheeks, cast even sharper than they were by the want of light, almost glowed in the dark with pleasure at her little *commedia*. Did I not prefer, perchance, the charms of *fausse* Anna? After all, she pressed, Joanna is close at hand and open in manner. I was reproached because I'd scarcely known her face and yet stood ready to stab her in the heart once more.

*What is there in my face that you may not spy more fresh in Joanna's with your lover's eye?*

My hands had begun to play the lute of love, and her whispered taunts were now slower and punctuated with slow gasps. But an all-important promise had been forgotten. There was no linen for the straw. Dear reader, know this: the old saw does not say enough. No sane lover takes a roll in the hay without his hose on him unless he has some sheets with him. The straw was sharply cut and pierced me everywhere, first in the knees and elbows, 'till I thought that I might bleed to death of love. There were some surprisingly sharp twigs in the straw, too. I rose above it then, but should have taken the turn of events for a proper portent of other pains that would come with the pleasures. She loved me furiously that night.

I tried always to keep her in the light because, though sadness ruled her face, her smiles, when they came, could blind you with happiness for a moment. It seemed she smiled to secret voices. At least she never would explain her smile, and she could say the merriest things in dour temper. Or smile to scythe you down.

Though I knew enough never to show myself troubled by whatever Anne did or said, our love possessed all the trappings of war. It made one of my better masques, *A Masque of Amazons*

167

*and A Masque of Knights*, which I staged at Court when the
French Embassador was received. Six ladies joust with as many
gentlemen, who all are vanquished. Those six ladies all were Anne,
not only in homage to her strange force, but also, sad to say, to
the number of love-causes [affairs A.F.] she would run at once.
Once she said that she would engage an army if they had my wit
and were handsomer than I.

*Am I but your monkey then?* I asked offended.

*In the heat of love, in fact, I always see you so. But in the main you are
my mirror-man. You see me as I truly am without alarum, and 'tis for
that that I am walked closer to thee.*

Wanton? Most certainly, but hers was, still is, an exalted state
of vice. As though God had turned His back for the moment on
a sinning angel, or a little devil had begun to pray. I tried to build
walls against her, but I could not stay away and danced along the
tops of those walls.

I had in those years a dear little cottage, too small to sell, on
the approach to London. It was of a size fit only for a widowed
farmer and yet had been given waxed walnut panels and radiant
white plast'ring. Doubtless 'twas a roadside stopping place for
crossroad lovers before we used it so. It was jolly there, with the
curtains and coverings made of Lipsbury pinfold [a fine material
modelled on rustic patterns A.F.], and its little bed and little
fireplace, though we would forget and knock ourselves silly
against the low doorways. *Seely* she would say in the old-fashion'd
way. We spent many nights also at Hampton Court, where I had
contrived that we be given the distant rooms that were connected
by the secret staircase.

There, one bright Summer morning, in a sprawling palace four-
poster I woke to find myself staring into the seat of my passion.
It was Anne's peculiarity with me at least to sleep head to foot,
which required a queer diagonal folding of the sheets. This
morning we were unsheeted, and her leg was thrown up as if to
climb some wall. A sash of tender and soft little black hairs was
laid along her cleft and seemed to reach almost to the small of her
back. Each hair was curled and set against the whiteness of her

skin like delicate dark lacework. The texture was a newborn puppy's fur, and the hand wanted to reach and stroke it. In this indelicate garden nestled a still-clos'd pink puppy's eye, and I was surpris'd to spy such beauty in so corrupt a place.

I did not wake her then but closed my eyes and slept on. Fate chooses strange moments to remember, and that was one when I loved her most sweetly. She had not won me yet to Hell and was still my friend in love. I did not see the fiend and fancied I was free. Anne ran to danger even more than I, and once called up Cupid by settling on my lap in a dress without hoops and with no underclothing as I sat behind side entrance curtains after marshalling the players before a masque commenced. She moved and wiggled on me like a playful yet solemn duck settling on her nest, and our little death that evening could well have come before our real ones, for we were not two pole lengths from the Throne as we co-joined.

I have gone too far and must mark this portion of my tale, at least, for burning. Anne measured me well. I am the mirror-man who sees all and still is blind. In thirty sonnets I've described our sometimes hateful love without a compromising feature save darkness, and here I've at once tripped on to all those things that never should throw their shadow on to paper. I do not want to swear against truth [Sonnet 152 A.F.], but is there no other way to paint her? These most offensive lines are the fundament of the truth of how we lived, and yet the lines I've writ do lie. Her unfeigned face, for surely no one could take up such a false appearance and play it so perfectly until the end, was a most uncommon admixture of nymphish sorrow and extravagant indifference to all the natural links and forms of ordinary life. She was a stranger from nowhere. With no past that seem'd to stick to her, she seemed indifferent to the future, and thus capable of anything at all in the present. Most rightly fear such an apparition as a cat fears young hounds more than experienced ones; others must be camp followers of such dangerous beauty even not knowing why.

She was for the good and for the worse a very English woman, and yet she had such queer ways and words that she spoke and thought like no one else in England. She always called me Vayr in the old manner and, in contradiction of all her own detailed accounts of her youthful frolics, was fond of mock-reproaching me for the ruin of her life. I wrote a jocular echo poem in which I teased her. It was publish'd under my own name on a dare:

O heavens! who was the first that bred in me this fever?
Vere.
Who was the first that gave the wound whose fear I wear for ever?
Vere.

It was a conceit I used again when Juliet hurls her lover's name into Echo's cave: Romeo. EO. Since Anne's inconstancy was constant, rocks themselves could vaporize and turn to stone again in her hands. No alchemist could wish more power than she had. I would compare her with the band of travelling players I came to know and drink with in Venice. Their set stories had become so much of a piece with their lives that what they acted every night was but a dream discussion of what they had done or would do or were thinking of doing before or after the play had ended.

I limned her in the sun for dark-ey'd Rosaline in *Love's Labour's Lost* and *Love's Labour's Won* [the lost play A.F.] and Beatrice in *Much Ado About Nothing*. I was the still-young fool who thought that Anne could rise triumphant and give us both a wild of joy. She warned me she would never change. I would not listen because I felt the sap and growth in me. After many years she sent me away for a twelve-month term after my distaff-wife died because, she said, I'd won her twice with false dice and now need give her time to lie fallow and revirginate. I came back and was a fool once more, though I was at least careful enough by then not to ask her again to marry me.

Anne's secret powers grew stronger with the years, and I watched and used them well, too. Though she did not much talk of my plays and masques, her crystalline glance could on occasion cut straight through them. *My hands are clean*, she told me quietly when she'd read the political play *Macbeth*, though I thought I'd hidden any trace or mood of hers from life in that portrait. *I shall not soon forgive you that*, she added, and didn't. *It will please the crowd and advertise a message useful to the Queen. But it also proves what I've always told thee: you neither know me nor love me, and now you know me not in new false hues.* There was nothing to be said. Her swift verbal tennis stroke had landed in France [slang for the forward left square on the tennis court A.F.], and I could only shrug and smile ruefully at her insight and my plight. Perhaps there never lived in any place at any time so sweet and doleful a malignancy.

Sing a song of sadness. Countless statues in a million churches could not rival the shadowy appearances that flitted across her long cheeks even when she was being witty. Thus it was that I was alerted by the simple stillness of her face before she told me, when one of our passions had ended: *You have cardinally known me too frequently, my pillicock* [cardinally, a pun on carnally; pillicock, a term of rough affection, 'sweet ratbag' A.F.]. *I am quick with child.*

The danger in the situation could not have been greater. I guess'd at once that I was done with daughters and that an illegitimate claimant to my title would drive the Lord Treasurer to any measures.

Anne was unperturbed. She stayed in Court in flowing dresses until January, when I took first place for the second time in a tournament, more in anger than in skill, and then retired to the country, considering whether it were meet to flee the country. Burghley, as usual, knew all, though I to this day do not know if the savagery of what followed belonged to him or to the Queen. When the first cramps of birth came to her, three guards appeared at the cottage in the middle of the night like malevolent wise-men from the Orient. A servant-spy, it needs be, must have shown a lantern at a pre-fixed place as a signal. She was wrapped tight in blankets, bound like a bunch of faggots and taken back to London in a jarring carriage ride. There, six hours later, early in the morning, on 21 March, she gave birth in the Maidens' Chamber on a bare bed surrounded by armed guards as though she were a dangerous rogue about to commit some dastardly crime. She was attended by only one servant, untrained in such matters until that night. Three of the guards stared idly between her legs while she was – her Yorkshire word – meaning, as if at the ready to catch an escaping prisoner, and only the fourth, who was a father and a man of some experience, took pity and advised the girl how to untie the cord and slap the child.

Thus was born, and nearly died, my son Edward on 21 March 1580. Anne had waved her hand each time I broached the subject of our flight across the channel and a new life abroad. It was exceeding odd, therefore, to find she'd named the boy Edward.

News of the event came promptly with ten soldiers at my bedroom door in the Savoy at daybreak. They expected a fight but had none. It might have been a grave error on my part, but the absurdity of it all disarmed me. Where would it all end? Arrest every nobleman in England who dares to fornicate outside his vows! O, then London would be a city of towers. I heard later that all the ports of England had been guarded against my escape. I was taken to the Tower, where Anne, still bloody, had been deposited an hour earlier. The same kindly soldier had sliced the babe's cord with his sword and handed him to a maid, who whisked the child away before his mother could hold or suckle him. Later, too, I learnt that all the retinue were awed by how the mother did not even cry out or reach for the child. That resignation or show of indifference, I think, worked to her advantage, for she was freed in just three days and took our child from the temporary breast to which he had been given. She claimed that she was a proper mother to the boy in all but that, for she had press'd the milk from her breasts in daily ablutions in the canvas-draped bath, to be whatever but not a cow.

We had no chance to speak while we were in the Tower together, but I could hear her songs each day at dusk floating down the stairs. They were songs I did not know she knew, gay songs of country courtship and Summer fields, but sung in a strange low dirge-like way. I think she'd gone a little mad, but, like me, was a little thus always. Time nursed her back. On the second day a man and a woman's voice joined in hesitantly, and by the next day the voices were like a good church chorus in a small stone Norman church. Those songs, those voices are remember'd. It seemed at moments that there were voices that I knew, and indeed 'twas so. Three friends, two servants and two courtiers had been arrested for their carnal knowledge, that they had known and yet not reported the state of affairs to Walsingham's agents. There were thus all the makings of a convivial weekend in the country, but through some error all the bedroom doors had evidently been lock't fast while we dressed for dinner. The Tower Guard did not much like the singing and on the third day marched up and down the stairs angrily rattling his sword. The singing would quieten where he passed and then take up again when he'd gone. His uniform's buttons were as polished as his wit was tarnish'd, but even he, I think, could see those ditties would do his office no good if reported to Walsingham as the stuff of conspiracy.

As Anne was in her disgrace given a nurse for her babe, so I was given a quill and crystal ink-pot and steady supply of fine parchments. That was my nose-herb from the Queen. I'd had the presence of mind to wear a fine suit, bring another and also a bag of linen. The soldiers waited in surprise. It was simply something that I knew to do. My clan had grown practis'd in that place; 'twas there that the thirteenth Earl's son had perish'd while his father was in exile. I sat precisely fourscore days, and it was then I saw clearly the advantages of exile and quietude. My mood was bitter and defiant, but in that time I wrote one whole play and a large portion of another, the third part of *Henry the Sixth*. She would have Her useful entertainment but for it would have to remember all that the Oxfords had done for England, and how the Tudors owe their very throne to the fierce loyalty of the thirteenth Earl.

I was released at the beginning of the second week of June, but not set free. Instead, I was given military escort to house rest. As I left the Tower the old porter came forward to demand my best velvet jacket as his traditional fee of office. I scorned his right in this instance because he had shown me no kindness whilst I was his guest and, besides, I was not there for treason or any criminal act. The house rest was worse than the Tower because, first, it was longer and, secondly, even with a guard at the door, my friends were free to come and go and dish me up all the vilifications being spread about me in the Court by those attached to Burghley, who was a mighty whisper-spreader. I was finally sometimes permitted to go out and even sit among the wits, but always watched.

The four years starting from 1579 were my lowest. At the end of 1578 my play *An History of the Cruelties of a Stepmother* was performed at Court [an early version of *Cymbeline* A.F.] and found great favour with the Queen, whose life had given her cause to beware of other mothers, though it seems to me that real ones often do greater harm. All hope was in my second investment in Frobisher's explorations and I had to sell two fine estates, but Her pleasure with me and my plays was such that, when She learnt of it, She granted me the Manor of Rysing for good, true and faithful service. It scarcely sweetened the gilt, however, that it came from Norfolk's estate. It was my payment for remaining loyal. But then She slighted good Sussex, for which I refused to dance on exhibition before the French Embassador. After that, things got out of control, though the reality of my situation was concealed for some time.

Churchyard, Lyly, Munday and I were working very hard to train our actors and our stage carpenters so that we could at last have a worthy theatre. The costs of maintaining my circus in that year [1579? A.F.] were such that for the first time neither by cleverness nor by my gold could I supply the Queen with a suitable Christmas favour and felt humiliated to be unable to show good quarter in the Court. She was the wise and tender Monarch then and thanked me in open Court for my Masque, which was, she said, the richest jewel laid before the Court that Christmas. I danced as though my very life hung on't, and in the Summer Court of 1580 the Queen once more had eyes only for me. Then in January I won the Tournament again. Leicester scowled every time she smiled, and I reaped enemies everywhere I looked. That was when the mocking poem about me, '*Were I a king*', was circulated. I wonder still who wrote it. Ben Jonson is suspected.

My ambition was more modest, however. I wanted stronger support for the theatre and did not get it. It appeared She wanted all England to be a stage, on £1,000 a year. On the one hand She let it be known that She would condone the public performance of plays, while with the other She commissioned Tilney to censure the plays more strictly. The two things, I suppose, followed one from the other. Tilney was indeed a strict censor but was fortunately unable quite to cope with the Queen's appetite for new plays and the rapid river of words that rushed from our long table. Much, too, he simply did not grasp. That was when Oxford's Boys were initiated as a troupe, and I took over Warwick's Company. At what cost! In 1579 five land sales had to be made; in 1580 it was thirteen more, and the money-lenders became my constant company.

It was then I wrote *The Merchant of Venice*, in its earliest redactions called *The Jews, The History of Portia* and *The Merchants*, which is my most misunderstood play. It was written in response, as is my custom, to a rough and vulgar play [Marlowe's *The Jew of Malta?* A.F.] that preceded it and means to show a whole stageful of calculating villains, not just one. Why, the money-lenders were gentlemen in comparison with some who sat in Elizabeth's Court. The de Veres have been here for a long time and know how the English Lord gave the Jew his right to lend with only one stipulation, no right to write a will, which reversion many debtors both low and high were often quick to hasten. 'Tis said in our family that in the times of Aubrey, before they were chased away, only the Jews besides the nobles had stone houses, of necessity, because often the mob preferred to attack them when the exactions of state grew too heavy. The thieving nobles preferred it that way, too. Now the story has begun again. The Jews did not hasten my end; rather, they prolonged it somewhat, and if those mock-Italians had been allowed to pay me a fair price and hold title to my lands, the which they much desired, then I daresay it would not have been necessary to give my avaricious countrymen such golden profits.

I should have played only with words, for I've never been lucky with money. I sold one more property in 1581, five months after my release from the Tower, in a bid to recoup all I'd lost with an investment in Edward Fenton's little private fleet, pirate fleet, not to put too fine a point on it, which intended to prey upon Philip's galleons. My hopes were high after Drake's sortie, which brought back many thousands of ducats. Fenton I trusted thoroughly. He would not misplace gold as Frobisher brought back false ore. But that very success of Drake's had so stung the Spanish that they had every boat on alert, and Fenton had to sail home sadly with several ships lost and no loot at all. At least my own ship, the *Edward Bonaventure*, was saved and served to give me my last moment of glory.

The Queen wavered long about what should be done with Drake's gold and cloves, but She herself had invested a thousand crowns and so stood to have back ten times as much. She could be, I fear, a greedy woman. Hatton and Leicester, of course, urged Her on, being themselves investors. Only Sussex and Burghley argued against, the former from principle greater than mine, the latter from quite justified fear of war, for Spain was even then a nation very inimical to us.

I am myself surprised we did not have a war, for salt was splashed in Spain's wound then, as a Royal Procession was mounted and Drake was knighted on the deck of the *Golden Hind* at Deptford. The Lord Great Chamberlain played his part in the procession. I walked to the pier at a remove of two behind the Queen, and I daresay it was my most successful role. Drake's men in the taverns had not kept hidden under a parrot cloth their Captain's most remarkable trait. The man who sailed round the world and singed King Philip's beard on more than one occasion had a certain affliction. On all but the smoothest of seas the stalwart Captain Drake had to retreat to his cabin with seasickness. With such a merry crowd lining the road on both sides the temptation was too great. Using my long white ceremonial staff for my mast, I heaved and drew in my cheeks, looking imploringly to the heavens, and stumbled and grabbed for the mast, and puffed out my cheeks and threw my hand to my mouth, and staggered with despair in my eyes. I possess'd the crowd, and I could see ahead how the Queen and Drake turned their heads back to see the cause of mirth that overflowed the music.

After the pirate became Sir Francis, the Queen reproved me at the feast because I had played lightly with the staff that my grandfather had respectfully carried at Her mother's coronation dinner. I think, though, She liked the jest in spite of Herself and was a little jealous that She had not been in a position to enjoy it. Besides, She still affected to frown on me at every chance. Sir Francis accepted my congratulations with a stony face.

There is another cause to remember the procession. That was the last public occasion when I walked without a limp. In debt and out of favour, with a theatrical regiment to support, I'd slip't back to Burghley's daughter once more, led on by her lachrymose letters, in which she begged my favour and sought assurances that I did not have some causeless misliking for her. Those reports, I'd guess, came to her from her irritable father anxious to explain why he could not simply order me to heel. I'd explained to Anne that she'd had my favour once but could scarcely hope to have it again whilst she remained her father's abject slave. The simple proposition was beyond her ken, though I'd detailed for her exactly what he'd done at Court to have me back, whipped. Here writes a man with the plague: the wrong family is life's worst pox, and a more kill-kindly one than my in-laws could scarce be imagined.

I'd been two months back at Burghley's house at Westminster. Each day I'd retire to the Savoy to write and direct our affairs. Farrant and Hunnis were working with me on the public theatre project, and Munday and Lyly were working to improve Oxford's Boys. Gloriana had set me the task of creating a Queen's Company, at the same time warning me that it must be the best in Europe. It took two years before we had people of sufficient skill to select from, which was the aim. Hunnis was upset to have his talent so skimmed off but was persuaded that it was a little price to pay for the Monarch's pleasure and continued indulgence. In the morning

I would write with Churchyard and the lads; in the afternoon, if there was time, I would rewrite by myself and send instructions to Gray's Inn for various necessary researches and texts. Late at night I'd write by myself.

After one such day in which much had been accomplished and in good humour, a band of us went to toast the day. This was the time of day when I ceased to be Lord Oxford or a vigilant taskmaster and became simply 'our pleasant Willy' for the men [the name by which Spenser refers to Oxford in a 1591 poem A.F.], my literary name, which, however ironic the sprout, I'd come to treasure almost as a lover's private name. Whatever just pride there is in name and rank, it is sweeter still to let them drop on the bank of circumstance and swim freely in the river of friendship. On this memorable evening my man and I came up the tavern steps to find Thomas Knyvett with his sword drawn. As soon as he saw me, he began to wave it back and forth and would have advanced to behead me defenceless in the stairwell if I had not managed to hurl my cape at his sword and thus obtain the time necessary to gain level ground and position myself for the fight.

Knyvett's star was lately rising at Court even as my own had been descending. He'd only recently been made a Gentleman of the Privy Chamber and Keeper of Westminster Palace, I wonder if to nettle me, for his hatred of me was no secret and even the jester scratched his head to see such a tough old fowl suddenly given preferment like a bright lad. Whatever the circumstance of his good fortune, his dastardly assault without announcement showed he was no gentleman and, indeed, lacked the gentility of a village lout born under a hedge. His face was full of fury, though I could see at once that he was not drunk, whereas I was not at my prime for a sword-fight.

My ears told me that our blades were meeting almost in iambic measure, whereas my eye wandered lazily o'er his profusely sweating neck and his ill-matched costume as though we were a picture for idle study. At one quick moment I counted with fascinating clarity in the moonlight the nicks in his raised blade. I was drunk but felt able to handle the knave without difficulty, when of a sudden he crouched to the ground like a washerwoman to avoid a blow he was not prepared to sally and then swung his blade at my leg as he rose. We both fell back. I cut him deeply on his unprotected shoulder, but his blade caught me above and behind my knee and slashed the muscle.

I was bandaged, wrapped in a blanket and carried by a crowd of players to Westminster on another blanket stretched out tight. I remember how their conversation floated to me in a haze as my tragic carpet floated along the night streets of London. Two wept and grieved as though I were already dead and destined for a tomb, some worried about my life, some about my leg, and one lone voice – I think I know whose it was – bemoaned the probable curtailment of our plays in progress and the uncertainty now of future finance. No one among the others answered him, but I heard his honest despair and chuckled in my delirium.

When Pondus was awakened at Westminster, the best surgeons of the city were quickly pulled from their beds to attend my wound, and that is why I limp today. I'd replenish the line: first let us kill the lawyers by placing them in the care of physicians. If the good doctor Arteslow had been there, he would have patiently knitted together the severed strands and bound them together with a poultice of fresh chicken gut. I'd once watched him do it with a favourite mare, and after three months it needed the most trained eye to see any break in her gait. My three worthy surgeons ministered first to their own vanities, with two squabbling over the best method of ligature until finally the decision was toss'd to their younger and quieter colleague to avoid the submission of the one elder to the other. My mercy was that as their dreadful restringing proceeded I was fed great spoonfuls of aged apple brandy from Normandy until I hovered in the air above their mending circle. The strange thing was that in my delirium I was a lad again and had evidently fractured a leg falling from the tower at Castle Hedingham.

My wife was my nurse for many weeks and, to do her justice, she relish'd the role, in part, I suppose, because I was her captive and not free to spurn her. Anne had wanted this reunion so much that she was unable to hold back the happiness in her face at my convenient misfortune. There began her second sorrow, because, in my sickbed and without the other Anne and my son, I was vulnerable and foolishly sought to atone for past sins. I took her between my sheets before my stitches had been pulled, and a son was conceived between us, who died unchristen'd shortly after he was born. She seemed to feel that she had lost her main chance and could find even less to say to me than usual. Her simplest sentences were punctuated with tear-storms. She wrote poems to her missing son. They were banal but no less moving for that. Poor Mouse.

Her father was disgruntled to have my former ties with Anne Vavasour made more public knowledge than ever, and his pleasure at the sudden reconciliation of his daughter and her husband just when it was least expected was dimmed by the keen awareness, which I'll grant he had almost as quickly as I myself, that I would be too proud now to limp back to Court. What gall'd me most was that the knave Knyvett himself was soon back in place, sporting an embroidered arm-sling far longer than he need have and playing avenged kinsman and triumphant swordsman up to his swaddled armpit. That was fortune's outrage. The place of my wound was known to all. It would have been a disgrace to him if he'd deliver'd it standing, much less without issuing a challenge and crouching in the darkness like a savage. The Queen's favour eventually returned after two years and even grew, for in several years Her secret commission to me was formalized, but my disdain remained and I made it a point for a decade to come to Court infrequently, only when I knew there would be no dancing. I was, however, often present behind the scenes when there was stagework to be done, until I finally quit the Court entirely and went back only a handful of times in six years.

I practised diligently until I could move my body in a gentle crescent as I walked to countervail somewhat my choppy stride. It meant I never walked but dipped and glided, most suitable perhaps only to lead fancy-stepping Morocco [Banks' performing horse A.F.] round a ring in a mincing walk. Now I am so tired and it does not matter in the least. My walk in Hackney is twenty paces back and forth, and I can do it as I please. But then I was just thirty-two, and raised weights with the leg and ran courses on a hobby-horse until I was still slightly awkward but exceedingly competent, though I preferred to be at sea or on horseback, where the lameness did not show. Only two years after the duel I was able, because Burghley now knew he had no hope of making Anne happy while I remained disgruntled, to go on the military expedition to the Low Countries and then later that same year [1584 A.F.] surprised everyone, and myself a little, when I took first prize at the tilts for the third time.

Anne had told me her uncle's dark secret. When she was but a child, Uncle Thomas had fancied her beyond the rights of kin. She'd fended him off, once with a ripped dress and refuge taken in the great barn, where she used to go to sit by herself and so knew every hidden cranny, and looked down on him searching for her from the dovecote. It is very likely that he guess'd she'd told me; or at least it is hard to explain such intensity of hatred to defend the honour of a grown niece who all the world knew was not always nice, and who was anyway the daughter of a sister with whom he was scarcely on speaking terms. The feud did not end with the attack on me. For two years, until the Queen at last intervened, bands of armed Knyvetts laid in wait for my men or even the men of my friends. The feud came into flower in a fine season, for there were already in the air the thicket of Sidney's anger at me and also the venomous accusations of Howard, Earl of Arundel and equidistant cousin to both Knyvett and myself, of which you already know something.

The first serious attack came in June, when my men Gastrell and Horsleye went to Blackfriars Stairs to take the ferry across the Thames and were met there by six of Knyvett's men, all fully armed. They'd marked their route and were lying in wait. Fortunately, they'd blabbed their intention at the water's edge and mightily interested the ferrymen and other rivermen, who anticipated a duel between the Lord Oxford and Mr Knyvett and stayed to watch, leaning on their long pikestaffs and staves, with many cast-iron hooks hanging from their belts. Though they were disappointed that the expected encounter was going to be denied them – I was not with Philip and Dan – the onlookers saw that the fight was unfair and began to take a part in it by cracking their staffs together and giving a mighty holla, after which they waded into the fray with their long poles as though they were separating river barges, and, further to our luck, the junior master of the fencing school that shared quarters with us at Blackfriars happened along at that moment and drew his sword to aid the underdogs. Things quietened down rather quickly. Swords were placed back in their scabbards and Knyvett's men quietly went separate ways as though they'd been strangers who'd come together by chance.

The feud was by this stage out of my hands. Gastrell's Irish temperament wanted revenge and he carried the fight to Knyvett's men several times, though I set another man to follow him and pull him away. In one such incident Dan was slightly slashed and after that the extremity of the matter worsened even more.

Knyvett himself coldly killed a young lad who had not even learnt to hold his sword properly. Another man, Robert Brenings, was slain in silent circumstances. Christopher Hatton was given the task of looking into the matter in the Queen's name and kept the thing out of court as though Knyvett were a nobleman. The verdict was *se defendo* and wholly unmerited. At this Dan Gastrell struck back and killed Long Tom Hunter, the most hated of Knyvett's retinue because he was a scurvy fellow and had once served me himself. Long Tom had wanted to draw importance from his size and, when he found himself without it, fomented little conspiracies in the kitchen, serving tales from one group to another like roast pigeon. I think he wrote reports as well. To the one judge good and true, the Queen now added another even worse, Leicester, to report on the matter, and here at last Burghley chose to step in on my behalf with protestations of my general guiltlessness overall in the feud and Gastrell's particular dumb innocence in the killing of Long Tom. But I knew, and the Knyvetts knew, too, that whilst I stayed in the Queen's displeasure all was permitted to them.

There was none the less some profit in it all for me, for in my season of disgrace I turned my childish play that I'd published under a close cognate of my real name [Brooke A.F.] into *Romeo and Juliet*. That was, I think, my most popular play, though it nearly wasn't staged. There was solace for my oft-spurned wife in fair Juliet and the only flattery I ever gave the Queen onstage in fair Rosaline, with whom Romeo, 'without his roe', was first in love but 'out of favour':

> She is too fair, too wise, wisely too fair,
> To merit bliss by making me despair.

That Rosaline all but wore the Crown, for I had her with

> Dian's wit,
> And, in strong proof of chastity well arm'd,
> From love's weak childish bow she lives unharm'd.

There was, however, tartness with the sweet. I reproach'd the Queen in plain-spoken fashion for Her jealousy of the black-eyed Anne when Romeo exhorts his Juliet:

> Arise, fair sun, and kill the envious moon,
> Who is already sick and pale with grief,
> That thou, her maid, are far more fair than she.
> Be not her maid, since she is envious.
> Her vestal livery is but sick and green,
> And none but fools do wear it; cast it off.

Tilney at once spotted the Tudor colours and call'd me in to lecture me. There are, in sum, not many colours to choose from, I protested, and chances such as this one must pop up. *Then take purple*, he told me, and I replied that 'twas too long.

*Well, red.*

*Too short.*

*Then we shall drop those lines.*

But inasmuch as he was evidently not privy to the underlying cause of my time in the Tower, he left the rest. The next day a messenger came with a call to appear before the Queen. It confirmed what I more than suspected, that Tilney merely made sure the ink was dry before he brought the sheets to the Chief Censor. The hour was an odd one, early in the morning, and She waited for me at the end of Her longest hall. My uneven steps echoed in the cold emptiness of the room as I walked towards Her. She was cross, and we were going to have an explanation. There were no Pages in attendance.

*I have been lamed by an oversized rodent ready to scratch or bite a man to the marrow or the heart and capable of anything except honourable conduct.*

*There are different versions of the man than your Tybalt, Edward.*

*That's true, but they are false, just as you know that I am lame only when I walk.* At this the Queen sighed, and I could see that the wind had shifted to the safe side, though the fuse of Her anger still burnt.

*Why have you dared to say that I was sick and pale with envy?*

*Did I say that about you?*

*You know you did. Is there anyone else in our land who is compared with Diana and called the shining moon?*

*Ah, but with my character it was the envious moon!*

*Silence! It is my privilege not to suffer such brazen dissembling. Do you recognize My Royal robe of green and white? I wore it just for you.* I remained silent. *The strings of my patience are very long, but they have snapped before.*

*Then send me to the Tower once more, one last time, but first I pray you change the guards that I may at least enjoy fit company for a nobleman to die.*

*If you were in the habit of seeing such things in your bed as I do in mine, you would not persuade me to take another head. Edward?*

*Your Majesty?*

*I wish that hurtful speech removed.*

*I'd wish the waters that flowed from the spring of your discontent had somehow been stopped. They were not.*

*You know I shall have that speech removed.*

*Indeed you may, but in that event, with or without my head, you'll not have another play from me.*

*Tell me why there cannot be greater harmony between us.*

I answered that our signs crossed close but at variance and, more than that, we were monarchs of two separate kingdoms and so could not escape small frictions from time to time, which differences should not mar our overall amity and mutual respect.

*Your King Richard [II A.F.] allows the dethroning of kings. They say that you have given up Rome. Have you given up kings as well?*

*When you put a poet in prison he may think such thoughts, but that is not the lesson of the play I meant for you.* I saw that it was time to soften and went to my knee, pledging unending loyalty within the prickly confines of my character.

*All except you lie to Me, Edward, and the awful thing is that often I prefer their lies to your artful truths, for which I reproach Myself bitterly, but I cannot help it. It is lonely here. I'll accept your envious moon, though it was not kind of you. I'll tell you only what you already know: I need your plays and so does My factious kingdom. I must also tell you plainly that the* Richard *has cracked my confidence in you. Do not, please, place such a play before me again.* She rose abruptly and said that there would now perforce be an exception to proper protocol because She had tarried with me longer than expected and Her Ministers were waiting. I still knelt as She walked from the hall and I thought I saw wetness in Her eyes as She turned Her head. She'd left in order not to see me limp back down the long carpet.

*At least I'll see that the lines are spoken swiftly and to the wall,* I called after Her, and She quickened Her step.

*Romeo and Juliet* was approved for the printer with no deletions, and thus we reached an uneasy accommodation and I was reinstated at Court, where I rarely went. From all sides the reconciliation was more apparent than real. She was quite right. *King Richard II* would stick for ever as a bone of contention between us, especially when it was revealed after the Essex rebellion against Her years later that many companies had been bribed to show the play in preparation for the uprising. It was played then not only in theatres, but also in private houses and on open streets in

London and twenty provincial towns and cities. One needed to be a bear in deep hibernation to miss seeing it. Before that happened I'd understood only the struggle of art with authority. Now I had occasion to watch how afterwards different meanings can easily be wrung from art in hostile hands.

I have not yet set down in detail the worst thing to befall me in those four years. My quiet Catholic faith had been a matter of personal conviction and discreet ceremonies in country houses where a little group gathered and a schoolteacher donned his priestly robe. It caused no difficulty within me to support the Crown. Indeed, though it was always and still is my greatest dream to see England join with France and flower with all the graces of Europe, I wished for nothing that would put free England, whatever else her faults and roughness, under a foreign thumb. I began to note that my Communions seemed to be like facetiae [entre-act performances A.F.] in battle strategy meetings. Thomas Howard and Charles Arundel were the leaders. Their ties were not to Mary but to the declared and covert agents of all the Catholic countries who were in London. At the centre of it all was Mendoza, the Spanish Embassador. It irritated me that Arundel especially assumed that I was one with them in intent, and it puzzled me that they seemed such a hodge-pudding of different purposes, now political, now religious, and often, it seemed to me, overly intimate even for plotters. They whispered in your ear and also kissed the ear. Every Catholic must make his peace with the earthly schemes and ambitions of Rome, but it slapped my soul awake to find myself at home in a covent of men who knew no borders. Did one form of treacherousness breed another, or did they all spring forth fully blown?

I was convinced beyond doubt that my fellow Catholics were traitors when I was shown Mendoza's coded letters from the rulers of Europe and their eager admirals. The only doubt seemed to be who was to have the honour of attacking England first and from which side. The march on London would be co-ordinated by a score of secret Jesuits who were skilled in such anim-adversions and keen to take vengeance on the daughter of Henry

VIII. If their numbers could be believed, every missing sailor or merchant was a Jesuit sent with a particular purpose to further the Romish invasion.

I did not bother with the spy-masters but sent a long letter to the Queen in severely formal terms, considering the somewhat distant state of our relations even before the discovery of Anne's pregnancy, because She'd known, of course, of our tie before that, in which I detailed all the plans and calumnies of Howard and Arundel that had been revealed to me. It was not the season to be a sentinel. It was then I was met with the fusillade of counter-charges that made it clear there were no private letters to the Queen in that Court. Fortunately, the Queen had marked both Howard and Arundel as dangerous with her own eye, and so what they said was only light smoke in the air above me that Summer, but the atmosphere darkened when Edward was born some months later, of course, and then all they said was accepted as common knowledge like tide and time by thrice-faithless friends who ought to have known better. It was rather a long time before I learned precisely what they were saying about me. There, in-deed, was, it appears, a conspiracy against the Crown, but it was led by the arch-fiend Lord Oxford, who acted on secret instruc-tions from Rome and took his private pleasures in little boys and farmyard animals. 'Twas said that an over-enthusiastic preacher had worked himself into a lather alerting his amazed flock to the grave dangers already lying in wait for innocent England within her shores, in particular a certain velvet Lord in league with the devil and Rome who'd been assigned to rape our Virgin Queen upon the rack before She was stretched to eternity.

Like a lonely oak in the middle of a field, I have somehow always been attractive to stray birds and lightning strikes. None there are but those who love me and those who hate me, and I have learnt 'till now to live with that and somehow survive in my busy solitude. Howard and Arundel were the worst, but most of the Cecils and, I daresay, all the Dudleys, not merely Leicester, and Hatton and Drake and Essex in his time, one loses count, they to a man dreamt of seeing me struck and split, perhaps reduced to a few cords of firewood.

Sometimes, let me grant, I myself will rage, waving my branches in the wind, where a wiser man would keep his peace. In this period I quarrelled with Bonetti, famous throughout the city for the deadly accuracy of his duelling. He was an Italian gentleman who'd lived among us for many years, an artist with his sword. He'd been paid well for his lessons and had his best pupil in me. I'd rented him quarters in Blackfriars at a peppercorn rent so that he could conduct his school of fence there. It did not happen thus, but his pupils and their diluted instructions to the foot-soldiers might have turned the tide if we had had to fight the Spaniards on the streets. Why did I quarrel with Bonetti? Simply this, that I discovered that he had also begun to give private lessons to some of my greatest enemies. I did not hesitate to front him with it, though he was the one man in England who could have treated any buttonhole in my jacket as a needle's eye with his rapier. Quick to love and quick to anger, I did not worry that he would have a double-vantage over me if we fac'd each other. To his credit, he did not press his advantage, though he might have weighed the fact that I was both Lord and landlord to him, and so there would be little profit except a few fees in a senseless quarrel and, perchance, much to lose. We were friendly again but never quite the same friends, for his friendship now seemed a mastered sport and such a repaired amity is unperfect however polished and can hold but a little moment. There was at least this profit: my actors took short lessons with Rocco [Bonetti A.F.] and, if they often could not say their words properly, their skill with swords could still thrill both the Court and the pits.

That quarrel is a fair sample of how I'd rush to quarrel against my own sense and interest, and could still if my body were sound. For the most part, however, my hatreds came uncalled. It took only a certain glance and I'd deserved another foe. I sigh my lack of temperance that I can so quickly bring frost to sun-filled rooms. Yet I'll still argue for myself that I would be disgraced in my own eyes if I were loved by such people as grace me with their hate.

It is not easy to rank the various woes whose weight I bore in those four curious years. The heaviest loss perhaps was also the quickest, to have the sun eclipsed as soon as day broke and to know that I could not be the father of Anne Vavasour's son or even acknowledge him lest my blackened name do him some further harm. He was raised at a short distance from me and by report for many years counted Anne's second husband – the first, a sea captain named Storm, vanished without trace after six months – Sir Henry Lee, as his father. But life has strange waftings and Edward grew up to be the true kinsman of Francis and Horace and a de Vere in many other traits as well. As I write these lines I have not too long ago had word from my cousin that Edward is serving with distinction and considerable bravery in the Low Countries and may now count upon a suitable place of rank in His Majesty's government upon his return. I have also in his own hand two recent letters from Edward himself, my first communication with him in twenty-two years, in which he speaks to me intimately and casually, as though I had always been his father, and describes his daily life with no word of his heroism. He is unknown to me, and thus I am only marginally his father if that word is given its proper meaning, but neither is he altogether a stranger. As I have neither power nor money to bestow upon him, I thus can meet him only in such sort as I am able, with a few poems and a friendly wave of my hand from afar. What is best in him is that he seems to want nothing more from me, which is not altogether common among children. That particular mal-transforming incident in my life, then, at least, has before I leave apparently ended well.

I must touch now upon another grievously sore spot in my life, which is also somewhat forward of the other events of this chronicle, but the place is as good as any and it will not get any easier to say it, so I shall have it out here and not spend too many words on the matter. In 1589, when Anne Vavasour had long and comfortably been married to old Henry Lee and had another son, this one in legal wedlock, though whether his or not there was some doubt I heard, against all my better judgement I once more swerved to bed with her again in just the same way that I'd slept again with my first wife. As I cannot fully explain to myself this vagary, so costly to me in so many ways, there is no point in trying to lay it out in many words. It simply was and lasted longer than it should have. Anne had become the devoted mistress of her husband's house and still was ever more the free woman.

Although Anne's appearance was full of calm, she had at last become the drab [whore A.F.] she'd once been unjustly accused of being. Her lovers by now had grown numberless, like the stars in heaven, and it showed upon her face. Such transformations must take place. Since I am widely despised, I have learnt to find much that is despicable in myself as well, however much I still disdain the motley view. I should not have gone with her again, but my eye could still see clearly the sad beauty of her spirit in the ruins of her honour and the Autumn-edging of her face. If she was a drab for others, she was not for me, though I admit that I was stupefied at first by the lessons she had learnt in life when we first became lovers again.

Anne entranced me now with another new skill, this one not practised. She put her hand upon my wrist and cried. Only then did I suddenly realize that her newly mournful visage was the least of it. In all the years I'd known her, I'd never even seen her yawn, and now she cried and would not say for what, though I had some idea. Our shames and losses were convivial. As once we were drawn together by our chatter, now we were bound by our silences. So we became Autumnal lovers, and I visited her in her lower quarters while her ailing husband slept upstairs. I'll say no more than that it was not a good idea. The wound was temporarily soothed but not removed. There would be no cure for our disgrace. If I was true to the love for her that would not be driven away, the cost of that amorous obstinacy was betrayal of a finer truer love, my only woman among the many, more beauteous than beauty itself. A fool between two lovers must understand that he will end with neither.

I'll rest here until the morrow, exhausted by the page I've finally written rather than by my plague. It was not my social shame but this later private one that mattered most and was hardest to put down. I have nothing worse to say about myself now. After 1584 all my youthful joys were far away and decay was beginning its work, but still my greatest loves and works of art lay before me, as well as ever-mounting grief.

# ∽ 37 ∾

I am little rested, but my fever has subsided and my pains have for the moment lost their pulse. Dull pains behind my ears position themselves with aches in my shoulder blades and groin and knees to constitute a constellation of soft agony. I can almost swear I hear my ribs move in and out like the salt-cased hinges on an oak sea-chest after a long voyage. The most wrackful [destructive A.F.] to my peace is still to gaze upon my face, which I shall have to do no more, because I have taken the small Venetian mirror and smashed it to the floor. Unfortunately, my strength was not equal to my anger, so now I have not one but ten small glitt'ring mirrors scattered on the tiles. No matter, they will soon be cleaned up and until then can reflect no more from where I sit than the beamed ceiling, the base of my dressing gown and the old willow that is dying with me outside my window. Spring has come, but the tree and I have not been invited to the fête.

Besides the mirror, my work this morning has been to read quickly through this chronicle. I had not realized it before, but I can mark my attacks of fever in the prose. The tale has none of the calm repose of poetry, and perhaps that is as it should be. My plan to tell my life story in two hundred sonnets went awry. Whatever their merits as poems, the sonnets have distilled me too far, and there are still the nearly fifty that I could not bring myself to write, though I made attempts again and again. In achieving pure feeling, too much was let become abstract for all but a tight circle. I plotted a play with a hidden story. Perhaps 'tis better with less art but more blood and feeling; perhaps I should not whittle away and polish what my mind and memory simply cannot contain and so spills out on to the page. Though I wish most to be renewed and shall not be, I feel now quite certain that if my lease be not long, at least I shall finish this story. The past cannot be cured; it can be related plainly and directly to ease the pain. Only am I still worried that I have gone too far in describing Lady Lee, who still goes about London followed by buzzing [gossip A.F.]. If through some mishap these lines were to be found and fall into some street pamphlet while she were still alive, then, though she be indeed black as night, my very worms would die of shame. When I finish, that part at least I shall rewrite.

## ❦ 38 ❧

My four unfortunate years were also the years in which my dramatic orchard first bore fruit. I was then much dissatisfied with the harvest whose faults cast me into one of my deep melancholies. I shall see if my memory of racing clouds is still sufficient to make a list of those I either penned myself or shepherded in tandem with the lads. In early 1579 *The History of the Second Helene* and *A Moral of the Marriage of Mind and Measure* were both performed at Court and greeted with great pleasure by the only audience that mattered. Her applause after each presentation was soft, but there was a glow of satisfaction on Her face and, as the play progressed, She would bounce in Her place at each witty line as though She were on horseback. *A Masque of Amazons and a Masque of Knights* produced pleasure for Her in a different way, but, in my judgement, plays were always favoured over the masque.

After that – was it in mid-year? – *The History of Murderous Michael* played at Court, and so did I, though after this year I began to tire of speaking in voices. I did not give much to that play in its beginning or when our table did it again as *Arden of Feversham*. My eye could see that its shanks were weak, and there was no likelihood that they would do anything but grow stronger in the same warp.

Similar problems were met with in the months after that with *Edward Ironside* and *Edward III*. I had at least that little bit of reversed power, to insist with the Master of the Revels that these weak plays not be signed with the false name they'd foisted on me. The censor was uneasy at the prospect that plays should go forth as nameless orphans. His concern was that a responsible party was required in the event that vexed questions should present themselves in a play after it had been given clearance. I replied that if the task of authorization were done properly, there

194

would be no need for second judgements and, in any event, it would be quite an absurdity to list the ten men who'd worked on the plays as authors. In such an event it would be necessary to interrogate and torture them all to find out precisely who had written the dangerous lines, and, what is worse, the guilty party would likely not even remember what had floated out of his ale-washed wits late in the afternoon. No, better to inform the Queen that her theatrical entertainments would not be ready to start until Christmas. That was always my best argument to win the match.

There was another set of plays o'er which I presided and which Tony [Munday A.F.] signed. These were *The Mirror of Mutability*, *Sir Thomas More* and *Zelanto*. These were weak-winged like the unsigned plays.

Towards the end of 1579 we staged *The Jew* at Court. The play was popular but I was not yet happy with it. After that came my year of troubles, mixed with a few petty triumphs, though I did have the enforced leisure to do *King Richard III* and to finish *King Henry VI*, and it was shortly before my time in the Tower that I did much of the work on my very first play, which ended in *Romeo and Juliet*. In 1582 I filled out and finished *Love's Labour's Lost*, working from the skeleton of *A Masque of Amazons and a Masque of Knights*, and in 1583 showed *A History of Ariodante and Genevora* at Court in the beginning of the year and *Agamemnon and Ulysses* at Christmastime. All of these plays pleased the Queen, and all depressed my spirits because they were all hasty quilts suited to give momentary pleasure and warmth, but not to store or even to last 'til another season. What I did not fully grasp then was how my skill at this new craft was growing. The potter cannot reset his pot, the painter repaint his picture, the poet rearrange his awkward rhymes set for ever in black dye, but the minstrel and the playwright can rearrange their tunes whenever they will. My players showed me that. With much experience and some solitude over the ensuing years *The History of the Second Helene* became *All's Well That Ends Well*; *A Moral of the Marriage of Mind and Measure* became *The Taming of the Shrew*; *The Jew* grew into *The Merchant of Venice*; the popular *Pleasant Conceit* into even better-loved *Twelfth Night*; *A History of Ariodante and Genevora* into *Much Ado About Nothing*; *Agamemnon and Ulysses* into *Troilus and Cressida*; *The History of Error* became *The Comedy of Errors*; *The History of Titus and Gisippus*, *Titus Andronicus*.

These future metamorphoses first flickered in my mind while we put our players through two seasons at Stratford by special dispensation. It was Lyly's idea and worked wonders in all ways. The players soon began either to know their lines better or to act with finer execution, though rarely did one man command both virtues. Our coffers filled quite smartly, for our rents were low, and a steady trail of common people from London and further afield, drivers and bakers and magistrates, made vacancies [took vacations A.F.] from their work and wended to Stratford with their families to see a series of plays over several days performed above the standard of the tavern theatres. All the rooms in the three inns were rented and then the hallways, and finally a little tent city rose up in the meadows round the town and along the Avon. Waggons of ale casks came in until the whole town smelled like a tavern. The players, joining in the spirit of things, played with merry gusto, undisturbed by the rhythmic crunching of nuts in the audience. We walked the streets and beamed at the throngs spilling about. They had not been called except by Mercury's free child of the streets, gossip. It meant that our dearest dream, a self-sufficient theatre of merit, even if leash'd in from afar, was near enough to see it in our minds fully built and bustling every night.

The other boon we brought from Stratford was young Shakspeare. I'll not begrudge him, who was innocent, my warmth, for in time he brought the solid virtues of the country to our enterprise and helped our theatre to survive. For long I worried that he must be one of Burghley's secret men, but time never gave weight to that thought. No twine was tangled in his simple soul, I think.

The end of my long courtly exile came when the Catholic conspiracy was, at last and unexpectedly, exposed to its full length and breadth after the arrest of Francis Throckmorton, who had been living in Paris and Rome under the guise of a scholar but who had, in fact, been conspiring with Papists both here and abroad to place the Queen of Scots upon our throne.

Throckmorton's arrest and his protracted soliloquy in the hands of Walsingham changed everything. Four years after my ill-timed report on the Jesuit conspiracy blackened my name so that easy friends cringed and turned away at my approach, it was suddenly perceived from on high that what I had written was truer than truth itself [a play on the de Vere family motto A.F.]. It also dawned on both Walsingham and Burghley that orthodox Lord Oxford had shown himself more loyal to England than to Rome and at some personal cost. My position became much lighter at once, to be sure, but the oddity was that the situation did not change that much.

In spite of the dangers to Her own head and kingdom the Queen had too much blood on Her mind to deal properly with the traitors. Many managed to go abroad the moment the arrest became known, though the main rogues, Henry Howard and his nephew Philip, dallied too long and were caught. Henry, however, sat in prison no longer for high treason than I had for impregnation, and then he was placed on surveillance in Sir Nicholas Bacon's house, where it seems he still lives, under a cloud but peacefully enough. Philip was questioned for two weeks in the Star Chamber, but Walsingham had instructions to do no more than question him. He obdurately denied everything that Throckmorton had said of him and was allowed all his dreadful lies. No sooner was he released than he took Catholic vows, and that was insufficient to disqualify him from competing in the tournament. Real punishment Howard only managed to obtain the next year, when he was apprehended on the Channel fleeing the country, which I can testify he did not love overmuch. As further information about him became known, it at last was impossible to release him from prison, and even there he committed high treason three years later by sending coded advice to the Spanish from his cell.

London had broken out in great dancing when the plot was discovered, and the Queen contented Herself with the warm wind of Her people's love, which blew away past deeds like leaves. I was happy for Her and for England. For my part, I discovered that if the Howards had been swept away, their slander seemed somehow to stick to me still. Often people are too busy to change their opinions, which, though hastily formed, become firmly set. It was now time to look back upon my headstrong youth with a more mature mind's eye, to find means to salve the long-grown wounds of my intemperance. Here I began work on *The Famous Victories* [*King Henry the Fourth, Parts I and II*, and *King Henry the Fifth* A.F.] in which I buttressed the cathedral of wise rule on all sides so that common people and courtiers could look into our past and see what they must do and with what they must contend. Though I did not take my limp to Court, this time was when I was most truly Her courtier. I lectured not only the Queen, but also myself in Prince Hal, whose rash youth would serve rich purpose in the end. My pleasure of low players and scribblers I then explained as best I could:

> The strawberry grows underneath the nettle,
> And wholesome berries thrive and ripen best
> Neighbour'd by fruit of baser quality

as being necessary in the true order of things for Her pleasure of plays and poetry.

I had ridiculed the match with the Duke of Alençon [the brother of King Henry III of France and for a period of some months in the early 1570s the declared fiancée of Elizabeth I; de Vere's reference may be to *Cymbeline* A.F.] in full knowledge that Diana had no intention whatsoever of marrying the fool. The more she gushed her admiration, the more one saw in her eyes the purposeful reasons of state. She put forward virginity as the Dutch show their cheese and spices and the Muscovites their furs, but, whatever samples She may have given, She never sold it, for it always held out to all the Kings and Princes the hope of a pleasant and easy victory over England without ships and troops. She may have insisted on it a bit too much, but it became Her story and could not be changed. That was something Leicester never grasped. But, whereas I had agreed with Her before and fed Her vanity, now I was a proper courtier and proffered a *melange* of sage advice with the compliments.

It was at this time I began to write sonnets in the spirit of Lord Vaux, my poet-uncle of blessed memory, who first used my sonnet form in English. He died when I was only six, but I do remember his hand upon my little head, his radiant smile and the passion with which my father spoke of the irreparable loss for England's traditions and her future with his death. My early sonnets all reminded Eliza of what She well knew but ever sought to avoid, the solemn duty laid upon Her by Her father and Her Council of Ministers, to which had recently been added the clamorous voice of Parliament, to produce an heir for England. The poems had the Court a-buzz, but She for whom they were written was more deeply touched by some of their lines than I'd anticipated. She bore the simple exhortations easily:

> Thou of thyself thy sweet self dost deceive.
> Then how, when Nature calls thee to be gone,
> What acceptable audit canst thou leave?
> Thy unused beauty must be tombed with thee,
> Which, usèd, lives the executor to be.

but broke under the strain of the twelfth poem [what follows occurs as Sonnet 3 in all editions of Shakespeare A.F.] which recalls Her mother, so briefly Queen Anne:

> Thou art thy mother's glass, and she in thee
> Calls back the lovely April of her prime;
> So thou through windows of thine age shalt see;
> Despite of wrinkles, this thy golden time.

She told me that it was not fair to touch Her with such lines: *I am sentenced to perpetual spinsterhood, as you well know, but I assure you again that it is not by prejudice or caprice but by deep streams in me that I do not fully fathom. Exhort me as you will and everyone now does, but pray do not cut so close to the heart. You have too much wit to be a redbreast-teacher* [one who tries to teach birds to sing A.F.]. *I see at last and after all the terrible things that have transpired between us and in the kingdom that you are worthy of my trust and are never just fair-spoken, but you must be more my humble-bee, dear Oxford. I am a woman and therefore weak. Though the very safety of my kingdom requires an heir, I strongly doubt that I can bring myself to it.*

It was then that I conceived a novel in poems using my own life, and I have no greater regret than that, to have written so much and still to have left the structure unfinished. It wanted another year. Let these last lines at least cast some light on my unwritten verses.

My exhortations to the Queen did have one rather unexpected result. They pleased Burghley, who wanted a safe heir to the throne as much as anyone in the land and who was already fair exhausted by the Queen's marriage games. I must confess that thoughts of a proper heir were much in my own mind at the time, as the sole means by which the de Vere family's rightful place might be gently snatched back from Burghley. I could not bring myself to mourn a son who'd not even lived long enough to merit exeguies [funeral rites A.F.] but much grieved the sudden closing of that window of opportunity for our name. I soon found myself in the daughter trade a second time. Another daughter, Bridget, was born on the first of April 1584 and snatched straightaway into her grandmother's care, as was the hastily renamed Susan almost exactly three years later in 1587. There would be no further chances with Anne.

I now had regular bouts of swelling darkness. The shock of the Jesuit conspiracy had leeched the last remaining faith from me. I am a man, an Englishman, an English poet but am too busy now with matters of greater urgency to waste time wondering whether to die by the rite of the Church of England or the Church of Rome. I need no further funerals and feel prepared to let those left with my bones toss them whichever way they wish. I shall not worry about my bones. They will be at peace at last wherever they are. My wife has faith in the new tradition. I do not object, indeed I cannot wait, and now wonder why I wobbled back towards life on those past occasions when I was balancing like a Turkish dancer on the tightrope of self-destruction.

## ❦ 39 ❦

To look at me, I had in those years seized upon the fortunes of fair times once more. It cost me dearly, but I sold some more land to acquire Fisher's Folly, a sprawling house in the centre of the city, with well-laid gardens and courts for tennis, croquet and bowling, that had been exuberantly constructed by the finest goldsmith in London, who one day'd vanished somewhere in Austria or Italy. I still kept Oxford House by London Stone. The new house, standing on slightly less than an acre, had a country air that was slightly out of place in dusty London. Its purpose was to rest the Queen, who'd given me clear hints in my new grace that if I was disinclined to limp in Court, She for her part would from time to time most enjoy sitting in secluded quietude with me as we'd done in happier times. Were any of my London quarters suitable to receive Her? They were not, and that is how I came to get Fisher's Folly. I, of all the Court, had always entertained Her not by my purse but by wit alone, and there was method in what I did. My debt stood at £6,000, and my three principal creditors were the Jewish money-lenders Baptiste Nigrone and Pasquino Spinola, and the Queen.

It is true that I had to sell seven more properties to buy Fisher's Folly, but it had its own value and helped me immeasurably. A repayment schedule of £400 a year was arranged, of which half was to go to the Treasury and the other half to the money-lenders, who gave assent to the proposal with stony smiles. They had demanded their money three times as quickly. More important than the debt holiday, it was in June 1585 that the theatrical subsidy that had been coming from diverse accounts for several years was raised and formalized at £1,000 per annum, with no stated purpose and no reports required by the Exchequer. So even with the debts at my back, there was now the assured wherewithal to go forward on my chosen path. In this at least I was very like the Queen: I was also too busy with my life to worry about posterity. If I recklessly sold such lands as remained to me, that was simply because I had to serve my fate out of what was my own. My needs were immediate, and it was I who said defiantly with old Timon: *Let all my land be sold*. In all, I have, in fact, ended with not much more than Lear or Timon.

It is sad that I shall not live long enough to finish my poems and plays, and also sad that I've lived long enough to outrun my worldly goods.

She told me that before She came to Fisher's Folly She'd heard that I was selling everything to place myself on a cushion of luxury and was being waited on by fifteen livried servants. In fact, She found me in near-humiliation with only two attendants, and was moved by pity for my dead son and my present state. But the house was grand and worthy of a Queen. The furniture and fittings were, fortunately, still in place, awaiting the distribution of Fisher's estate. I made the third servant on afternoons after I had written, as we all brushed the beeswax into panels and floors, allowing it to sit for a day before we polished it with soft cloths until we could see our cloudy faces. If a nobleman may print poems and plays and even act, what is there to stop him from shining floors? The house grew smart and tranquil, even if the pantry was sparsely stocked. I'd bribe the serving men to bring food from the palace, which they would do gladly enough at a price. Whereas She never went into the country on a progress without three hundred waggons, She would come to Fisher's Folly with only three. A false queen would be sent out after several hours and return to the palace in the carriage until it was time to send the false queen back again a day later so She could exit on Her business. London knew how often She went there but not how long She stayed. She did not even bring Her bed, which elsewhere was Her wont.

The conversation was always intense, the entertainment elegant but simple. Usually five or six of the best and most trusted players would do a scene in uniforms of unadorned velvet. Then one or two would play the lute or zither whilst the others danced the Earl of Oxford's Galliard as I used to do it more than a decade ago. When the entertainment was completed, they would exit to the Earl of Oxford March.

Eliza's red hair was now a wig. Her little mouth seemed shrunken in her squarish face and, worse, her teeth had grown quite black from chewing Byzantine nuts. It was understood without words that there'd be no more tussles between us. And yet I loved Her, then more than ever. In spite of all, She was often a great Queen. It was convenient to our conciliation that we both blamed Burghley, as though the death of dear Norfolk was all the result of the unseemly haste of middle-men, which I did not believe, and as though the bad faith about me had come to Her as a result of Burghley's irritation with me and his schemes, which I did and do believe. But looking back upon it now, the main thing was the revelations of Throckmorton that brought me out of the shadows. Eliza volunteered that my father-in-law had struggled between his vexation and his natural desire for my good repute, but that the decisive word for my restoration had been spoken by Ralegh. I had enemies I did not even know, but also a few unknown friends, it seems.

I am not proud of it, but, as it is my purpose to give pride only small place in this chronicle, let me confess that I'd also begged help not only from Burghley, but also from Walsingham, and let me add, too, that in my so-called maturity I have come to see the necessity of spies such as Walsingham for the safety of the state. What I can never forgive is the endless facile questioning with which Burghley ever surrounded me. He questioned me. He questioned those with whom I had intercourse. He questioned my servants. This was the constant in our relationship, and for this, through all the years I knew the man I never ceased to reproach him to his face and in hot letters to inform him that I was not his child and no longer his ward. Walsingham at least had a reason and went about his work quietly, whereas with Burghley it was merely the pattern of some sorrowful and peevish emotion. He was like a hen pecking for imaginary grains from habit on a smooth marble floor, and the process itself pleased him more than any pieces of stuff he found.

The sign of my new position of trust was my freedom at last to travel once again and take part in combat. A plea had come from Sturmius that I be sent with English troops to help the Protestants on the Continent. That was denied, but at the end of August 1584 I crossed to take command of the English horse and prepare them for possible battle against the Spanish in Holland. We had to pay a small ransom to pirates again on the way. Once there I found the horses were ill-fed, the men overfed and that martial discipline had been left behind somewhere on the pier at Gravesend. I sighed and set to work, covered with summer flies in conditions of sudden rainstorms and steaming heat. I had just left players in London who at last were learning to execute their lines with wit and polish. So now I would train horses and resty [sluggish, perhaps rusty – used in Sonnet 100 A.F.] soldiers. Then, after only six weeks of work with the regiment, a message came from the Queen: return to London haste-post-haste. I could not tell what the message might portend, but I left at once with the messenger and found a bawbling [small, trifling A.F.] vessel with its sails fully hoisted waiting to transport us.

*Reason not my need*, was all that I was told. *I decided that I did not want you in danger, and I am sorry that all the same you might have been at risk.*

I bit my tongue and my heart surged, because now I knew that it would be, if anything, even harder than when we were younger to leave England or to accomplish the exploits I'd been bred and led to perform.

There were other annoyances in that year, which was the time in which Anne Vavasour's young nephew insulted me. I would have responded had he been even four years older, but I was powerless, and it was also then that I fell into my third investment in an exploratory adventure, still seeking that same North-west passage to the riches of Cathay, still sinking further into debt. Yes, I was but mad North-North-West [a reference to a line in *Hamlet*, Act 2 A.F.]. What a wondrous thing, to give a nobleman gold and then expect him to know how to husband it with a merchant's soul. With it without it, I never was at ease with money.

## 40

I know mainly my own ignorance when I look back on the decade immediately after Europe. What I see is a young man ever full of changeful potency, never able to understand himself as well as he could understand the world. Ever-Never de Vere was the name with which my closest friends teased me. What made me then, when I had seen at first-hand the dangerous vaulting earthly ambitions of the Bishop of Milan, hurl myself into secret Catholicism – and with friends like Arundel, Howard and Southwell? Likely it was the same force that made me come forward to repent of it and announce their conspiracy in the wrong season, drawing down upon my head prodigious buckets of lies, not only buggery, but also supposed speeches late at night against the Queen.

It all began quite differently, as I was courted for my pen because, whilst I'd been away, the Entertainments had seem'd lumpish to Her taste. After one at Woodstock, in which Gascoigne had the leading hand, She'd even called for the script and tried to mend it, but it was ragged beyond repair. The conceit of the show was that the little piece had been quickly replayed in Latin, French and Italian, which was sterile facility. It did not gain anything from that but only became three times the worse.

The Queen asked me to supervise the Shrovetide shows, and they were particularly successful. My mind was teeming with the styles and devices I'd seen beyond the seas. In addition, two of my earliest works, *The History of Error* and *The History of Titus and Gisippus*, play'd very well in the early months of 1577. Eliza was virtually one of the players, because at every sharp sally She would quite audibly call out: *Excellent! O Excellent!* It made me wince to see my play turned into a rehearsal, but it is necessary to admit that each interjection gave such encouragement to the players that their diction and verve steadily improved. Improved, in fact, to such a point that they bumped into one another's words in their eagerness to speak. To have the words by heart, to have the words in heart, to tame the audience so that each whispered word rings out clearly and can sail through halls and walls, to restrain one's arms from turning like a windmill, all these are necessary aims. But the highest sign of virtue in any player is his skill to listen to the other player and mark the empty space of the pause so finely that each speech has the careful natural spill from line to line of a true poem. This tiny skill, in life and art, requires every talent of one's soul. It cannot be taught, or learnt, as I discovered in sad time. Many's the time in the past three years I've had to hear Hamlet's instructions to the players rendered badly.

The comedians seem to have this skill more than those who play the tragic parts, though Edward Alleyn and his great rival, Burbage, had the gift for it in the main. Comic Will Kempe was best of all in his timing and his silences, and, though I have not seen them often, young Dick Cowley and Rob Armin in recent years have given me pleasure as Lear's Fool or Touchstone or Dogberry.

These were the years when John and I were working hardest to establish the Euphuist creed, not only to make our language flower, but also to establish adherence in fashion to certain values. The Queen wish'd to be in the kitchen to help cook the scenes, and it took some persuasion to make Her see that Her fresh eye was needed on the night. My audacity would be prais'd by Her, but there were always certain differences on the question of how the play should be put together. She wanted a play to be like a box, with sides that are plumb, level and square. I was not in the business of making boxes and can see only two of my plays in which I've even held the classical frame of time and place: one, because it was written very early [*The Comedy of Errors* A.F.] and the other because it was so wild in other ways [*The Tempest* A.F.]. In art I once more drew Merlin's magic circle, which I could never do in life. What we always easily did agree upon was the need to be able to find meanings no less hidden than uttered, and no sooner uttered than demanding a second consideration, even by those who dispose their hours to the study of great matters. That knack is perhaps simply of our age entire, when so often there has been need as well as pleasure to seek shelter and obscurity. It serv'd me well to withhold explanations from Her for a while. The Queen was nothing if not critical, and so it became my part not to provide any hidden meanings until the play was safe.

The talk of Court in the time of which I speak was that I might soon surpass Leicester in Belphoebe's affection. I daresay those who watch'd whose eyes rested where and for how long had no notion how right their surmises might have been had I wish'd it. But I had by then my own third layer, which felt sweeter and deeper.

I played, I wrote, and I gambled on ships. After my first investment in Frobisher scraped bottom, I went in again for three thousand ducats [a reference to *The Merchant of Venice* A.F.] and well and truly dis-grounded myself. I was in bond for £1,000 and further invested by underwriting the £2,000 worth of stock purchased from my fellow-investor, the merchant Michael Lok, who thus grew rich from me rather than the expedition. The company of Cathay gave our language a new word, Cataian, for scoundrel. It is a concept for which we cannot be over-supplied with words. I started with just £25 but, four days before the first sailing, lunged in with all the rest, to be the biggest loser in the land. As pirates and explorers brought more and more gold back to England over the years, the coins in all the purses of London grew in number and sounded ever more gaily. I was not to be among the happy holders of new gold. My ships never came home laden with true cargo.

It is a false compare to set the same plays of Court against those of The Theatre or The Rose. Players pass'd back and forth between both spheres, yet the craft was always better practis'd at Court, where even the boy players were only the most talented. That said, my best memories are of our private performances at Blackfriars Theatre, where Oxford's Boys and the Lord Chamberlain's Men, together with Warwick's troupe, eventually regrouped as The Queen's Men and The King's Men for the Royal performances.

The admission charges at Blackfriars were rather higher than at the public theatres, which meant that there were always fewer spectators, and less drunk as well. But above all the other venues stands King's Place here, until the plague and finance broke us up, where, as in days of yore, only friends could come and the players always outnumbered the watchers. The promised end would have been the play as poem with each word in its proper place and player and spectator finally one.

There were higher hopes for public theatre in early days at Avon and at The Theatre. I merely cooled on the thing as it came into its own, for reasons perhaps not altogether sensible or thought-out. Let us say that that dream in me was o'ertaken by rough reality. But however rough they were, it was sometimes a comfort to me to be able to go into the city and see my plays, still living if sorely wounded. They tell me, and I believe, that The Globe on a good night can seat nearly three thousand, and that is proof that The Theatre has grown up since James Burbage, Richard's father and a much better joiner than he was an actor, dismantled England's first theatre, which I'd helped organize, with his sons and made its wood cross the Thames to Bankside, where The Globe was built of it. I must have a certain reserve about the reputed new polish of our players' skills. Let us grant they have grown better. They could scarcely have grown worse. I can well imagine The Globe in a century, when all the talents of Court have come down the river to dwell there and it is no longer a circus where the stage manager seeks to show any new trick that flits through his head and use as many jugglers and acrobats as he can. But who knows? Perhaps when that time comes the public theatre will once again have lifted up its skirts and gone further down the Thames or even, restless town-girl, crossed back over again.

Certainly it is awkward for her where she is, because on still nights the sounds of two dreadful competing neighbouring theatres can make the most ardent player's tongue freeze on the moment. When the patrons have paid enough for double beer and wine, the manglers at the Paris Garden, where they keep the bears and which is less like Paris than anywhere on earth, begin to poke the beasts with long sharp poles. There is supposed to be an arrangement between the managers of The Globe and the Bear Garden whereby the bear-baiting will not commence until the play has concluded. After all, the Paris Garden is run by Edward Alleyn. Often, however, the patrons grow too rowdy waiting and the roaring begins early. One night at The Globe I sat and shivered in pity while Feste fooled [*Twelfth Night* A.F.], a radiant full moon was shining through the thatch in the centre part of the theatre roof open to the sky, and outside a beast in torment roared in wildest rage from a distance.

I myself visited the Paris Garden only once, in disguise. The drinkers glow'd with pleasure at their safety near to danger and there was no want of merry women there.

The other even crueller theatre is The Clink, where every new torture imported by rumour from abroad is promptly tried out. In his quiet way the Englishman loves torture. Fortunately the prison is just far enough away that the screams and moans are rarely heard. But they are heard. When the performances and tortures are finally over each night, the carousing begins at The White Hart and The Tabard. From the days of Chaucer, The Borough [Southwark A.F.] has been the rooky wood near the city where all the most colourful crows have come to crowd and drink.

I still play'd with Entertainments at Court occasionally because I enjoy'd the company of Sussex, who was most active in constructing scenery and staging. Unlike the plays, the Entertainments were thin of substance when they fell into the printer's hands, as sometimes they did. They were meant not to print but to shine and pop like bubbles. There was fun in *A Paradox, Proving by reason and example, that Baldness is much better than Bushy Hair*, for which we gathered together all the thin-pated courtiers. That was 'Englished by Abraham Fleming', one of my less well-known non-names. George Gascoigne, I think, was working with me then. Such things were a most convenient place to use the skills of the Queen safely. She gave them gladly.

The idea for public theatres came from the Court itself, when the Masters of the Children declared a need to rehearse their charges before they appeared at Court. The experiment was kept at first at Blackfriars until the time was right, but 'tis a nonsense that it had anything to do with rehearsals. It had to do with an eye for money in the streets, and I still cannot slake my ire with myself for not having had my own eyes open to invest in the lands and buildings of the several theatres of London rather than in the far-off follies of Greenland and Cathay. If such wisdom as I have had only had had more constancy.

I'll give myself one small excuse. At that time I was furiously writing, fending with Anne, deep in a most serious conspiracy and playing leader of the Euphuists against Sidney's grouping. Their credo was, firstly, chivalric, an ideal better suited to deeds than to verse, and, secondly, opposition to me. There was not much serious in any of them except Spenser, and he always refus'd to quarrel with me. Notwithstanding that, their club, The Areopagus, had Leicester and Essex in it as well as the Puppy, and so I gave more energy to the paper war with them than I should have. Petty spirits lure us into petty traps, and we end in a wind-storm counting the leaves from an oak tree on the ground.

## 41

Lyly, my minion secretary, as he liked to call himself, and my fiddlestick, as others call'd him, was well paid to do three jobs for me: to write, to pay my players and other writers and to co-ordinate the plays. He presided over my purse with perfect honesty in pursuit of our shared goals, but I'd chosen a man too much like myself in worldly habits. At first it was all my money that went to pay the wages of Evans, Churchyard, Munday, Greene, Nashe, Leveson, the Dutton brothers, Wilton, Tarleton, Wilson, Laneham, Bentley, Mylles, Towne, Cooke, Johnson, Adams, Garland, Synger – I'm sure I've left some out. There were also printers to be paid for worthy volumes that needed my patronage. In my new leisure I've counted them: seventeen. Later, with the Royal grant, it was easy to pay the outgoings for eight months after Accession Day, but it was rather difficult after that. The number of men for whom I had to pay wages doubled. For all his good and faithful services, I of myself gave John £80 worth of land every year for four years in the beginning and assigned the lease of Blackfriars Convent to him that he might have some relief money from the rents. He solemnly took my gifts, being a mad lad in his humour except where money was concerned, and husbanded his own new resources well, I've been told. Then, when my funds were strained, he gradually drifted away from me and from the theatre. Though we did write several splendid high comedies under his name, John at last became what we together had always mocked, a parliamentarian. He and Moth had used their wit wastefully before that in the Marprelate exchanges, answering a secret press, probably Throckmorton's, that served the purposes of a number of Puritans. Though he's not as wealthy as Alleyn or even Shakspeare, he's added to his substance, because there is, of course, no such thing as a poor parliamentarian.

Perhaps these are times when all sensible people opt for vulgar station. No one has ever accused me of being a sensible person. Tony [Munday A.F.], who took up John's tasks, cost me less and perhaps managed the money better, but he put down his pen as well and now arranges parades and other pomp for the Lord Mayor. In these days, however, I fear there are no parades but quick ones to the cemetery. Only poor Churchyard of all our merry band has kept his pen, but his brain has become addled with confusion between his name and his purse. He thinks he owns the language in the air and has composed all the lines he used to supervise, which have been stolen from him. Unless you are also a printer like Field, shareholder like Shakspeare, or a greedy landlord like Giles, your words are like food. You cannot eat them twice, and count yourself lucky if you are in a position to have them paid for at the eating. Thomas had printed under his own name when I was still in my baby cap, but he never amounted to more than a most prolific groundling. He was on the verge of becoming a ramping old fool with his thought-sickness when the plague released him two months ago. As if there'd have been room on my skin for one more carbuncle of calumny. How could I have stolen what had no value and was not even signed with my own name? However that may be, he escaped my retribution through his age, as Knyvett did through his youth.

This good news was conveyed to me by Henry [the Earl of Southampton A.F.] with all concern and sympathy. As he reported it, the question came to mind: would he have even thought to bring such news to me five years ago? I know it is an ill-taken suspicion, but strong for all that. I alone saved him at the trial. Have I all the same been judged for having let him come to trial? Awhile before he'd also brought me information from Norfolk's children, saying that, in his last conversation with them before his execution a quarter century ago, Thomas had blamed me severely for not having had the *Grace of God* ready on time to take him into exile. You could not ask a better friend, he'd told them, when he remembers to think of you. That did hurt, because the fault had not at all been mine. The Captain was a coward, and there had not been time to hire another ship. What difference did it make anyway? The fat-bottomed hull of the *Grace of God* would have bobbed and brushed against the pier for a long time waiting for him to come. It was Thomas himself then who would not flee. I was furious with him for that, as he well knew, and so he defended himself in his own weakness by besmirching my name and our friendship as he went to the block. As for old Churchyard, he was just a common carp in a garden pond that has taken it into its fishy brain to leap and thrash like a river trout before it dies. And I, too long the furious and ecstatic trout, would now so prefer to be a comfortable carp, at rest.

## 42

I've lost all feeling in my hands. Will Death, which I've been sure will at last consume me in a blaze, come instead sneaking up on raised toes as a creeping chill? I am fire and ice, as I've always been, but now run riot. There is my pen held properly in some strange hand. My arms have married themselves to puppets that still move and prance at command yet no longer quite belong to me.

## ❧ 43 ❧

That London wants its theatres there can be no doubt. We have five now, and the noble badges of the players are worn on thousands of blouses in the streets. The aspiring hired players who do the minor parts and have other jobs wear them most proudly and trade in letters of entry whene'er there's to be a restricted performance. The seal of their lord, who in most cases has never laid eyes on them, can also be of use for a bit of credit at the shops, though that is happening less and less now that the risks of the courtesy are becoming better known. Other employees are the book-holders [prompters A.F.], stage-keepers, tiremen [wardrobe keepers A.F.], and the people-gatherers, who circulate through the taverns and chat enthusiastically about the plays, sometimes giving well-studied amateur improvisations of scenes. The people-gatherers never wear badges. This device works well, and it is sometimes impossible to tell the paid gatherers from the unpaid enthusiasts. I visited the taverns to hear what the public was saying but gave that up when I understood that the unpaid opinions rarely departed from the paid ones. When I'd asked someone whose play it was, the answer would always be: The Globe's, The Hope's, The Swan's, The Rose's.

I never met a spectator from the shouting plebeians who thought my plays were anything but true. They had neither training nor inclination to ponder what different coats truth may wear. All the plays were wonderful or terrifying pageants, and none of them, of course, not even *Coriolanus*, had anything to do with their simple low-born lives. Once I heard a smith with half-mask'd face ask his mate if he, the smith, had seen the play that was being recounted to him. The favourites of all were the plays where in the more profitable theatres they'd fire an uncharged cannon.

Even though Lyly diligently administered and watched over everything for me, matters soon got beyond control. Players slipped back and forth between the theatres so frequently that it was impossible to keep track of players who drew double salary by sending a hired man to play for them so they could pocket the difference in the fees while playing somewhere else themselves. It was difficult to see, finally, why theatres manifestly so profitable should draw the amount of buttressing from the Crown and my pocket that they did. John's explanation was that if it were done otherwise, soon the theatres would be nothing but juggling and song houses, which would scarcely please the Queen or suit Her needs. Belphoebe Herself, if memory serves me here, never went to a public theatre and only once attended a private one, when the Burbages built their fine new theatre at Blackfriars after I'd gone into my retreat. I went to that play disguised as a money-lender and did not announce my presence. I'd guess it was the audience more than the players that disturbed Her. They freely took sides in the story, and that came as rather a shock, especially when they cheer'd the treachery of Brutus. She found it easier to be satisfied that the plays were knitting the nation together if it was not necessary to observe the stitching too close at hand. She provided the finance, and that was enough. In a rare gesture of confidence Burghley had shown me years before the minutes of the Privy Council in which the Queen had squeezed notices of rewards to the longest-serving members of Her recognized companies between urgent judgements on high treason and heresy. It was a consolation and a distraction to Her. While it is certainly true that She took note of particular players of mine, such as the Dutton brothers, it is equally certain that players who'd never performed before Her were sometimes given small bounties, thereby offering yet another proof that the theatres were being carefully observed.

As at almost any given time for a decade there were always at least two theatres staging one of my plays, it might be assumed that, money and acting skill apart, I could not be too unhappy with the state of the theatre in England. But no, there was no peace even in their freely nominated popularity. Inevitably there would be a fray between two companies, with one claiming that the other was showing a play to which it had sole rights by virtue of having shown it to the Queen, though there was no law or custom that granted such proprietary rights. It very much reminded me of the bridge quarrels, as I often had to adjudicate and conceal the fact that I had interests in the play and both theatres.

The Duttons delivered me into much difficulty of this and other sorts. 'Twas said their family boasted the longest lineage of The Castle Clink. The Court would have been surprised if it'd managed to find out where else they'd played. They were, all the same, extremely good players, and they could juggle and tumble as well. They play'd before the Queen on many occasions, once when they were out on bail.

The very success of all endeavours in the theatrical sphere threatened to distract me from my proper labours. John was highly irritated with my decision, but the exhaustion that follow'd too many efforts on too many fronts was making me grow sour. It was no longer my place to be a secret intermediary between the Office of Revels and the theatres. The colleges of Oxford and Cambridge alone were now staging between thirty and forty plays each year. A madness of dramaturgy was abroad in the land.

It was in such a mood, after a foolish masque of Moscovites with blackamoor torchbearers that I'd been called in to rescue from total disaster the night before, that I lash'd out at the Puppy, not to humiliate Sidney but to show the Queen that I could not for ever be hemmed in and pulled this way and that by little men and little tasks.

## ⤜ 44 ⤛

Gabriel Harvey, the rope-maker's son from Saffron Walden, is, more than most, both a natural scholar and quarreller. He has a place here in my chronicle because he almost dragged me into a second quarrel with Sidney. Harvey wrote poems only in rare fits, and some few of those were even fit to hear. But he championed the Latin hexameter, ill-suited to our language, and would not desist from it. He could not sit at the long table with us when we wrote plays chiefly, though, because he was more peevish than poet, and his conceit was a sponge that first created and then soaked up hatred and converted it by strange internal alchemy to self-esteem. He was a difficult man, and methinks Thom Nashe did not journey too far astray to say that he was known to the world for a fool, though all the world does not know Gabriel Huffe-Snuffe. Those who do know him, remember him as the almost-junior-proctor of Oxford, brought down by the Queen's long memory from the time when his college enemies put him up to dispute publicly with Her on Her visit to the university in the summer of 1578. I was there and smooth'd over my frown with disdain. He lost then and lost later, too. Well, yes, an impudent academic fool, I suppose, by most measures.

Harvey was never my man. He first belonged to Spenser and spent many years pushing very hard to shepherd his genius on to the rocky meadows of hexameter. After Immerito, he passed to Sidney – I'll tell you how – whom Harvey first tried to flatter and make his own, but he was not over-skilled in pleasing anyone. Then Huffe-Snuffe suddenly came to me for favour. He had like as not himself forgot what he'd hissed at Cambridge high table. I'd heard of it and have not forgot either:

> A little apeish hat pressed fast to his pate like an oyster
> In deed most frivolous; his every look Italian
> Delicate in speech, quaint in array, conceited in all points.

But even so the perfect fool babbled on about me in words not cut to suit and hang well on Sidney's pleasure:

> For gallants a brave mirror, a primrose of honour,
> A diamond for his nonse, a fellow peerless in England.

That was at least the mixed wool I had by report, and it was better than the war-like turn he did to my face in his Latin address to the Queen. That is an English illness, to insult and then to turn for favours with a sunny smile.

So here stands the double-tongued fool wagging at each end in his own winds and seeking my offices to carry a manuscript to Her Majesty.

A Burghley with neither estates nor caution. I can still almost laugh myself out of my woe to think of it. The title was *A Nobleman's Suit to a Cuntrie Maid*. 'Twas a short tale performed without a wag. That was the thing. The matter was stated as bloodlessly as any lawyer's tenour, though the question was the honour of Huffe-Snuffe's own sister Mercy, and the brown egg of his indignation had been left to hatch in his pantry full ten years.

The villain of the piece was Sidney, who must somehow have prick'd the poor fellow's pride to bring forth such a mighty and o'erripe denunciation. The outline of the man would be clear to all who'd but glimpsed him, though he was not at first named. Harvey knew the power of Sidney at Court and was of an age and stage to fear the sting of his own barbs returned once more. Yet his rage must have been such to fear as much the chance of too successful concealment. Before the end he'd slipped grossly, as if by chance, and called him Phil and, lest there be some other noble Phil in England, he spoke of Sidney's aunt as well to cap the allusion.

What was droll, though I daresay Huffe-Snuffe saw it not, was that, first, Sidney's man bade Mercy to share a couple of roast cunnies with him in the town, which evidently she did willingly enough, and, later, some sweet wine and little cakes when he followed her and her peasant girl into the fields as the two collected faggots. Then the servant showed that he was not a hunter but the field scout for his Lord and sometime coney-catcher [whore A.F.]. Mercy did know who Sidney was and told the servant that he should not expect her to believe that his master had noticed her, or would turn to any other than his famous and goodly Penelope Devereux, Lady Rich, the Stella of his soggy sonnets, who dropped him unused when she saw him well and wearied of his courtship.

Sidney might have been a little forewarned by Mercy's rather precise information on him. Only fancy the sublime misfortune for a nobleman to chase Gabriel Harvey's sister for a coney. The servant and Sidney fed her foods and letters for weeks, Mercy always protesting of her chastity but partaking until she found herself at last one day shoved into a very tiny parlour at a house that was not her home. And there was Sidney in all his lowered glory, his doublet and hose still on, but just, and his codpiece already a freely hanging garland, with his shirt liberated from his belt. He had to have her and said he would make her his wife. He gave her kisses and readied to lay her on the bed, but the maid would none of that. The good wife of the house came to her screams, and she escaped. Mercy knows what finally became of her chastity.

All of this Huffe-Snuffe conveyed to the Puppy as a batch of letters and accounts 'conveyed to a sister of his by a mere chance' from he knew not whom. He offered his services. It was a gentle enough extortion that worked for a little-awhile but not for ever.

What Harvey could not grasp was that it was not for the Earl of Oxford to be his messenger, however I enjoyed the message. I'd placed Sidney in the dry castle-ditch of the Queen's discomfort and did not propose to play another set of falling out at tennis o'er him. An Oxford does not traffic in base denunciations. Yet it was a text worthy to be examin'd near the Throne. I dismissed Harvey with a show of indifference and watched him leave with the face of an unfee'd lawyer, but swiftly sent ahead to have Lyly suggest it was a correspondence worthy of Sir Francis. I knew well that Walsingham was Sidney's friend but guessed correctly that the Queen's secretary for secrecy would feed a friend to the Monarch. The news indeed did not tarry on its way to the Court, and Elizabeth kept back even more of her favour from Sidney, who'd already intruded too far into his Queen's business. But then, as all the world knows, two years after that he caught a bullet in his thigh on a foolish skirmish in Holland and became an instrument of state, a false hero given a king's funeral at St Paul's and valour and poetry he'd ne'er in fact attained.

I've escaped his fate in every direction and dimension. He did little well in his life but proved a perfect fiction on which to pour passionate admiration. Every man's hero must not be over-real a hero, so every man can say, *With different luck I could have written those sonnets and fought those battles*. I saw Sidney radiant and lovable in the circle and saw, too, his perverse and vile nature when he thought himself safe. His friends blamed all the irksome moments on his chief man Cuffe without a moment's focus on what it means to employ such a chief man many years. Sidney never had trouble with his servants.

They tell me Fulke Greville proclaims Sidney was our true model of worth, and he will write his life. For me, he was a whole strolling company of affected virtues and gestures. In a word, a professional, I'll grant. Is it not proper when the performance is concluded that the actor has his points untruss'd and plays another part? We have many such well-graced perfect actors in England. These most noble hypocrites exceed in talents the humbler players that they watch. And Sidney was their Prince.

## ❧ 45 ❧

A year after Sidney's impudent challenge a weightier threat hove into view. King Philip seized Portugal, which meant that in an instant he possessed the greatest fleet in Europe and could now even challenge the Sultan. But since Drake had captured the Spanish treasure-ship *San Felipe*, Philip faced North instead, with mounting anger as Elizabeth gave great oaths that She had no knowledge of such actions at all. It needed no wisdom to see that conflict with Spain would occur sooner or late. I did not conceal my displeasure at what Drake had done. Was I near the shadow of low envy before their towering profit? Their circle was tightly closed against me. But no, I would not have come with them even if called!

Though I was supposedly restored to favour, there were numerous frowns and warnings directed at me. The ways of Court are reptilian. It was tolerable for me only when I could speak openly and defend my friends, such as Sussex and Lumley, who'd very nearly lost his head for involvement in the Ridolfi plot and had retreated to Oxford to spend his days in study. Of all my consanguinity from boyhood, he alone was by then left to me and had not made further, more profitable alliances in life.

Since I had stood against the Ridolfi faction and yet fiercely defended some of its members, it is not surprising that I was part of no one's band in my efforts to have the Queen's heavy fine on Lumley lessened. His father, John Lord Darcy, had defended me when few others had. I would stand in temporary alliance on any question I supported, but free and bound only by personal loyalty. If it proved necessary to stand alone, I had no fear.

Some friends worried about me in those years. They did not understand the pulse by which I live. While I fought with Knyvett, young Thomas Watson, a fair poet who'd joined our Euphuists, wrote of wishing me *the continued increase of your Lordship's honour, with abundance of good friends, reconciliation of all foes, and what good soever tendeth unto perfect happiness.* Let us take count of how things stood as I entered my fourth decade: my honour was real and recognized once more; my esteem was high amongst those who love books and plays, shaky to dark with all others, save the odd physician, soldier or gardener with whom I was warm. I did then have an abundance of good friends, though most were not of the lasting variety. Of these, the best and worst was probably Chapman, who praised me thus:

> The most goodly fashioned man
> I ever saw: from head to foot in form
> Rare and most absolute; he had a face
> Like one of the most ancient honour'd Romans.

There was something else, which I've forgot, and

> Spoke and writ sweetly, or of learned subjects.

Such speeches reverberate from the deep voice-boxes of empty purses. But since I speak of honesty, again let me pause here to register the necessary lines from one of my own simpler and better sonnets:

> Sin of self-love possesseth all mine eye,
> And all my soul and all my every part;
> And for this sin there is no remedy,
> It is so grounded inward in my heart.

That, alas, is how I was, in the Court and in the country.

There was no hope or even thought on either side of reconciliation with my treacherous and strutting foes. I read with quiet pleasure but did not reply to Arundel's whining letter when he was released from prison, in which he asked me now to desist. From what? I was not the attacker but had been attacked, and would not even then have sounded the alarum had England not been at risk. As if I had the time or mind to interest myself in their fates after they were caught. Watson makes no mention of money, which, of course, would have been impolite in the dedication of his poems, but harsh pecuniary letters were then already arriving with a press of people at my door virtually every day.

And last, Watson's tendency 'unto perfect happiness'. That was to come to pass, in a fashion, though it would be several years yet before this so bitter-sweet last act of my life. When I was thirty-seven my lot was still two Annes, a hundred debts and a desk overtopping with plays, some trash, some played, some half-polished, some to be and nothing more than a few quick scrawls on a piece of paper as yet.

The years 1586 and 1587 were the deep bottom of my miseries, but then the Queen formalized the theatrical subsidy for my work. Anthony Babington's plot to murder Elizabeth was discovered, and I was called as one of the Commissioners to judge him, which meant that I was trusted, if not fully in favour. Mary was executed, Arundel died, Sidney was mortally wounded at the Battle of Zutphen, the weather was lovely. But war was about to start between England and Spain, and in the stillness of enmity that always precedes war the Armada was being prepared. I waited with keen anticipation and dread.

With every reason to expect it as my right, I asked to be made the Governor of Harwick after the victory over the Spaniards, that I might mend my fortunes. She refused, whereupon I sold both Fisher's Folly and Oxford House in London, serving notice at least that we should spend less time together and hinting that I was preparing to retire to the country.

What followed shortly nettled and stung me, though I remember thinking I'd always known somehow that it would come. Pondus sued me for unfulfilled mortgages, and, after the usual legal delay of several years, took, among several other things, the land where ruined Castle Hedingham had stood. *It is all in the family*, he tried to joke. I did not even contest the action, nor in those years did I pay any attention to the House of Lords, where in the past at least I'd gone regularly to the opening and closing sittings, as was the duty of every Lord. In my experience rank does little to remove the smell from a scurvy politician.

Because I was selling up my houses in London and letting out my leases, too, it was necessary also to break up Oxford's Boys, but at least here there were many theatres eager to have and needful of my players. Not that I could cut completely clear. I'd made more promises to my players, scribblers and servants than I could now afford. One debt of prolonged annoyance was the commitment I'd given to pay for the quarters of old Churchyard, lately a grumbler, in rooms on St Peter's Hill. The impulse had been to do the kind thing and at the same time gently remove him from my retinue. The instruction had been to rent two rooms at £1 a week and have the landlord send the weekly account to me. What he did instead was to search out three particularly fine rooms at £1 a week but in doing so bound me to a bond of £25 without telling me. The insupportable vexation of the affair was that the landlady was Mistress Julia Penn, who was the mother-in-law of Hicks, Burghley's private secretary. Not only did I have to pay it, and by then my affairs had reached a stage where such a sum was no longer trivial, but also I had to endure a correspondence of sweetish threats from Mistress Penn. She was a very model of the common London landlady, Mistress Trusteme. I thought I could detect the odour of Hicks, if not of Pondus himself, in the letters.

226

## ∞ 46 ∞

I've saved a bit a savoured story, my last great moment. Philip
had sent his Invincible Armada – beware the names you give, for
they will mock you forward or back! – in exasperation at our
Queen's invisible armada. She had for years closed Her eyes to
Her unacknowledged navy of rovers who looted Spanish ships
on the sea and sometimes Spanish cities, too. Once only She paid
Him back, but after so many years and subsequent offences as to
be a mockery. I would have struck back before He did. She
opened Her eyes and smiled when Ralegh, Drake and Frobisher
and the other knightly pirates came to Court with bags of ducats
and bars of silver and gold. So if our ships were manned by
volunteers, those volunteers were better seasoned at sea than the
masque of naval uniforms that we later would watch stumbling
on their ropes and colliding smokily with each other on the decks
of Philip's galleons. They did not seem sailors, more an army sent
to sea in heavy boats.

Yet it could have had a different outcome had a breeze or two
come sooner or later or from a different direction. The *Ark Royal*
was ringed by Spanish ships and five hundred men of Madrid
deliriously readied to clamber aboard when a strong gust gave it
the power to break away. Howard, too, found himself at the hub
of a watery wheel with spokes of Spanish cannon shot. There was
no wind, and so we dropped all the small boats overside, and
hundreds of Englishmen jumped in, grabbed oar and took the
ship in rapid tow, quite mindless of the hail of musketry that
spattered down upon their backs.

The *Edward Bonaventure*, a cast-off which I'd purchased cheaply
from Leicester unbeknownst to him through a secret agent,
rubbed up against its foe and I was able to board before the
grappling hooks were even fixed. The *Edward* was a good ship,

built by Henry Ughtrede in Hampshire. The Spanish sailors meekly formed an audience while their Captain and I engaged by sword in light armour. I placed my thrust with speed and to the point, entering the fatal chink between armour and helmet at the neck. He went back and never tasted the sea into which he fell, at which one of my men grabbed me from behind and propelled me towards my own deck as the ships had begun to separate entirely. It cost me the better part of my armour to make the leap. There were witnesses to that fight and it commanded some notice afterwards, though I am bound to say not as much as it might have, because nowadays strategy is all and single bravery does not count for much. Like much else I bore it with a patient shrug. I never knew the Spaniard's name.

On the Sunday after Victory I walked after the Queen to St Paul's and carried Her Golden Canopy, as was my duty. Afterwards, across the square She visited the Children of the Hospital, as was Her duty, and I threw open the windows to lighten the air. She was not, in fact, that fond of children unless they could sing or act.

We won the war by wind and clever mischief. August weather on the Channel is often up and down. This August it came perfectly to heel, like a well-trained field dog, and flew out when it suited us. The Spanish had lost many of their first and even second anchors as our little boats came in to nip and run, leaving them to fly against the wind with moth holes in their mainsails. They feared our tricks and our airy impertinence after the damage done them by our fire-boats in the harbours of Holland and Zealand and Drake's comet-like flying squadron down the Spanish coast in the spring of 1587.

We did not guess how corpse-weary the Duke of Parma's Armada was, though it was easy to surmise that they were as short of powder as we. The plot was laid on a Sunday evening in the *Ark* by Drake, Frobisher, Seymour, Hawkins and Howard. Though my friends Seymour and Frobisher wanted me in the company, Drake assigned the *Edward Bonaventure* to guard the captainless ships while the plot was laid. I was to be thankful that the Queen had given me leave to see service at sea at all. Before that, at Tilbury on the Thames, a little village not far from the sea, I'd had to endure receiving the Queen's commission from incompetent Leicester, whom She'd made Commander-in-Chief of the army. At least he was no happier than I and told me to my face that he'd be gladder to be rid of me than to have me.

There was a rising wind from the West sufficient to carry our eight big vessels down Channel towards the Spaniards. It was not a hard choice to make, as all our largest ships were already half-sinking. They were the only ones that had not been able to evade the Spanish balls. The ablest of our seamen navigated them in total darkness until the ghostly hulls were several spans from the enemy. Then they lit the ropes and spars, all well-steeped in pitch, till the night was day with burning smoking crosses and lace. The ferrymen lowered their diminutive boats into the water and scudded off like water-flies.

The Spaniards remembered Antwerp and turned all boats to flee before the fire was among them. But they were hoodwink'd, for the truth was that they saw almost all the fire we owned. There were too few barrels of gunpowder to cause devastations as had happened in Antwerp, and it would have been a light matter to send their own launches to tow the gently burning wrecks away as softly as they'd arrived. Instead, they fled and were very pleased with their escape, except they'd left so much anchor behind that they were now a fleet fit for nothing but flight. Drake's joke was to send two more boats the next night, which were now treated casually by Parma and Sidonia but had the whole last four barrels of powder that we possessed. Most of the Spanish fleet broke away again, but for those who had stayed death reigned upon the sea for an hour.

The Queen in armour, half silk, half steel, waited with Her troops at Tilbury like Joan of Arc. They had no way of knowing which way the battle would turn. I had helped Her write Her address to the troops, which was read to them at twenty stations by their officers from distributed copies. They say that the courageous smile never left Her face as She rode from rank to rank. That day

She was Gloriana and never more truly the Queen of England.

It was a memorable Summer, 1588. A daughter born, the country saved, a wife dead. I baptized the child Francesca and would have taken her to be raised a de Vere, but the women snatched her and even changed her name, fearing the taint of my influence and Mediterranean sympathies. Thus my third daughter became Susan, and I did not protest too much except that I would not call her by their name and soon, which was their plan, did not see this child overmuch either.

When Autumn fell, the Queen sent word that I should come to Court. I had no heart to go again but went all the same. The same tilts and pageants would be staged by old Sir Henry Lee, the father of the royal fairs, who could now not walk without weaving. He was always treated with such deference. I wonder if the stories were true that he was the Queen's bastard half-brother. Though England still rejoiced at the victory at sea, the Court was a strangely gloomy place. Its colours were already old and could not hide the onset of fading. I went to pay respect and detail further withdrawal for my writing. Everything was as quiet as though they all were hedge figures in a garden. What had they been talking about before I entered the Court? Or had it been a mass mid-morning nap?

## 47

I did not, at least before the plague, count myself old except in spirit on clouded days. Yet all around me they now lie dead. Not only friends; even my choicest foes have crept away: Burghley, Leicester, Walsingham, Warwick, Hatton, Knyvett. As I look about me only Burghley's son Robert and Amis remain. The former blocks me at every turn but does not otherwise meddle with my life; the latter reports on me once again, but it no longer matters. The middle-men are out of luck and work when the time for scheming and control has passed. What fatal softness or deadly attraction was there in me to take Amis back, like Churchyard, when he was down on his luck? Pondus said he punished him when he was caught, but then it was probably Pondus who sent him begging back to me. Why do I do these things? When the stage is empty, the last player's exit speech should be short. In health I would have gladly stayed ten thousand days with Beth and my ink-well. I regret we could not keep the theatre, but acting's now a thriving profession. They say the players will soon be a proper Guild. It was only fair. We could not pay them properly and did not want them to play for charity. The Rose, the new Globe, and the King's Men use most of the stipend now. It would have been easy enough, of course, to hold some players fallow in Hackney and work them to improve their skills, but, to tell the truth, we'd reached a point where we did not need the stage. Beth prefers, preferred to hear me read the plays aloud, and I myself found them more and more becoming dramatic poems as I worked on them. If my lot had been even ten years more, I'll wager every play in its third and final draft would have finished nearly unplayable, a poem.

Should I live beyond the end of this chronicle, it will be necessary in the rewriting to fix upon which time I wish to stand in. More than ever before things slide away in my fever, and I cannot be sure whether I am here or there. The cord of my dressing gown, the rope at Castle Hedingham, the rigging of the *Edward Bonaventure* are all the same between my fingers now. The jagged pattern of my bed-cover, which has cut me like a saw and made me look away for many weeks, now draws its teeth apart like a great shark and prepares to swallow me into a terrible darkness. No, surely there will be no revision now. My son-in-law William will have to attend to the plays as best he can, continuing our friendliest of quarrels as to whether poetry is better turned into prose or prose into verse. He'll do the job well, though I'm cross I'll not be there to make each struggle end properly.

Let's hope at least that Will will be quick enough to spot all the tired old bits of Court tittle-tattle and take them out, all except my proper allusion to the just union of England with Scotland in *Macbeth*. It is meet that it was said then before others dared say it, and it will serve our cause well with James. Our cause? Shakespeare's cause.

The blazing star with fiery tail should be sent back into darkness, the earthquake made placid, the price of fish adjusted for the new century. Such trifles need careful attention in any work of art, for the spectator notices them without noticing and if they are old, a certain faint air of staleness will arise. In 1604 who cares any more about the quarrel between Southampton and Willoughby seven years ago? To my nose, the plays smell too much of the past two decades. Whether the scene is ancient Rome or modern Verona, there must be some fresh home-grown herbs, too, scattered on the stage.

My mind runs everywhere now. I must stop this discourse here and write a sheet of instructions for Derby whilst there is some time and energy left.

That's done. Why was I rammed full of passion for the plays once more? How many more times must I change my mind again before I die?

The very air is pink-hued.

232

I've lived long enough to see the sad histories of Court begin to repeat themselves. Not only Henry, but also Lord Pembroke's son, rash William, composed himself a predicament not very different from my own. It was in 1600, after my Bridget had refused his hand, though I had much favoured their match. She was then, foolishly, my favourite daughter. Bridget later married Francis, Baron of Rycote, who counted, I think, on coming into some Cecil money. There was no sympathy between us. Not that the marriage was mine to approve, for both Bridget and Susan had been made wards of Robert Cecil, whom the Queen had called Her little elf but who, for all his twisted spine and dwarf-like stature, was happy for any opportunity to try to imitate his father's supposed high stature and good offices. As it happened, it was Susan who proved the truest of my three daughters. She is set to marry rash William's sweeter brother, Philip, as soon as he gets his title. Because she came so late she seems to have escaped the baneful influence of the Cecil women and may come good. I worry that she will marry too quickly at her mother's age. The wheel turns. Susan and the two brothers have begun to pay me wholly unexpected obeisance from a distance.

William understands my life; Susan and Philip are sympathetic to my art. Such family loyalty, not the highest reward life has to offer but one that is all the same very sweet, caught me unawares and surprises me, as I've never known it before, save from Beth, and had frequently found it ill-received when I myself tried to give it. They say they'll be my editors in the new reign. They mean after my death.

William's misadventure arose when Mary Fitton, the ward whom old Sir William Knollys had in mind to wive when his Lady was ready to be cull'd and carted away, grew tired of waiting for this promised clearing, as the Lady was in disgustingly good repair. Mary said for her part that if the grass is left to grow too green, the horse may starve. That is when she took young William by the hand and other parts, and together they had a merry chase through town, country and Court, with Mary often tucking up her clothes, wearing a large white cloak and marching about with

William as though she were a man. They came to Hackney to visit, and I saw them prance proudly together. There was reached a point in due course when no amount of folding or draping could hide the ripe September pear and finally even the Queen, who was not noticing much, saw the pregnancy.

There were differences, to be sure, for bold Mary was hauled away to Lady Hawkins' house, where, more or less at her ease, she had a still-born son, whilst the Earl was not even sent to the Tower but to Fleet Prison. From this middle prison he at first sent low verse, not of the kindest sort, to his paramour:

> For if with one, with thousands thou'lt turn whore,
> Break ice in one place and it cracks the more

and then, I know the feeling when your reason races wildly out of control, he had a change of heart and was ready to take her back, but her raging father, who saw no good in Pembroke, sent her to the country like an errant child, and William did not follow. In revenge, she lashed out at both of them with her legs and built for herself such shame as never had a Cheshire woman, ending with an illegitimate son by Sir William Polewhele, though her father had stuff'd her full of garlic to mend her kissing.

This story, told sadly to me by my future son-in-law about his brother, is not that different from my own. Mary play'd both Annes, and William took my role, though he did play it somewhat lowly. I'd not have written verse like that and I'd not have married for money, as he finally did when he took the Earl of Shrewsbury's deformed and shrewish daughter, by repute the ugliest woman in England and thus too dear a purchase even with her vast fortune.

O, there, there is my defence at last! He threw his money away, refused to live in peace and subordination under the broad shade of the great Burghley tree, he spurned his first wife because she was under her father's thrall, turned his back on his children, lived in England but lusted after every breeze from France or Italy or even ancient Rome, thought himself more noble than the monarch, sought any excuse to quarrel with anyone who made him frown, loved women beyond measure, spurned some women to whom he then crept back, betrayed the woman he loved, loves, will love most in all eternity. But for all these grievous faults with which I lean upon my desk here panting like a weary monster, there are two small but rare redeeming virtues: I did not lie, to others or myself, I did not marry for money. Wherever and however I could, I gave; I did not take. For these shards of rectitude I'll not be sanctified, but neither am I entirely without merit in the ranks of our nobility.

I heard William's story in a few minutes, swallow'd it with a grimace, digested it and thought of other things. Why then, after so many years, can I not do the same with my own so-similar tale? Is this sullen romance to be repeated endlessly, with players yet unborn?

If you in the library of your monastery have followed secret studies as far as I have to see the skeleton of things, then you may understand why I've been willing to neglect worldly ends for aerial and bookish glories higher than an earldom. Even if I've erred, soon it will not matter. I'll not choose silence as Iago and Prospero did, but I'll have it all the same, and a good thing it is. My rough magic ends, and kingdoms and follies slip from my sleeves unused. For many weeks I have drawn my breath in pain and my dumb hand across the pages to tell my vile story to a vile world. The magician begins to melt, his last trick, and with him melts all creation, too. It is Sunday and time to rest.

## 48

These sections, as I promised and forewarned you, will be brief ones, even though they concern the best decade of my life as an adult. For in them are my only real wife, all of my best writing and rewriting, and my truest friend, young Henry Wriothesley, Third Earl of Southampton. Both of these friends have inner lives that should remain in the warmth and understanding of those that know and love them, lest some storyteller someday cast their shadows askance to make a better story, which is what we are all wont to do.

Solitude was always my destination. One is a man or a woman, a city person or a country person, and you strain against nature if you try to make the two be at peace with each other and live in lasting harmony within yourself. Mingle your life, but with others, not in yourself, which is good and free advice I myself took long to take. In one of the poems I wrote as de Vere, I stated precisely who and where I was:

> Nature thought good
> Fortune should ever dwell
> In Court where wits excell,
> Love keep the wood
>
> So to the wood went I,
> With Love to live and die,
> Fortune's forlorn.

And that, more or less, is my story.

This little I can say with safety. Elizabeth was as fair as Anne was dark and as much of a piece with herself as Anne was tangled. She was one of the two most beautiful of the four new Maids of Honour, and probably the most intelligent person in the entire Court, though this was known only to a few, since she was not talkative by nature and kept her own counsel. I first became aware of Elizabeth when her droll witticisms about past events at Court reached me and intrigued me at third-hand.

When I came to know her, I found that Beth possessed profound knowledge about many subjects except herself. That was only because she was quite complete and there was no need to flail about in search of who she was or even think about it. She did, however, think herself uncomely and a compliment on her dress would bring only a pained query about the defects in her previous attire. No amount of opinion from others could ever shift her opinions on the things that matter, and yet on all the things that do not matter she was timid to a fault and always preferred to take advice. She was unlike me in every way, including age, for I am too much her senior.

I might have simply sighed and admired Beth from afar. After all, I was forty-two years of age, lame, balding, no longer as slender as once I'd been, a notoriously bad husband and father of children whom I did not see, conspicuously poor, and kept, indeed preferred, bad company, and was the object of general scorn and derision in the Court. Yet somehow we were at ease only with each other, and so I delayed my departure for the country by nearly a year until I could take her with me.

There was no need of a proposal or explanation with Beth. It simply became understood between us that we were destined to be man and wife. What was a shock was how quickly consent came from the Queen. Let me explain, if the annals of Court life should perchance forget to note it for our time, that for a courtier to carry off a Maid of Honour was not a minor crime, and many more powerful than I, such as Sir Walter Ralegh, have gone to prison for the mistake. It made me wonder. Did She herself play the mother I never had and make the match?

Beth is the daughter of Sir Thomas Trentham. The Trenthams own considerable land in Staffordshire, all of which is so carefully supervised and tended that it produces the yield of holdings twice the size. Sir Thomas has studied the conditions of insects and moulds within the country so that he may early attack the causes of bane, and, though he is old, he makes it a point on several days at harvest time to mow the wheat once at each of their fields that the men may see that he does not simply live at his ease in his manor house. Apart from that, he possesses all the dignity of an old-fashioned knight in retirement, and I feel a profound ease whenever I am in his presence. He is a poet of the ancient kind, for though he has a pile of poems and has promised to show them to me, I have still not yet read one. His daughter is the same. But Sir Thomas knows what I have done, and I am of the opinion that I won his permission by virtue of my writing, which comforts me considerably whenever I feel dark and question the point of everything.

Beth, who's like her father in many ways, which is a good sign in a woman, quietly set about mending my fortunes after we were married. I wanted to make the politic gesture and have our marriage in St Paul's on 19 May, which is the day the Queen had been released from the Tower to go to Woodstock and hence always considered a lucky day in the calendar. But Beth exercized her own queenly power and the marriage took place as quietly as could be imagined in the smallest chapel in Staffordshire A handful of cousins and uncles and an equal number of Trenthams were all that were in attendance. I grieved that I could not have my old fellow ward Rutland as my best man, but he had died quite unexpectedly four years earlier. In his place I was happy to have my cousin John, Baron Lumley. The July sun had been mitigated by an early morning shower and a cooling breeze. I can recall no finer day.

As the vows were exchanged Beth first said that she would take me as her lawfully wedded wife, and so our union was blest by a warm and well-meant wave of giggles.

The Queen had sent Her regrets that She could not attend because of Her health and the distance, but sent as Her wedding present the deed to a house, which was King's Place, Hackney.

Hackney near Stoke Newington is the Court end of town and the first fine suburb of the city. The Queen herself kept a house only a little more than a mile away in Canonbury, though She did not have much occasion to go there, and I visited Her only four times at Canonbury in a decade, three times at Her calling and once when I knew She was in residence and went to present myself. She never came to King's Place. By now we were forever querulous old friends, happy to see each other though neither of us would admit it. In the country She was much better. Terrible tales would come from the Court as the Queen engaged in mortal combat with her Maids in vying for the attention of handsome Essex, who wanted a new conquest with every meal. After he had made Elizabeth Southwell pregnant and got Elizabeth Brydges cheap, Lady Mary Howard set her eye on him and flaunted herself in lavish outfits. The prospect of a Courtful of pregnant maids was not to be excluded. The Queen was so outraged by one voluptuous gown which Lady Mary sported that that night She had it taken from her dressing room. She wore it to Court the following day, but, unfortunately, Lady Mary is rather small and the Queen was rather tall, so that Her breasts, which were no longer quite suitable for display, were too well-presented. The Queen stormily announced that She would have no more ungracious flouting wenches, but, even so, it took all of Lady Mary's friends to calm her, get her to forswear rich clothing and bring the ageing Queen Her cloak for Her morning stroll next day.

The Queen, as always, wished to be mostly moral, but little by little over the years, on the theoric that what is good for the Queen is good for Her Maids, the lusty God of Gallantry had come to rampage in Her Court, led by Lord Lack-Beard, manful Essex with his wispy chin. He was a fashion-monging boy who went in pursuit of a Queen too willing for awhile and nearly twice his age. He was an ambitious scambler who could have ruined England. But, after all, there were some worse. Essex was finally just a handsome young stirrer who came to Court and to grief, an episode in the life of our proud and elderly Queen.

I am not Coriolanus ready to set fire even in my heart to the Rome he loved so much that has rejected him. England has grown richer. She has escaped and confounded her enemies. We have our theatres and our poets. France, they say, is still being harried and spoilt by civil tumults, and often there is a dearth of food. Italy is as ever pinched by the Pope, the Turk and the Spaniard. It is just that, an all its faults, I prefer the England I once knew, where honour was not merely a game.

In Hackney all was in order. It is a large brick mansion with proper entry hall, a chapel, a substantial gallery, where the private theatre was installed, and a library with shelves to the ceiling. Beth's need and her delight was to re-establish the garden and fill the house, which had been left standing empty for some time before it was given to me. Her style in the garden was to mix the fruits and vegetables most cleverly, so that the fennel provided a green muff for the columbines. The well needed cleaning, the paths needed trimming and fresh pebbles. All of this Beth supervised with great energy, and sometimes even helped do the work herself with a sure Trentham hand. Robin Christmas, the last of my faithful servants after Tony Munday left, divided his labours between tending the garden with Beth and making fair copy of my previous day's writing.

Every play in my mind wanted to be written three times. In fact, only half of them reached that point, and even for most of those I'd still prefer one more time. A sonnet could easily take three weeks.

In the mornings there would be rough and new writing; in the afternoons I'd do rewriting, which was light work that could be picked up and put down if we wanted to ride or friends visited, and only at night, after the late supper that became our custom, did I do my most important composition to the steady low light of the whale-oil lamp until dawn came and I lay down to nap. On many nights I'd lay down twice, the once before or after dinner with Beth.

Life was in repair. I would work to reconstruct old notions to function better, as when I joined Hollenshed's Sir John Fastolfe, who 'from this battle departed without any stroke stricken and in the same year for his valiantness was elected into the Order of the Garter', with my sudden recognition of the courtier Nicolas

Dawtrey, who, given half a chance, would have been Fastolfe's equal. It made a better Falstaff and pleased the Queen more, too. I joined the money-lenders with the foreign doctors Fenatus and Lopez, who'd been unjustly persecuted, to make a stronger Shylock.

I found the means to re-do *Telemach* and lighten its gloom with savage laughter when I suddenly remembered Guiderstern, the Swedish Embassador to London when I was a boy and it had been my father's duty to meet the Swedish king, who'd come to woo Elizabeth. I hadn't thought for decades of my father's story of how Guiderstern had taken him for a dumb organ, whose pulls, stops and keys could be play'd at will, and defeated him precisely by playing dumb. That play journeyed some distance from Greece to little Denmark in its new version, where my brother-in-law Lord Willoughby had been sent in 1583 to try to soften King Frederick's control of the Northern seas. He was a good man and a good friend. I still wonder at the inexplicable way I held back permission for him to marry my sister for so long. Once in Denmark it was easy to fit foreign Telemach out with Hamlet, a good English sort of name even if no one ever had it, which I took from Hamnet, the slightly pretentious name of Shakspeare's poor short-liv'd babe. That was my private jest, except from Shakspeare, who had a letter written to me from Stratford in which he complain'd that I'd offended his poor infant's Christian memory. I was amaz'd. *Hamlet* is my private play, although, when it was made right, others found sufficient in it to understand, and it was heard with ecstasy at Court, in the city and at both Universities. I fear that I repeat myself, or boast, or both.

Life was in repair in other ways as well. In this benign Hackney atmosphere I was calculating new weights for love and trust and passion. Henry Wriothesley, Earl of Southampton, an addict of the theatre and England's new golden boy, fell into our orbit and rode with us so often in the country that when our son was born on 24 February 1593, we named him Henry and nominated Henry as the boy's godfather.

Beth's great feat was to march through the whole disarray of my debts, deeds and accounts and find therein three fields, two houses and a provincial gravel-yard that I'd forgotten to sell. In truth, I'd never known I own'd the gravel-yard. Her management of these assets was so good that our situation quickly eased, and Beth began to talk about the time when I would take her to France and Italy for my new Grand Tour. For four years we shuttled back and forth in season between Bilton Hall on the Avon and King's Place, until, but of that in a moment ...

With all of these fruitful events Hackney bid fair to be the promise of mortal paradise. But there were from the beginning worms on the leaves and cancres on the fruit, even before the snake arrived. The world would not stay away.

My former father-in-law had a new project, to marry his eldest granddaughter, Elizabeth, to Henry. Suddenly I fear'd his illness was more serious than I'd ever guess'd, that he was a hermit crab on the beach waiting to collect his next shell. Young Southampton was handsome, had money and was much thought of by the Earl of Oxford, who'd vexed me so by trying to disown my granddaughter. What, then, could be a better match, with the bonus of perhaps drawing obdurate Edward back into the net as well? He must surely have been thinking something very like that. It cost a fair bit of work and explanation with Henry, but in the end, thank God, I saved him, and he withdrew his offer. Pondus was even happy, since he exacted a fortune, £5,000, from the boy in compensation for the injury to his granddaughter.

Hard after this difficult passage, Pondus was at work again, this time to engage Elizabeth to Henry Percy, the Wizard Earl of Northumberland, but now Elizabeth herself did not fancy him. With his steaming scientific experiments, the Wizard Earl would not have made a bad match. Whatever she did or said, he'd hardly have noticed her. Here Fate played a most intricate trick: in 1594 Burghley made the match that Elizabeth wanted, with William Stanley, after his just deceased brother's widow had given birth to a girl, which meant that he became the Earl of Derby and the wealthiest man in England. Naturally Pondus waited until the earldom was assured, and my views were not sought. Now

William's brother was both a poet and a patron of drama. Though our group stood apart from him, we recognized his pen as showing promise of greatness. He was thirty-four years old when he was poisoned, six months after he had become the earl, thereby producing a most eligible bachelor in his young brother. Another Cecil was well-provided for.

William, who had done the Grand Tour and even been to Madrid and Constantinople, also wrote and loved drama, even more than his brother. Strange turn, the boy was unruffled by the marriage and ended spending more time with me than with my daughter, who eventually came straggling after. Elizabeth and I established a kind of distant wary amity. Wondrous Beth treated her as warmly as she did Susan, whom she really liked.

## 〰 49 〰

Will became my apprentice and worked with me in the gallery-theatre. First he worked with Edward Halle's *The Union of the Two Noble and Illustre Families of Lancaster and York* to flesh out the history plays, for which I had leaned too much on Hollenshed in the early versions. In the beginning he did small insertions to the history plays. Fairly soon he was writing himself, eventually whole speeches and even the odd scene. So there we were, two Willies at one table. Much of our work for a long time consisted of rooting out shag-hair'd or shallow-rooted lines from the original long table. Some were so bad that it was hard for me even to believe that I'd been present at the table to pass on them. William, more than anything, wanted to be able to sit beside me as an equal. I let him have his head, knowing that he had sufficient self-knowledge to rein himself in at the proper time, which he always would. Then I might tease: *From a prince to a prentice?*

William was at his best and happiest administering the plays and players. I saw my young self as I watched him and came to the conclusion that he did it better than Lyly and I had managed it, allowing, of course, that the Chamberlain's and Queen's men sometimes reached the smoothness of clocks that wind themselves. All the same, some chain always snapped, and the theatrical enterprise had flourished so well that the best companies kept costume wardrobes of £3,000, and there were rumours that secret holding rights were being paid for some plays. In different ways it was still not easy.

All this activity I watched with pleasure from my little distance, either at King's Place or the simple Bilton on Avon, where I would go to write when I needed to be alone, which was sonnet time. We felt bless'd with safety in the country in 1593, 1594, 1602, 1603, and, until I was stricken, this year, all severe plague years. They say that if the pace of plague continues, all the theatres will be bankrupt. I went to the city from time to time in season but did so less and less because the boy players, whom I particularly liked to watch, were falling most swiftly, and only the very best of them. Heavy was the loss of translucent Salmon Pavy, who died at thirteen two years ago. As a man he would have been an actor worthy of any play. I have not heard lately of Nathan Field or Israel Jordane, who is but a book-holder, and yet he speaks so clearly and beautifully above the players that many go especially to listen to his readings from the pit. Many of the boy players seem to cluster together to live in St Giles, without Cripplegate near The Fortune. It is a dangerous parish in such times.

My idyll came to an end once more when ... I do not have to set this down ... No, I shall say it: when I met Anne by chance in the city one day and lapsed into her experienced arms once more. Worse, such was my love for Beth that I told her of my lapse. She encouraged me to continue if I must but only not, please, to tell her about it.

With erudition I had not suspected that she had, Beth cited ancient Philotimus on the Massagets, who visited their wives but once a week in order not to hear their chidings in the day time, nor their complaints in the night time, and she offer'd that it might be better for me to habit Hilton and come to her when I felt I loved her and needed her, which I do always. Only from her slur of Bilton did I understand the degree of disturbance she felt. I did go to Bilton Hall, in guilt, and like a drunkard forswearing his bottle have fought my way back against myself to King's Place.

I have a natural son, an infant son and heir by Beth, and a chosen son in Henry, his godfather. Why should we allow ourselves to be held in prison by blood in such matters? Henry chose me as his father as I chose him as my son. Look not at his beautiful face and graces, but at his life. He'd been another of Burghley's wards, and one, moreover, with the same slur of illegitimacy hanging over his name. He, too, had been sent to St John's, from which he graduated in his fifteenth year, and passed to Gray's Inn, where he was intoxicated by the potion of drama. Henry was proud and hot-tempered, sweet and learned, a patron by nature, sometimes more myself than my voluntary son. He'd been in trouble with a Maid at Court. He'd been in prison. There was no chasm between us an our twenty-three-year distance of years.

The strain came in his youthful friend Essex's rebellion, in which he'd faithfully implicated himself as I had in Norfolk's. And how had he been involved? By arranging to stage Shakespeare's *King Richard the Second* on the eve of the rebellion. And whom did the Queen appoint to try him and Essex? The Lord Great Chamberlain, chief among the judges. It was bizarre. You wouldn't have believed the situation in a play. I led him in the questioning, never quite sure if he had my gist and knew that I was leading him. His face seemed to focus on me as the source of his complaints.

He and Essex were duly sentenced to death, which had to be, given the jury She'd appointed, and that also was somehow taken to be my fault. Damn the law. Damn this rotten land and time.

I went straight from the verdict to the Queen and argued for his life with more force and eloquence than I'd ever argued for anything. I won, and She commuted his death sentence, even released him when Essex was beheaded. I had the feeling that the release was taken as Her grace, having nothing to do with me.

Thus we live in awkward, bruised love among friends at King's Place. I have even accepted bounties of £1,000 from both Henry and William. Disgrace without end. William, Beth and Henry seem to cluster together in love and injury. Elizabeth stands at a distance with her grandmother's face, as if she knew it had to be thus. Francesca looks at me with sympathy and sorrow through her mother's face. It is too much. When will it end?

246

## 50

I returned to Court by Royal invitation yet again. It was, in truth, a visit to the Shades. I could hardly refuse, since the portion of the £1,000 each year that Elizabeth could husband was all that stood between us and the poor house. The Queen waited and feared the one subject in Her land whom She did not want to invite and who would take the Throne at last. The Court sat quietly, one on a throne, the others on their stools, whilst outside there sounded the impatiently waiting horse hooves of mortality and some new age. She knew the sun was setting and that everyone at Court was taking care to send respectful greetings to James, waiting for the dawn in Scotland.

There was one young man there but not there. He was John Donne, whose poems a friend had recited for me at Hackney when he was invited by Henry and Beth to join our little audience and sit for *Measure*. The poems were full-rigged ships. The shipwright, I found, was but an elderly lad, who belonged better among the Spanish godly theorics than in England's Court. We chatted as a dance went by, more slowly than in my time, and I heard him task first the Catholics, then the Calvinists. Nor, of course, had he overmuch affection for the English Church. His grandfather was favoured as a boy by Henry, but the family had waned under Elizabeth. Young Donne's poems make duty and godliness a face of love, while the world is a strumpet. I did not tell him that my ear had been touched by the soft flesh of his love poems. He did not seem to know of my other self, for he spoke coldly of the new Shakespeare he'd seen at The Globe. There was the blood of genius in him, but perhaps too much brain for his fancy to outrun time. As we spoke his foe seemed the foul devil who was quite real, mine mere de Vere myself. He thought he had time outfox'd. I guess'd he'd not. *Know thy foes rightly*, I advised. He listen'd cool and contemptuous. Against all logic we had no marriage of true minds. He owned a sharp sense of humour, yet I only smiled. There were no truculent words, yet he was truculent. He said nothing with arrogance, yet he was arrogant, nor anything immodest, yet he was immodesty itself. I thought, will this John be the Queen's new poet, greater than Immerito or Shakespeare? No. I doubted that his luxurious stiffness would stop even at the Throne. For different reasons he, too, would surely not be Laureate whilst She lived.

That night I was exhausted and frightened in the safety of my bed. I should have stayed at home. King's Place is my Court. Outside it now my poems and plays seemed broken-winged and toss'd to die into the muddy flats beside the Thames.

A barge glided down the river in my dreams. Good Spenser waved regally from it. A smaller bark came after, and on it was young Donne, the ever-confident heir apparent. I felt my tune could never change, nor could I pick up the new ways and parry and thrust with them as once I had. Better if I had known to do it, for what I had written shows my face as much as this deskbook. Still I dip my pen.

In the morning I wrote two sonnets all at once and without correction, which very rarely happens with me. I do not like them much for their self-abasement, though I shall not quarrel with their art. The simpler and better of the two sonnets is remember'd:

> Why is my verse so barren of new pride,
> So far from variation or quick change?
> Why, with the time, do I not glance aside
> To new-found methods and to compounds strange?
> Why write I still all one, ever the same,
> And keep invention in a noted weed,
> That every word doth almost tell my name,
> Showing their birth, and where they did proceed?

The other one, a lesser poem, imagines my own death and plucks at once the strings of Queen and mistress and even the unborn quarrel with Donne, with a side glance at the light and airy verse of Sir Henry Lee for dark Anne, which is nothing but risen sugar and egg-white well-whipped in his buttery for two days. Such things I should not explain. That poem reeks of pity and has more emotion than verbal jewellery, but let it stay and have its word against me, too. Jealous Ben Jonson has begun already to satirize and cut me. The Amorphous indeed! I'll be outstripped, but not by too many pens. I like, at least, the poem's wonderfully ear-offending broad English ending:

> But since he died, and poets better prove,
> Theirs for their style I'll read, his for his love.

True love in my life never once made a proper butt-end rhyme.

I went to the Queen's Court again several times when it could not be avoided, but always as a distant visitor who could not stay. She treated me kindly, like a minister dismissed but kept on pension. This was not revenge but plain hire. I would now be ever faithful primarily to my own home and song. There is but one enemy in that private Court at Hackney, and I am he in remembrance of my own past.

*Have you been true to yourself?*

    *The question is banal, you know.*

*I know. Answer it.*

    *At most times, but that faithfulness has had to be weaved and entangled with the oddest circumstance as much as my life itself has been. A true soul when most impeach'd stands least . . .*

*If you please. Let us conduct this inquiry without hollow literary echoes. There will be confusion enough for us if we are to pass judgement without draping plain statements of fact o'er with rhetoric. I think you often let yourself go mamm'ring on too much.*

    *I think you haven't understood how my mamm'ring has been the only wind to push us through Scylla and Charybdis.*

*Which rocks are they?*

*Sadness and madness. You know that.*

*Through night's middle darkness a poet did walk . . .*

*Now it is you who're tempted by literary phrases.*

    *Oh, you may protest. I'd have sooner said 'twas between sadness and the state.*

*And which was the greater?*

    *A state has sadness of its own. And a person may also be enormous and dispatch embassadors of the spirit to distant colonies, although he be but a seed ground by the barren rage of the state's stone mill.*

*And yet live for ever in the hearts of the heirs of all eternity.*

    *On that at least there need be no quarrel. The state is soon or late a puny thing, and such promise of eternity as it has hides furtively in little-noticed lips and eyes. The only hope, however, lies in the lines if they survive; the lip will never be reported aright.*

*But will not eternity be ever-peopled exactly as it is now?*

    *Please stay close-lipped on that score. That is a beast that dwells beyond the mesh of reason. Think too much on that possibility and there is only* murky Hell. If there are unborn Burghleys, at least I shall not know them.

It is not a matter on which it is profitable to think too much when all round in this time, this place, aspiration lies on the ground like rotting fruit, and dreams have been exhausted.

Some were realized.

Not enough. Some poems, a play, no two, three if we are softly dispos'd. All the rest is Entertainment and Pageant. Be grateful for the few hours of sleep that did come every night, or else the wild and wand'ring flood of words with its merry and melancholy currents would have been even greater.

That is not the fault. The fault is that 'twas never dar'd to speak against our own capricious order and instead a harmless and endless saga of all that monarchs do was written.

Endless perhaps, but not so harmless. How oddly situated and what a crooked frame of sense 'twould have been if the Lord Great Chamberlain had taken as his task to mock five centuries of his forebears' loyalty. That would have been a corruption to shame all the vices of these abusing times.

All's obliquy.

What? Was I a dog to smell out stenches? I gave sufficient hints, methinks. The high-born and the public people together are cloth'd in vice well-sewn to give a show of virtue. Their raiments reek, and they are drunk with the smell. To say as much needed only a short poem, which properly understood would by itself have put me outside the city's walls as a truth-telling idiot or inside the Tower as a rude traitor. Immerito had a close call with his poem against Burghley. Whatever tipsy clothes I have worn, I have not gone that far.

You exaggerate.

Always.

You are too soft, and then you are too hard, by which you harm both you and all you love.

Rage and scruples are ever intermix'd in me. That is the soft and then discordant music of my soul in the same way that my pen must blend the common rhythm and the delicate music of metre. There is no explaining that. It is my voice. I am . . .

. . . that I am. It was agreed that this internal inquisition would proceed better without self-citation.

I am a poet. I've chang'd my mind once more. Why should the frivolous *world know this my secret tale? I no longer wish it. When Jane appears, I'll have the fire lit and that will be the end of it.*

*It is an uncommonly warm June. She'll think you mad and press cold balms upon your forehead. This intensity of scribbling has now lasted more than a month. You don't need that fire to drive out this fire. It will burn itself out.*

*And besides, from sufficient distance your fire may yet be a star to another.*

*It does not matter. Near or far, I doubt the retort will be sufficiently hot to burn away the bad in sulphurous fumes and leave only the good behind in the crucible.*

*The process might proceed otherwise.*

*We are getting nowhere with this superfluity of interruption. Witnesses await.*

*What sort of witnesses are they?*

*Unapprov'd witnesses. There is no point in having the others. You bought their praise and good will in salaries, plays and books with your many estates. Besides, players and writers are never fair witnesses. Look! The cloudy mass above the distant oaks once again rolls towards your window. They must be heard. They will not go away.*

*I do not have to listen.*

*You always must, dearest friend. Well you know that in this theatre there is no curtain, and the play will proceed even if you lower the shutters. Pray be seated. The last act ends as usual with sunrise.*

At that a woman walked towards me through the window from the cloud-bank and stood pensively in the middle of the room. She wore a plain and simple old-fashioned smock, wet and stained with gore. I could not recognize her at first or even tell her age, which seem'd to shift from moment to moment, until she put a wet handkerchief to her mouth and I could smell the heavy perfume with which she was trying to smother her foul odour. I motioned the Lady first to my chair and then to my bed, but She shook Her head.

*You are my Queen, are you not? Or else Her ghost?*

*Do not be ridiculous, Edward. I am neither. You are a playwright and over-inclined to setting ghosts upon the stage. I've told you more than once that I do not like this dangerous foppery or approve of it. I am no real or unreal ghost, but merely one of those affable familiar apparitions with which you people your rich sleeping-hours. I am ill-dressed and ill-at-ease. Hear what I have to say, which is only what you know already, and thus I need not warn you beforehand that you will not like it, so that I may leave your fever'd imagination. My reproaches will likely be the mildest that you hear tonight.*

The censure was for the way I'd turned our friendship into money; that I'd even tried to exchange my £1,000 a year for a once-only sum of £5,000.

*Never mind the theatre. Can you imagine how much more quickly you'd have come to a worse state than you're in if I hadn't exercised some restraint on you? Only that and your wife's good charge over you has saved you from sprawling in a tavern like a drunken yeoman. You wanted me to grant you monopolies. Did you think you had a thousand pounds a year for pure respect? You wanted me to make you President of Wales, Governor of Harwick, ruler of Jersey. Did you think such things were mine to give? Can you imagine to yourself the ruin that your lax rule would have made of that little isle?*

*Can you conceive of what a million pounds is? It cost me five times that to administer my kingdom and wage wars that Parliament applauded even though it had not supported them. Against that my revenues were but three and a half million. The difference, my Lord Great Chamberlain, was made up of subtle fees for governorships and monopolies. When Ralegh went to sea for England, he was stealthily financed by the monopoly on wine I gave him. How did you, with £1,000 a year plus other frequent signs of my favour, come to think yourself deserving of a bit of every piece of fruit eaten in the kingdom? You were a true-telling maker with a place in the scheme of things, but even more you were a too-demanding friend of my purse. Through all my reign I was surrounded by little, little men. It hurt me then to see you sometimes grow small, too.*

*Were you aiming to embellish a title that was rich before, or did you seek to become more rich in matter than in words?*

*When Burghley was dying, I came to his bed and sat four nights feeding him porridge with a spoon. I know you did not like him, but he secured the England in which you were able to play your frolics and follies. Yet you were too busy to attend my funeral, though that was an obligation of your office. Thank you so much. We frequently quarrelled, I'll grant, but I was in heart your friend. You were not mine enough. I, silly Queen, ended comfortless, though I was not deposed. I hoped for more from you because you are your father's son. I thought that you had the imagination to have some compassion and respect for the circling shadows in which kings must seek to sleep. Goodbye here, then, in case we do not have occasion to speak there.*

I strained to breathe and make reply, but there were no words in my throat to answer the ghost-Queen's strident accusations. It is always what happens when I dream. I move freely in unknown spheres and have but that one iron constraint: I cannot speak. There is thus rarely pleasure in my dreams, and I dream too much. Strange 'tis how my mind should give the dead leave so to berate me whilst withholding my sword, my pen, my tongue. Still I should not complain of my dreaming overmuch, as my shrewdest doubts always come to me during sleep.

The phantasma shifted slightly and was my first wife Anne, in whom distress and dolour dwelt as cozily as when she'd lived. I stepped back, and she followed every pace, no more and no less, but gave way before me to the same degree when I took a step towards her.

*Whose was the first fault, Hap? Probably 'twas mine, for, though I've never told you this before, I went and begg'd you from father like a toy, and when he said that I might have you, you were given before you knew of it yourself. I was the most daff'd of the daffodils that dared to come before the first swallow. But once in the hedges you did say you loved me. You might have said 'no' before you did, or after kept your resolution when I wept to have you back. What did I do? Nothing with which you charged me. I think that now you know that, too. I stand guilty of being a constant accessory to my father, but can you say that you steadfastly resisted his manipulations? I see that now you've even let yourself write fawning letters to my brother, seeking the same favours you asked of our father. Shame on you, Hap. Even if I did not know it then, my spirit was bound and gagg'd in Hatfield House like yours. What would it have cost you to lend a stronger helping hand? Why did you not spirit me away to Italy as you once said you would?*

*Often was I cold and had need of you, and you were not there. Often as I strained to give birth, I wanted your hand to hold, and you were not there. My flesh, my blood you often forswore, and then had of it to give me greater woe and early death at last. When I was sick and most sorry, you would not visit me. You call'd me a whore, and I became the ale-house talk of every carter. Stranger, wild man whom once I loved when I was young, say prayers for what you've not done as well as what you have done before you go.*

*I am nothing because I had no love. I suffer'd long, I thought you no evil. I hoped, I endured, I waited to rejoice in the truth with you in spite of all one day, a day that never came. My only consolation was a nameless son.*

*Was it me you hated, or was it the common gateway of womb that brought you into the world? You had a mistress, who drove you crazy, and then another wife, who's been loved with a tenderness I never glimpsed, and yet you've treated her badly too. No, it must, then, have been my own fault. I, I am to blame. For loving you too much. I humbly do beseech you of your pardon.*

*If you did not want to pass your life with me, why did you not help me in my first youthful passion to escape to a nunnery like your Isabella? I saw the world through childish eyes and can scarcely blame you for that. Now, after death, at least my eyes have repaired and I am come out of blindness. What was I, who was I for you, Hap? It seems to me that I was not quite a person, just a gesture of youthful arrogance on your part, and later nothing more than alternating occasions for guilt and anger, yes, and a warm, wet hole that became a grave. I cannot in my heart even blame you for the words you said after you'd straddled me and taken my maidenhead: 'So now I've tupped you* [barnyard terminology for animal copulation A.F.], *and you know how to make the Beast with two Backs'* [*Othello*, Act 1, Scene 1 A.F.]. *After all, my father and I had entrapped you, and so I deserved the words no matter how terrible. The very thought of you makes me burn with shame beyond the grave, and yet, I cannot tell you why, in my prayers for the past and my crippled soul, I still remember you softly.*

This apparition was not easier on my heart, but more savage. There are truths accessible to mediocre minds, and these are harmless, and there are those that rip and tear and make unbear able noises within the brain, and these unclaimed truths are the stuff of which my dreams are made, my dreams that teem with blood and gore and quiet words, which are worse. I called out with all the energy I possess'd, but could manage no more than a bare hanging vowel. I reached out. The cloud moved off. I knew that this exhibition of my worst self-accusing fears was no more real than my over-rich imagination, but that was real enough, and knew, too, that the line of accusatory dolls had not yet ended its march along in my mind like the Strasbourg clock.

I must have fallen in a faint within a dream, for I awakened falling like a ghost through the ceiling on to my bed, where, as I half-expected, old Pondus awaited me impatiently. The oddity was that I was cloud, he was flesh.

*See now where you stand, prodigal stepson. Did I not fit you out in mind and body for a great life? Did I not give you my favourite daughter's hand? What did I ever refuse you that was not for your own good?*

*Our family takes in hand £4,000 a year from lands alone. Under this great canopy of sufficiency you might have lived in peace and honour and been physician to the arts, the state or our own estates, however you desired, or better still, with all your manifest ability, to all three at once. Yet, though every gallant heart at Court envied you your luck, you would not have these things. O no, your destiny was for higher and lower things. Instead, you unroofed the safe world and chose to pass windy nights with your reckless manuscripts and friends.*

*Now you've destroyed yourself and are not much better off than a country reeve. There is no truth when they say I left you stranded without money in Italy, or that I've taken all your land. That land was largely given by you to others. I took only what you pressed upon me, and that only for the safety of my daughter and granddaughters. It cost every skill that I possessed to defend you and keep you from pulling me down with you.*

*Would you know the worst thing about you, Lord Oxford? It's simply this, that one can never guess from one moment to the next what you might say or do. I do not doubt that your character is difficult for you yourself, but know that it was horror complete at times to stand beside you in life, which I did almost to the end.*

*You remained blithely unaware whilst my daughter and my wife and my mother-in-law swooped at my head and pecked me like daws after mating season for what you did.*

At this outrageous speech my guilt blew away and I was now filled with fury. These were damnable lies made up entirely of half-truths. I wafted menacingly towards Corambus [the Burghley figure in *All's Well That Ends Well*; in the first quarto of *Hamlet*, Polonius was named Corambis A.F.], who looked at me and said in his usual queer senseless speech: *Nay, come your way if you must*, and then vanished like all the others, leaving me in a solid heap on the floor.

I dreamed a dream of youthful remembrance, of how not long after my father's death I wandered in the wood at night near Saffron Walden and was frightened by a severed human hand tied to the lowest branch of a tall oak beside the largest of the lanes leading from the town. It was not hard to imagine the person to whom that had once not long ago belonged. I even thought I vaguely remembered a lad a little older than I in the town square with a menacing face and bloody gauze on his right wrist. The punishment was owling, specifically reserved for those who break the monopolies by bringing goods into the cities and towns on little-used roads under the cover of night. The punishment was, of course, designed to frighten owlers, but it was stupidly chosen because it rendered them unfit for any other work and so converted a part-time occupation into full-time brigandage in most cases. This particular hand, which even had a bit of sleeve, was lit from behind by the moon, and a small bare branch came down behind it to give the appearance that it was holding a pen. And now I dreamed of that same oak, but this time a hand holding a pen was hanging from every twig of every branch. I started and wished to run away, but every vault I took away somehow brought me closer to the bloody tree. As I came to the edge of its branches, all the hands dropped their pens, which floated lightly to the ground. In unison they pointed at me, and I woke up.

I looked up and as I did a disembodied voice began to speak in a flowing clerkly quiet way.

*This indenture is made in the seventeenth year of the reign of our Sovereign Lady Elizabeth, by the grace of God Queen of England, France, Ireland, defender of the faith, etc. between the right honourable Edward de Vere, Earl of Oxford, Great Chamberlain of England, Viscount Bulbeck and Lord of Badlesmere and Scales, of the one party, and the Right Honourable Thomas, Earl of Sussex, Viscount Fitzwater, Lord of Egremond and Burnell, Knight of the most noble Order of the Garter, Captain of the Gentlemen Pensioners and Gentlemen-at-Arms, Chief Justice, and Justice in all matters of all Her Majesty's forests, parks and chases on this side Trent and Lord Chamberlain of Her Majesty's households, the Right Honourable Robert, Earl of Leicester, Baron of Denby, of the most noble Order of the Garter, Knight Master of the Queen Her Majesty's horse, and Her Highness' Most Honourable Privy Councillor, Thomas Cecil, Esquire, son and heir apparent unto the Right Honourable Sir William Cecil, Knight, Lord Burghley, and High Treasurer of England, Sir William Cordell, Knight, Master of the Rolls, and Thomas Bromley, Esquire, the Queen Majesty's Solicitor General as the other parties ...*

The incantation proceeded with the lulling rhythm of Homer, in which the sentences become a song above their sense.

*I have come to know if you will give me tidings of my father. My holdings are being devoured, my lush lands are being ruined, my houses are full of malevolent men with rude ways and manners who slaughter the broad flocks, and these same men are those who woo my mother, arrogant out of all measure. I have come to kneel before you on my knees in the hope that thou may tell me of my father's pitiful death. I pray thee, good Odysseus, now remember all and tell me truth.*

The boats sway in the harbour and are listed in solemn glory before they sink or burn or land in every particular.

*The lands and fees which had been for the lonely use of the said Earl and his heirs for ever as manors, Lordships, farms, tenements, hereditaments, and their attachments are called by several name or names of Greyes in Hedingham, Sibley, Peppers, Prayers, alias Bowerhall, Over Yeldham, alias Yeldham Parva, Mauldon, Flounderswike, Bunches, Flexland Stansted, Mount Fitchet and the park there, Bentfield, Bury, Bury-Log-in-Standsted, Netherhall in Gestingthorp, Brown's Tenement in Topsfield, Parke's Tenement in Gestingthorp, Chelmissey Wood, Nether*

*Yeldham, alias Much Yeldham, Barwick and Scotness, Shrewes in Gaines Colne, Tilbery, Iuxta Clare, Perers Estonhall, Fingrith, and Bumpstead Counts in the Country of Essex, with the Manor of Esberchold in the Country of Suffolk, and the Manor of Aston Sampford in the County of Buckingham, and the Manor of Eston Mawdit in the County of Northampton, and the Manors of Hornwood, Barkway, Newsale in the County of Hertford, and the Manors of Swappham, Bulbeck, and Abingdon Magna in the Country of Cambridge, and the Manor of Fleet in the County of Kent.*

All of these lands came to me from my father, John, and were to pass sideways from the clutches of my wife Anne at Much Provided, and go to my Vere cousins and their heirs. And even though that Will did not live to be executed, I notice with a smile how all the same they have fallen out of the old family tree, the most ancient in Britain, into the aprons of those very same right honourable guardians that were nominated over me, the Burghleys and the Leicesters and their runners, which is why I'm saved the bother of writing another Will. The water in the harbour is dark green with slime and stink. What they did not steal I tossed away in disgust.

*Mill's Farm in Earl's Colne, Chalkney Crofts and Bowersfield, North on the highway from Colne to Great Tey, the site of the former priory of St Mary the Virgin and St John the Evangelist in Earl's Colne, Ingesthorpe alias Insteps at White Colne, Colne Engaine, Wakes Colne, Pebmarsh, Lamarsh, Stansted in Halstead, the Manor of Bretts in West Ham, Burwells in East Ham, West Wickham in the County of Cambridge, again in Essex, Sible Hedingham, Great Maplestead, Bilton Hall in East Warwickshire* ... You have forgotten *Bentley and Great Bentley in Essex.* When I was very small it was my duty and my game to recite all the de Vere lands rapidly and grabbing breath before my father. It was necessary for a future earl and for a boy to strengthen the muscles of memory. Once I could seize a full page in a few minutes, now there are always never places and holes where words used to be. *Shipton-under-Wychwood in Cotswold, Langham Park alias Lavenham Cockfield in the County of Suffolk, the Manor of Elmsthorp in the County of Leicester, and Earlshelton also in Leicester, and in the*

*County of Essex again, Colne Priory, Playstowe, Hawstead, Colne
Comitis, Belchamp Walter alias Beauchamp, Court Harwick, Cool Alba,
Messing, Waterdower, Havering-in-the-Bowerie, Castle Hedingham.* Help
me, father!

The names had been soothing me and rocking me to sleep.
Though the lands were gone, the names remained and could be
heard in place of prayers. Those lands will stay for ever in England,
though my heirs and ancestors will now have no need to learn
the litany. At the words Castle Hedingham I woke up with a
scream in a crumpled heap on the bedroom floor. Cold sweat
streamed down my scalding face. I then looked up and heard my
father's ghost speaking gravely. The vision at the window with
first light streaming through it had no face, but there was no
mistaking the mellifluous power of his voice, though its tone was
deeper than I'd ever remembered hearing it.

*Hap, I come to lead you to what you've been too dull to find yourself.
You were a boy surely even then too read in ancient tragedies not to question
the cause of your father's death more closely. I have no power to tell you
things you yourself do not know, but think of the sudden nature of my death
and your mother's departure, contemplate the copious gardens of Kenilworth,
in which all rare plants, including poisons, grow and then consider to whom
our lands fell. One smiling friend, one over-pious enemy poised to wrestle
each other for power but perfectly united for a time to manufacture rich
orphans and shift them to good use. There was no way for you to know the
nature of the vile sores that covered my body as I died, but I wonder that
you did not guess the unseemly haste of their rush to the window.*

*Weeds may make flowers most lovely and most deadly. In Leicester's
glorious gardens at Kensington there is a special alcove that few have seen.
John [Garrad? A.F.] told me of it. Tempting* Atropa belladonna, *the
deadly nightshade, grows there, with exceptionally large and shining scarlet
berries, more like cherries. It gives a gay death with mirthful delirium.
There are many beautiful blue varieties of* Aconitum napellus: *the
common blue rockets, wolfsbane, monkshood, and their French cousins the
various Casque de Jupiter, Capuchon-de-moine and Char de Vénus. When
these are ground together with the sap from yews, one obtains the most
diabolical poison of all, the deadly hebenon, so strong that one warm portion*

*of a single drop administered in the ear of a sleeping man will be fatal,
and fatal in the slowest way, with great depression of the heart, paralysis
and intelligence unaffected until the very last guttering of life. This rare
produce of Kensington Gardens was never sold at market but given away
secretly.*

*You had your chance to guess about all of this. 'Tis pity you were so
slow to summon me up, for it is now rather late, when all the villains who
participated in my most foul murder are safely in their graves. How now
can you give me the revenge I need?*

'Twas Leicester, I said to myself, 'twas Leicester. He was the
serpent in our castle before my father's death, he was the young
gallant with whom my mother fussed obscenely and mysteriously.
[Robert Dudley, Earl of Leicester, was thirty-two years old in
1564; in 1560 his first wife, Amy, had been found dead at the foot
of a staircase under mysterious circumstances in Cumnor Hall,
Oxfordshire, and during the next decade, following a period when
he was sentenced to death for plotting on behalf of Lady Jane
Grey, Leicester's wealth grew greatly and inexplicably. A.F.] A
play, a play's the thing to bring at last revenge upon his memory.

Blackbirds on the lawn scattered to the sky from some unseen
early danger. So menacing and fair a morning I'd never seen.
There was no need now for juggling ghosts. Let artful reasoning
do the rest, I thought.

Death take my maddened head. What I thought would be bravery or fear or, at worst, run-a-tilt with death within a bed is instead a storm of fragments, scraps and bits and relics of a life. Endymion meant eternal sleep. John Lyly put it out to market in his play and leased it for a term of only forty years. I laughed, but now I see that time has taken its usury at fifty in the hundred. If death should be a never-ending storm of scraps, that is Hell. Life is a chaos that spits forth death and mountains, rocks and poets, noblemen and peasants. Then all resides in its natural order until the storm swirls up again and everything scatters like poultry in a yard. I want the silence of the hanging heavens outside my window, cold, bright, silverly, unperturbed. Those stars will not blink at an occasional rash comet, nor will they hear low slander. 'Tide life, 'tide death – I am ready to come without delay, but still you are tardy. I crave death more now than even honour or truth, which has been much over-rated.

Death, after all, is no stranger to me. It's preyed upon the outward parts of my life for so many years. Crabbed memories are in my mouth. I cannot spit them out. A marriage died before it was born, and with that death my life was marred. My parents' life was a living death. My daughters. They bring to mind my amusement in Venice when the silver lids were lifted in unison to show artfully arranged snakes. The jest of it was that they'd defanged and scorched the snakes to stun but not kill them. The hosts laughed merrily at our consternation as the stirring snakes were whisked away and the garnished giant fish was brought in to our delight and relief. Would that my daughters could have been so removed. One, at least, has been most tolerable, and another's husband has been one of my truest friends, so there has been a little benefit. It was my sons who were swept away from me by circumstance, and so I've had no life and little life with them. How could Henry love the father of whom he had to learn to be silent and ashamed? Was not dark Anne's constant insistence upon our end from the beginning a promise of death? To love her and death were almost one thing.

Today Beth and Henry came to see me together. It was the first time I'd seen either of them in a fortnight, and never before together since I've been to bed. It meant they've been told again the end is near, which does not now need a soothsayer, with all my black carbuncles and my heavy cow's tongue that I can scarce keep in my mouth. They'd dressed too brightly. I was alarmed at their visit, since I have grown used to seeing only Jane, the tinker's wife, whose husband still waits, now impatiently, to finish off the service. They spoke lightly of how Henry intended to follow his successful revival of *Love's Labour's Lost* for the new Queen, who's declar'd herself enchanted by it, with another of *The Merry Wives of Windsor*. They well knew those plays were out of season for me. I was living in *Timon*, *Lear* and *Hamlet*, but because we loved we all lied on. Henry said he hoped to print the Sonnets and then scowled because he knew I'd know that meant my death had occurred. Beth prattled about a trip to Italy when the illness passed, but her whole face spoke against her. It always did. You were a grown woman who'd never learnt to tell even the most necessary lie, and that is one of the reasons I love you. In every silence as we spoke the air screamed *Death! Death!*

As she spoke, I inwardly repented all my faults before her but could not find words for them. After all, I'd known Anne longer, and she had been no secret when we met. Her power over me was a fatal spell against all reason, but is not all love a tyranny? I've had three such loves, two women and a man, and each has generated love's wrongs, which are heavier than hate. That is all that I can write, more than I could say. Had I said it fully, it would not have been true. I was grateful for their silence, too, because that estate I shall hold, to enter my grave without knowing how it is between my true love and my best friend. I love them so, I shall to the last minute image only the best. That, at least,

I'll hold as I prepare to surrender my last property, which is my death-bed.

They very nearly frightened me to death as they took their leave when they bowed down in unison to kiss my head. I screamed and tried to push them off, but I was too weak and it was too late. When they'd gone, I sobbed. That there could be human kisses beyond the power of any poet! One prayer only to God before I die: let them not be plagued like me, or by me.

My infection came days after I dressed in costume as of old and went from Hackney to watch my play from the pit at Southwark. I should not have gone, but I was never strong enough when the matter touched women or art. A lout laughed like a horse at one of Anthony's base smirks and covered my face with his beery spit. That surely was it. It was not a successful evening. There was not one word aptly spoken, there was not one player dressed or fitted to his part. As the heads of traitors were once exposed on London Bridge and then sent on provincial tours, with odd limbs dispatched to the smallest hamlets, so will my plays travel abroad. I'll hope more on my poems. As I rode back to Hackney, I passed over melancholy Moor-ditch, once the moat of ancient London, now a wild bramble of weeds and rats, and returned home half-flea'd with the wolvish things.

Death is just a familiar theme. I have been the poet of the sad stories of the death of kings. I'll not now chant a doleful hymn to my own death, which I'll know only from the doorway. Death I do not fear thee; I fear me, for ever and ever. Amen. A thousand souls this moment prepare to die, so I must wait my moment like any man. I'll now put all the players and knaves out of sight. *All hid! all hid!*, the old infant's game.

Die like a poet. I can hardly hold the quill. The trumpets must sound three times as the play begins. The maggot will now be my Lord. Out of my mouth, my eye will fly eternal darkness like night swifts. For sorrow have I sung. 'Tis strange that even in Death's song there is misunderstanding and malice. Only after pestilence can there ever be peace. *Quaelibet orta cadunt, et finem coepta videbunt.* My Ruin ran apace with Glory.                     E.O.

# Editor's Note

*The rage of parallelisms is almost over ... Shakspeare wanted not the stilts of language to raise him above all other men ... [Moreover] it is indeed strange, that any real friends of our immortal* POET *should be still willing to force him into a situation, which is not tenable: treat him as a* learned *man, and what shall excuse the most gross violations of history, chronology, and geography?*

(Father Richard Farmer, Master of Emmanuel College, Cambridge, and Principal Librarian of the University in the preface to the second edition (1767) of *An Essay on the Learning of Shakespeare* at a time when stirrings and vague uneasiness about the attribution of authorship to the actor and stage shareholder from Avon had first begun to bother scholars.)

Those who are familiar with the literature pertaining to Lord Oxford will be aware of how deeply indebted I am to three books in particular: *Shakespeare Identified* (1920); *The Seventeenth Earl of Oxford* (1928), and *The Mysterious William Shakespeare* (1984). These books everywhere stand behind my own research, conducted primarily at Cambridge University, The British Library and the Colchester Public Library. However, *The Lost Chronicle* is, of course, just a story, though it may have different degrees of verisimilitude for different readers.

A final word should be said about chronology. A reader who has command of the traditional dating of the plays must raise an eyebrow at the number of works that first appeared after Edward de Vere's death. However, several very strong cases have been made against assuming there is any link between composition of the plays and their first dates of publication. The only reasonably sure clues we possess (remember that there is no extant manuscript of any play!) are internal references to events and personages of the time, and all of these references support different and earlier dates of composition. Belief in de Vere as Shakespeare does not require any suspension of disbelief, because nothing that we know contradicts the theory, and everything that we know supports it, even granted that there is much that will now never be known; but it does demand a slight bit of historical daylight-saving time, allowing that the plays were written, and in some cases performed in court and private theatres, a few to many years before they first reached print.

A.F.